The War Revealed

Karl K. Gallagher

Thank you for reading!
Karl K. Gallagher

Published by Kelt Haven Press, Saginaw, TX.

Cover art by eBookLaunch.com.
Editing by Laura Gallagher.
Audio Recording by Laura Gallagher.
Lyrics for March of Cambreadth used with permission by Sea Fire Productions, Inc and Alexander James Adams. www.faerietaleminstrel.com

Interior art by Kelt Haven Press.

Previously in this story (spoilers for <u>The Lost War</u>)

Newman Greenhorn and his girlfriend Goldenrod planned an entertaining weekend with their historical reenactment group, The Kingdom. Instead a magic spell pulled all two hundred reenactors into a unknown world. Shock turned into a scramble to find enough food to survive.

(ALL THE SPOILERS)

The woods were full of orcs, which considered humans prey and hosts for their parasitic young. An elf sorcerer watched from afar, giving and removing protective spells according to his unknown plan. Many reenactors died, including the original king and queen of the kingdom, succeeded by visiting monarchs King Ironhelm and Queen Dahlia. Some people discovered they had magical abilities which range from trivial to useful to a mind control power abused to the point the owner was murdered. A massive orc attack on the camp was smashed with many casualties. Newman and Goldenrod were honored for their part in the victory by receiving noble titles, and celebrated by getting married.

The land surrounding the Kingdom's camp.

In the Wilderness

Newman had Cuirass as his partner because he didn't want to stick any of his men with the new guy. Even after a few lessons on how to walk quietly he was crashing through the woods like a truck.

Well, they were supposed to flush game toward the rest of the hunters. Being noisy by accident would do that as well as on purpose. Just as long as they found some game. There'd be a lot of hungry people in camp if they didn't.

Cuirass squeaked as a spear hissed past him.

Newman nocked an arrow, trying to spot where it came from.

Then it was obvious. Two green-skinned orcs charged through the trees at them, spears level. They'd been a rare sight in the month since the orc attack on the camp was smashed.

Cuirass screamed as he ran away.

There was no time to curse at the fool's cowardice. Newman put an arrow into the left orc's belly. It kept coming. A second arrow hit it in the eye. It crashed to the ground in a flurry of dead leaves.

The other orc was almost on top of him.

Newman dodged behind a tree, throwing his bow away to keep it safe.

The orc came around the tree, spearpoint thrusting for his thigh.

Newman had his knife out. The Ka-bar cut at the orc's hands on the shaft.

The spear fell as the orc let go and clamped both hands on Newman's forearm.

The hunter grunted with pain as the bones squeezed together under the grip. He kicked at the orc's knee but the orc leaned into him and they fell onto the moss and leaves.

Newman twisted, keeping the orc from landing on him. He kept his grip on the knife despite the pressure on his arm.

His free hand punched the orc twice but with no weight behind it the orc just grinned. Flailing about he found a dry stick. He swung hard. The stick snapped over the orc's head.

The monster laughed.

Newman snarled as he drove the broken end into the orc's eye.

It slapped his arm aside with one hand and clutched at the wound with the other.

His now free knife drove into the orc's neck.

Orange blood sprayed out.

Newman twisted the knife, digging deeper until the blood stopped flowing.

Breaking branches told of someone else charging toward the fight. It was fellow hunter Deadeye, bow ready.

"Hey. New guy said you'd been killed and eaten."

Newman sat up, wiping his face. "Yeah."

Deadeye looked over the bodies. "Nice work."

"Guess so." Newman didn't feel like gloating. "God damn it, I was only supposed to be here for a weekend."

"Cheer up. You've been here six months and you haven't been eaten. What more do you want?"

***

The clearing had been used for meetings before. Boulders and a few rough-trimmed logs provided a loose circle of seats. Its site on the bluff edge provided a pleasant view of the river. The afternoon sun gave it warmth.

Goldenrod sat on a blanket-draped boulder. Facing the river kept her from staring at everyone as they approached. She didn't want to scare anyone off at the last moment.

The attendees trickled in, one or two at a time. The last was Lady Burnout chivvying on someone with cold feet. Everyone had shown. Goldenrod felt honored. They'd finally been bringing in enough food to start a stockpile for winter. The Autocrat was allowing people to take one day off a week to celebrate. Everyone invited was using their day for this.

Despite Redinkle's efforts there was no small talk going on among those waiting. Too nervous.

Goldenrod couldn't blame them. She was nervous herself. She

stood.

"Thank you all for coming. Please, take a seat."

She waved toward the circle. Everyone found a spot. A couple preferred sitting on the grass. Goldenrod sat again when they were settled.

"We are all the people who've expressed some talent. Call it magic, psychic, or just a gift, we can do something that we couldn't before arriving here."

Goldenrod let that sink in among the ones who hadn't realized the purpose of the meeting. She'd kept it quiet to avoid attracting curiosity seekers or hecklers.

"Think of us as the Council of Mages. We're the first people with these abilities. We won't be the last. We need to help each other learn to use them. Learn the strengths, the costs, how to protect each other, how to help those without magic.

"We'll need to talk through them. Brainstorm. Do experiments. Find a way to make the most of our magic.

"Because, let's face it, if we're going to survive here we need all the help we can get."

Goldenrod put on a grin at the last part. Her tension eased as more grins reflected back at her.

"This isn't official. Or mandatory. It's just a way for us to organize to help each other. If you don't want to be part of it that's fine. Do you want to form a council?"

Affirmatives in various forms came from everyone. Not a single no. Someone asked, "Where do we start?"

"With introductions. I'm Goldenrod."

Redinkle interjected, "Baroness Goldenrod."

"Hush. That's not important here. My power isn't well defined yet. I can say something. Sometimes it comes true. We've been experimenting to find the limits of it."

She looked to her left.

"I'm Lady Burnout, the Chiurgeon. I can make blood clot. Even internally. It's made me shy about touching anyone's chest or head."

The next was a teenage boy. He held up his hands a few inches apart. Sparks flashed between the fingertips. "Sparrow. I do things with electricity. Recharge a battery. Or shock a grown man hard enough to fall down."

Several people stirred at that.

"Yes, I'll charge your gadget. If I have time. The Autocrat has me filling laptops and tablets for him already."

The next was older than Goldenrod. She said, "Marjoram. I can make birds change direction as they fly."

Goldenrod watched the reactions as the introductions continued. Some were taking comfort in not being alone. More judging each other on the usefulness of their powers. A desire to toss out suggestions for their use, shushed to not interrupt the introductions.

Many used their powers regularly. At the other end was: "I'm Aster. I flew into the air to escape the orcs in camp."

She flushed and ducked her head.

"Did you do it again?" someone asked.

"No." Her voice dropped. "I'm afraid of heights."

Most people were polite enough to stifle their reactions. Only one laughed out loud, and that was cut short by an elbow in the ribs.

"Helping each other with that sort of issue is exactly what we're here for," said Goldenrod.

***

Newman had meant "Sounds like a guy I knew who kept freezing on the rappelling tower" as casual conversation. Instead it turned him into the chief of Aster's training. Pointing out he wasn't a mage won Goldenrod's assurance that as a "mage in law" he could participate in Council business.

He hadn't expected this consequence of marriage.

"Here's the tree," Newman said to the group. It was the most climbable tree he'd seen within miles of the camp. The trunk was knobbed with handholds and tilted back and forth, no part of it vertical. Branches sturdy enough to hold an armored knight poked out every few yards. He'd be willing to climb it with one hand tied behind his back. Both hands, if he had a safety line.

"Okay," answered Aster. She'd brought three friends for moral support, none mages. Goldenrod and Redinkle represented the Council.

"The formal term for this is desensitization therapy. The idea is to expose you to a little of what you're scared of until you're used to it, then a little more, and so on. If you had a fear of snakes we'd show you a picture of one, then show you one in a sealed tank, then be in a room with one.

"To help you with heights I'm asking you to climb up the tree, just as far as you're comfortable with. We'll have a safety line on you so you can't fall. Going up and down a few times will give you a chance to get used to it."

Aster managed another, "Okay."

Newman gave her an encouraging smile. She hadn't volunteered to do dangerous stuff. This was much more out of her comfort zone than that acrophobic soldier had been.

There was a fork in the tree trunk thirty-some feet up. Newman scampered up and fed the rope through it. As each end hit the ground one of Aster's friends took hold to keep it from pulling through.

Back on the ground Newman tied one end of the rope into a harness around Aster. Fortunately she wasn't one of the women who'd only brought dresses to the event.

"Right. Now I need to test this to make sure it can hold your weight."

Aster nodded.

Newman grabbed the rope hanging from the harness and lifted his hands over his head. She squeaked and lifted onto tip toes.

"That's good. Rest for a bit while I get the anchor set up."

Newman picked the heaviest of her three friends to tie the harness on to. The other two were to hold the rope and make sure they were gentle in taking up or releasing slack.

"Remember. Don't pull. She needs to go up on her own. You can help her go back down, you can save her if she slips, but never pull her higher."

When Aster took position at the base of the tree the anchor team took up the slack.

"Sit down on the ground," Newman ordered her.

"Eep." Suspended by the rope, she fell against the tree trunk.

"See, the rope will hold you. Now climb. See how far you can go."

Aster grabbed hold of the trunk with both hands. Her right foot found a spot to brace on. Then she paused. She looked down spotting a foothold, but needed to gather willpower before lifting the foot off the ground.

Watching Aster move made Newman realize how freely he could climb. He'd balance on one foot while reaching for a handhold, the other hand and foot waving in the air as counterweights.

She would only move one hand or foot at a time, the other three anchored to the tree. Then he realized she kept her torso pressed against the trunk as she shifted hold, firmly enough to be another grip. That slowed her progress even more. Each time she found a new hold she held on with all four as she slid her torso up the trunk.

He composed himself for a long wait. Monitoring the anchor team as they shuffled back to take up slack from Aster's movement kept him from being bored.

"That's it. This is as far up as I can go," said Aster.

Both her feet were even with his shoulder. Newman suppressed a sigh. "Good work. Grab the rope with one hand."

It would easier for him to just reach up and grab her off the tree. But training her to trust the rope was a key objective of this exercise.

"Now bend your knees to put your weight on the rope."

This was the act of faith. If she wouldn't let go of the tree the exercise was futile.

Still with both feet and a hand on the tree, she moved her body down enough to take up the slack.

"Good. Now both hands on the rope."

When Aster was properly braced Newman signaled the anchor team. They shuffled forward, lowering her down until she stood on the ground. Redinkle met her with a mug of water. Aster chugged it down, pausing halfway for a gasping breath.

Newman studied her. Face flushed, breathing rapid, jittering as she stood. Clearly she'd hit full panic at the top of the climb. But she hadn't lost control.

"How do you feel?" he asked.

"Tired," said Aster. "Let me catch my breath and I'll go up again."

The second ascent went two feet higher. The third was faster, not because she was moving any faster but because she remembered where more of the hand and foot holds were. The fourth gained another three feet in altitude.

As Aster drank Goldenrod took Newman aside. "Is this going to work? She's holding on to the tree so tight her fingers are bleeding."

"I think it's going well. She's stretching her limits. Making good progress. My worry is her arms giving out. It's a lot of work for someone with her build."

They went back to the climbing tree.

Climb five brought Aster to a new bend in the tree. Newman would have rotated around to be on top of the trunk. Aster stayed on the side she'd reached it from. That left her traversing diagonally along the trunk.

Her left foot had to brace against the underside to hold her weight. That worked for a few steps. Then a bit of bark peeled off the wood. Aster's foot shot into open air.

Her hands clutched at the trunk but were too tired to hold her whole weight after so many ascents. She fell, screaming.

Newman opened his mouth to tell the anchor team to draw up the slack and hold her.

Then he closed his mouth.

Aster clung to a branch, well away from the trunk.

Newman looked up and down the tree. The branch was at least ten feet above where she'd slipped off the trunk.

He'd seen her dart to the branch through the air. As pure an example of magic as Redinkle starting a fire or Goldenrod slaying orcs.

"Help. I'm stuck," said Aster. She was on the underside of the branch, her arms and legs wrapped around it.

"Help," she repeated, a little higher pitched this time.

Newman called, "I'm coming up to get you." He scooted up the trunk.

Aster's branch was thinner than the ones lower down. It visibly bent under her weight. There was no danger of it breaking for now but Newman didn't want to risk putting his weight on it as well.

They were thirty feet off the ground. She was a dozen feet out on the branch, head toward the trunk. The anchor crew had taken up the slack in the rope. Still, if she let go of the branch the rope would swing her toward the trunk. She might hit her head. Would her magic work if she was knocked unconscious?

The good news was the branch was straight, no laterals sticking out to get in her way. "Okay, you can shimmy along the branch to the trunk. Then I can hold you and help you come down."

"I can't move."

"Just move one arm a few inches, then the other. It's like climbing the trunk."

"I can't! Get me down!"

Minutes went by. She wouldn't move. He couldn't go out there without breaking the branch.

"Get me down!" she demanded.

Well, getting her down he could do.

Newman carried his multitool even though it didn't see nearly as much use as his knife these days. The saw blade was still sharp. He unfolded it.

Aster noticed the vibration in the branch right away. "What are you doing?"

Newman didn't answer.

"Stop that!"

He kept sawing.

"Don't you dare!"

He was less than halfway through the branch when it snapped. Aster screamed. Newman braced to catch her as the safety line swung her against the trunk.

Instead the end of the broken branch smacked him on the head. He lost a foothold and slid down the trunk. The multitool spun into the air as he hooked his arm around the stump of the branch.

"You asshole!" The branch hit Newman's shoulder.

He pulled his other arm over his head to protect it from Aster's blows.

"Bastard!" That swing landed on his triceps, which would bruise but have no serious damage.

The curses and blows continued. He found a foothold he could brace both feet on. Newman felt secure enough to look out at her.

Aster hung in mid-air, holding the branch with both hands as she flailed at him. The safety line was slack, hanging down to her knees before rising up to the fork in the trunk.

A blow to Newman's ribs stung. Fortunately for him she didn't have the leverage to do any real damage. A broken bone would make for a rough climb down.

She paused for breath.

Newman lifted his head. "I'm sorry."

"Like hell you are. You did that on purpose."

Aster dropped the branch. Goldenrod and Redinkle dashed out of the way before it hit the ground. She floated in the air vertically. Then she drifted down. "More slack!" she called to the anchor team.

Newman watched her descend. It was very graceful until she put her feet on the ground, lost her balance, and fell flat on her face. She brushed dirt and leaves off as she stood.

Then Aster rose into the air again. She floated straight to where Newman was hanging on the tree.

"Fine. It worked. You were right. But you're still an asshole."

The reply that sprang to mind was, *It's my job to be an asshole.* But this wasn't the Army, he wasn't a sergeant, and he didn't have any authority to do things like that. Plus she might be able to carry him up half a mile and let go, so he just nodded.

She landed again, managing an intentional-looking hands and knees this time. "Would somebody get this damn rope off me?"

Her friends gathered round and tugged at the knots. Newman watched quietly until one drew a knife.

"Don't cut that! It's the longest rope we have." He scrambled down the tree less gracefully than he'd gone up. The new bruises made themselves felt.

Aster glared at him the whole time but didn't object to his hands undoing the knots of her harness. When he had it off her he undid the anchorman's.

She led her friends off without a farewell. Goldenrod and Redinkle joined Newman once the rest were out of earshot.

"I totally agree with what Aster said," said his wife. "I can't believe you did that."

"It wasn't the plan," said Newman defensively. "If she'd just gone up and down the trunk she'd've been fine. But once she flew into that situation she had to get out by flying."

Redinkle shook her head. "It's not my place to say bad things about my best friend's husband. Which is saving you from being called an asshole again."

***

"Your Majesty wished to see me?" Autocrat Sharpquill looked around as he entered King Ironhelm's pavilion. The two of them were alone.

"I did." The king's grip was tight on a pewter tankard but he didn't take a drink. "I thought I was serving the remainder of Estoc's reign. When I mentioned that to someone at practice, he informed me that Estoc's reign expired before he did. Why haven't we had a tourney to select my successor?"

"Ah. This again."

"Again?"

"I had a similar conversation with your predecessor." Sharpquill pointed at a canvas folding chair. "May I?"

King Ironhelm considered keeping the Autocrat standing, then relented with a nod.

"Thank you. Bluntly, Your Majesty, I don't think we could survive a crown tourney. We're too close to the edge. The man-hours it would take would put us back at least two months.

The king scoffed. "It's one day."

"You've kept your sword-fighting skills in practice. So have some other peers and their squires. Every other contender would need at least a couple of weeks to bring their skills up to par. Consorts will cheer them on, gear will be repaired, and the injured will need time to recover. Many of them will be our most productive workers. We can't afford it."

"How many contenders are you expecting?"

Sharpquill's voice rose. "Everybody! Everybody who can swing a sword. It's not a ceremonial position. It's life and death. The right to replace me, replace Lady Justice, order people exiled or flogged. Everyone who wants power, or has a buddy who wants my job, or wants to keep somebody else from winning will enter."

"Thinking on the gossip around here," said King Ironhelm, "the last group might be the biggest. I see the problem. But we still need to have turnover. It's what keeps kings from abusing that unlimited power we give them. If I'm tempted to do something stupid, I know the next king will undo it a few months later. That lets people not worry so much about my power."

Sharpquill nodded. "I agree. We need turnover. When we can do it without starving."

The king flung up his hands in exasperation. "If we can afford to give everyone a day off a week we can afford the tourney."

"We can't afford it. I declared a day of rest because people were collapsing from exhaustion."

Ironhelm stood up, eyes locked on his vassal. He took a deep breath, went around his chair, and rested his hands on its carved wooden back. "Can't afford how?" he said with perfect calm.

"If you'll pardon the expression, winter is coming. We don't know when. At our current rate of building up a food reserve, we'll need fourteen months to have a three month reserve. If we get that much time, fine. If not . . ." Sharpquill shrugged.

The king's fingertip traced a carving. "Your weekly status reports were more optimistic."

"I've been keeping it secret to preserve morale."

"And secret from me because?"

"Your Majesty, your mood always affects public morale."

Ironhelm lunged around the chair with the speed which won four crown tourneys. His face contorted in rage as he stopped inches from Sharpquill. "I played Othello and Richard the Third in front of a thousand people! I can keep a fucking poker face."

Sharpquill recoiled, his chair tipping back until it hit a table. An empty goblet fell over and rolled off.

The king replaced the angry expression with a calm one as if changing a tunic. He dropped into his chair as relaxed as a sleepy cat. He waited until Sharpquill finished righting himself before speaking.

"Your next status briefing will be complete. We will discuss who will attend. We will hold it some place safe from eavesdropping."

"Y-yes, Your Majesty."

"Good." The cat was now alert, not sleepy. "If I understand you correctly, when we have enough of a food stockpile, we may safely hold a tourney?"

"Yes, Your Majesty," said the Autocrat.

"Calculate how much is enough. We'll mention it to people, let that number go through the grapevine. At court we will announce the size of the current stockpile. If people can't count down days to the end of my reign, they can count up pounds."

***

Rivet could levitate rocks. Only rocks. Not sticks, coins, tools, clothes, food, or clumps of dirt. Size didn't matter. Pebbles, gravel, stones, boulders all moved through the air. A multi-ton crag shifted under his will but he was too scared to actually lift it until he had better control.

Tying anything to the rock kept it from moving. So did wrapping it. Dropping something onto a floating rock produced a spin that flung off the intruder. Sticking something to it made the rock fall.

For the next set of experiments Goldenrod was working with Rivet on control. They were in the meeting clearing, home of several boulders conveniently sized for sitting on.

She produced an egg and sat it on one. "This is a raw egg. I want you to hover a rock over it just close enough to crack it without squishing it."

"Ooh," said Rivet.

"You can do it," said Marjoram. Half a dozen mages were present, supporting the effort or getting ideas for their own experiments.

Another rock, about twice the size of Rivet's head, lifted into the air. It moved over the egg. Then it moved down in short jerks, a few inches lower each time. Then a "clack" sounded as the stones touched. Yolk squirted between two mages, who flinched and giggled.

"That's why I brought more than one egg," said Goldenrod. "This sort of thing takes practice."

She shoved the smaller rock off and put a new egg in place. Aster had brought her five. She hoped that would be enough to make some progress.

The second attempt had a smoother descent but ended in about the same way.

"The yolk only went half the distance this time," said Marjoram. "That's progress."

Goldenrod replaced the egg.

Next try Rivet put the stones close together, hovering close enough they couldn't see the egg. When he moved the floating one away Goldenrod checked the egg. "No cracks. I don't think they touched."

"God damn it," swore Rivet.

Goldenrod said, "There should be errors in both directions. That way you know you're centered on the target."

Rivet made a growling sound as the stone lifted up again. The movements were jerkier this time. The stone overshot the grounded boulder and had to move back to be over the egg.

As it got closer to the egg the rock bounced up and down.

"Behave, you piece of shit," snarled Rivet. His face was flushed with effort.

Cracks appeared on the floating rock. Goldenrod opened her mouth to tell him to drop it.

Then the rock shattered.

Shards of quartz flew across the clearing. Goldenrod felt a sting as one cut her arm. Everyone was screaming.

"Calm down! Who's hurt worst?" she demanded.

The volume decreased as the mages recovered from the shock. Rivet was still screaming, lying on his back and thrashing. Goldenrod crawled over to him, looking for wounds.

A shard of quartz was embedded in his right eye socket. She grabbed his arms to keep him from dislodging it. He kept screaming in her ear. "Help! Rivet's hurt bad!"

Another mage grabbed Rivet's shoulders to hold him still. Blood was pouring down the helper's face but he wasn't bothered by it.

"Marjoram was stabbed in the chest!" someone yelled.

"I'm not dead, damn it, stop screeching," she retorted.

Rivet went limp. Goldenrod felt relief, then guilt as she realized what a bad sign passing out had to be.

"We need to get Rivet to the Chiurgeon," said Goldenrod. "Right away."

Two mages started bickering over how to make a stretcher.

"Dammit, we can carry him. You and you, grab his legs."

Four of them managed to lift Rivet off the ground. After some fumbling for better grips they began to walk.

Before they reached the edge of the clearing some hunters burst out of the woods. The lead two swept their nocked arrows over the clearing, looking for targets.

"No orcs!" cried Goldenrod. "It was an accident. We need help with the wounded."

Deadeye relaxed his bowstring. "You're wounded, my lady."

"We need get Rivet to camp."

The sight of the shard sticking out of the mage's face drew a low whistle from Deadeye. He turned to his hunting party. "Leadsmith, toss that venison over a branch. We need the travois for the boy."

Marjoram's wound caught his eye. "We'll need to make a second one for her."

"I can walk," she said. "It's not as bad as it looks."

"You're about a minute from going into shock," said Deadeye.

Leadsmith insisted on converting the travois into a stretcher. "Too many jolts could drive that wedge into his brain."

As they neared the camp they encountered fighters returning from patrol who took over the stretcher. Deadeye kept carrying Marjoram over her protests.

The side of the chiurgeon tent was up to provide ventilation on a warm afternoon. Lady Burnout was reading on a tablet, being high on the list of people Sparrow provided charging for. The tablet flipped into the dirt as she saw the wounded approaching.

"Orcs?"

"Exploding rock," answered Goldenrod.

"How the hell did that happen?" Burnout stepped up to her examining table as the stretcher bearers set Rivet down on it.

"Magic gone wrong."

"Okay." She raised her voice. "If you're not bleeding, put pressure on someone who is."

Her hands went around the ruined eye socket. Magic let her sense the bleeding even where she couldn't see. No time to worry about causing strokes now. She coagulated blood around the shard, working from inside the skull out.

When he was stable she ordered the stretcher bearers to roll Rivet onto his side. The shard was small enough she could only grip it with one hand. Gentle wiggling broke it loose from the socket. She pulled it straight out. A gush of blood followed, flowing over Rivet's nose. A bit more magic stopped the bleeding where the shard had torn scabs loose.

"Okay, put him on his back." The bearers complied.

Elderberry, Burnout's apprentice chiurgeon, arrived. Burnout greeted her with, "Treat him for shock," then turned to the rest. "Who's next?"

"She is." Deadeye stepped forward, Marjoram in his arms.

She'd recovered consciousness. "Put me down. I can stand."

"No."

Burnout pointed at her chair. "Put her there."

This shard hadn't done nearly as much damage as Rivet's. The chiurgeon wrapped her fingers around the wound. "Didn't reach the ribs. The muscle should heal. You'll lose some milk production, if and when."

Marjoram chuckled bitterly. "No more wearing bikinis for me."

"Oh, don't let that stop you. If we make it back to Earth you'll be amazed how many guys think 'That's a cute scar' is a good pick-up line."

***

"Lady Yarrow?" Goldenrod addressed the oldest of the women in the tent, hoping she was the head of the Green Stag household.

"Who wants to know?" The woman's hands had the ground-in dirt of someone digging up wild vineroot for a living. Not a crafter, or at least not practicing one useful for survival.

"I'm Baroness Goldenrod."

"What do you want with us?"

"Was Belladonna living here?"

"She paid for her food and her share of the floor for the weekend, and gathered food while she lived. Never bothered anyone in the household. I'll not listen to complaints about her, true or false."

Goldenrod was not used to this kind of hostile reception. Disdain from nobles, yes. But ordinary members of the Kingdom thought of her as the lady who found food. They were grateful.

"Belladonna used magic. I want to examine her personal gear for any evidence of how she did it."

"What gives you the right to search her stuff?"

Now she was getting angry. "I'm head of the Council of Mages. We're researching how magic works in this world."

Goldenrod stopped before saying more. She wondered how much it would hurt to say, 'You are a frog.'

Either the title or the thoughts of frogs got through to Yarrow. She led Goldenrod to a pile of bags in a corner. She pulled a couple aside. "That's everything Belladonna had."

Goldenrod sorted through it. No bedroll. Hardly any clothes. Well, those would find new owners easily. The candles, altar cloths, and other paraphernalia for the neo-pagan ceremonies were complete. *I guess no one had the nerve to steal that.* A ritual blade, possibly made of real silver.

Unwrapping the altar cloths revealed a notebook. The pages were three quarters filled with diagrams and cryptic text. In the middle was a piece of thin leather.

Goldenrod took the leather out. It was scraped smooth on both sides and densely marked with symbols burned with a thin implement. The symbols were rune-like but didn't look like any she'd seen before.

Yarrow and her tentmates had started a game of spades.

Goldenrod stood by the table for a moment waiting to be noticed but none of them looked up from the game. Finally she interrupted. "Do any of you know what this is?"

They glanced at the leather rectangle then went back to their cards. "Never seen it before in my life," said Yarrow.

She gave up. "Thank you for your help." Goldenrod picked up the blade and notebook and went home.

Mistress Tightseam had no insight on the writing. "See how it curls more easily to this side? It's a scroll. I bet this dent is where a cord was tied to hold it closed."

"Okay, I can buy it's a scroll. But what's it for?"

"Dunno. Try Lord Parchment. He's fond of ancient alphabets."

Calligraphy not being in demand, Parchment was gutting fish when Goldenrod found him. He cheerfully washed his hands of it to help her.

Once outside the common pavilion she handed him the leather scroll and explained how she'd found it.

Parchment traced every line on both sides before looking back to Goldenrod. "I hate to say this, but I think it's just a movie prop."

"What?"

"It's certainly not any writing I've seen before. No resemblance to Ogham or Futhark. There's only a dozen different symbols in the text. I'm not counting these diagrams. There's single strokes vertical, horizontal, and left and right diagonals. Then two stroke combinations, plus and X. triangles in four different orientations. Square. And diamond. That's twelve characters in the alphabet. The only human alphabets so small were created by missionaries for illiterate cultures.

"No, I think someone made this up to be handed from one actor to another in some sword and sorcery flick. Then it was given away or auctioned off and Belladonna wound up with it."

"What would she want it for?"

"As a prop. The lass had a gift for showmanship, whatever else she . . . well, *de mortuis nil nisi bonum.*"

"Oh."

And she'd been thinking this was a clue to how they'd all wound up in this Godsforsaken place.

"I'm sorry, my dear. Show it around. Someone might recognize it. I certainly don't know everything."

"Thank you."

Goldenrod took his advice. But after a half dozen archaeology and movie buffs disclaimed any knowledge she gave up. She'd try Belladonna's notebook next.

***

Belladonna's notebook wasn't encrypted. But Goldenrod had to use some basic decryption techniques to figure out her handwriting. Once she had the vowels the rest came easily.

The first half was the routine notes of a church leader. Contact numbers for reserving sites. Teaching plans for students. Brainstorming for rituals, followed by step by step scripts.

Less routine were records of completed rituals. Prayers sent, deities contacted, and sometimes messages received from the divinities. Some from specific deities addressed. Some were annotated as "name and pantheon unknown."

The leather scroll's arrival had an entry to itself.

I found a leather thing in my booga box. It's covered with some kind of code. I don't know how it got there. Someone could of dropped it in when we were packing up from Imbolc. But that was two weeks ago. I think I would have noticed it

sooner. I can't see someone breaking into my apartment to leave a mysterious object.
Unless . . . he was trying to convince me it had appeared by magic. Which is exactly
the kind of stunt some of those jackasses in the Sept would try to pull. So I'm not
going to tell anyone about it. Let them wonder if I found it or just threw it away.

Belladonna had been curious about the scroll. She'd transcribed the
whole thing into her notebook. She did a frequency analysis of the
different symbols (simpler were more common). The diagrams were
analyzed from multiple aspects, starting with the hypothesis that they
were intended as descriptions of a ritual.

The dates on the scroll-related entries grew farther apart as she
failed to crack the puzzle. Regular business and planning for a Beltaine
event filled the pages again.

Then she fell asleep holding the scroll.

Oddest dream last night. Felt astral, but not in the way when I try to contact a
god in dreams. Not prophetic. Mystical, yes. I heard a voice speaking to me in a
language I didn't recognize. Musical speech, almost as if he was singing to me. He
wanted something. Badly. He heard me answering him. I could almost perceive a
figure. It was fuzzy, like there was thick smoke between me and him. I woke up
holding that leather thingie. I'd been brooding on it. Guess I fell asleep.

Then there was a page of notes on some of the words she'd heard
in the dream, annotated as rising or falling in pitch.

Six pages after that were all devoted to the upcoming Beltaine
ritual. No reference to the scroll. Goldenrod looked from the sketch of
the ritual to the unrolled scroll lying next to her. It was not identical to
one of the scroll's diagrams, but close enough to give her a chill.

Goldenrod tucked the scroll into the notebook to mark her place.
Then she shelved it with the cooking gear. It was getting late. She
didn't want that near her when she fell asleep.

***

Peers had the right to demand a private audience with the King.
When two dukes, two master organizers, and a master crafter requested
an audience with King Ironhelm and Autocrat Sharpquill they made
time. The Autocrat's pavilion was chosen as the location for privacy.

Both dukes were also knights, so all the councils of peers would be represented in this meeting.

Duke Mace was the spokesman. When the pleasantries were over he knelt before King Ironhelm and offered a scroll. "Your Majesty, I present a petition signed by twenty-three peers begging you to disband the unchartered entity called the Council of Mages. We further beg you to order that no magic shall be performed but by the order of the Crown."

"Please rise. We shall read and consider your petition." King Ironhelm took the scroll, read through the list of names and passed it to Master Sharpquill.

The Autocrat read through it more slowly and nodded to his liege.

The king asked, "What moves you to make this petition?"

"Your Majesty, the Peers we represent are greatly concerned by the actions of these self-called mages. When it was just a few people practicing little tricks there was no reason for us to be concerned. Now . . ."

Duke Mace stepped back, took a deep breath, and began the rant. "Now we have someone who can kill with a word. A secret group meeting in the woods where no one can see them. One smashed a rock so hard a dozen were wounded and his eye was gouged out. When someone wasn't willing to use her magic as the Council directed, they chased her up a tree, sawed off the branch she clung to, and let her fall."

He looked at king and autocrat to be sure he had their attention. "And now these mages have used the fear of their magic to begin stealing from those without it. Baroness Goldenrod invaded the House of the Green Stag and took several items. She claimed her magery gave her the right to do so. We pray Your Majesty will take proper action to end these abuses."

The duke bowed and took his seat.

"These are serious charges," said King Ironhelm. "I swear by my crown that I shall not allow the gifted to abuse those without gifts, magical or otherwise. There shall be a full investigation and all appropriate action taken."

The delegation all offered thanks for the king's time and attention. After more elaborate courtesies they left.

King Ironhelm waited to make sure they were clear of the tent then looked at Sharpquill. "Talk."

"I don't know. Well, I know a few things. First from what Mistress Tightseam told me Goldenrod's magic is so flakey she might not be able to kill anything but an orc. She tried to kill a squirrel as a test and couldn't.

"The Council did get a guy's eye ruined. Lady Burnout reported it as an accident. I think I would have heard about the tree thing if it happened.

"Third, the theft. I have a hard time believing it of Goldenrod. And a hard time thinking the victim wouldn't come to me or Duchess Roseblossom. Theft is always a crime."

King Ironhelm began to say something but Sharpquill was still talking.

"Fourth, this list is a bit less than half of the Peers who came with us but they produce eighty percent of the complaints I deal with."

Sharpquill pointed at names on the list. "'The privy by the royal pavilion isn't cleaned often enough.' 'Peers should have more variety in their food ration.' 'Why does my squire have to work shit hauling duty?' And so on. I'm tempted to blow off the petition in hopes they'll be so mad they'll march off and form a new camp where I won't have to deal with them."

The king was laughing. "Okay, I feel for you. They're a pain in my butt too. Queen Camellia's biggest fans."

"But you want to do the investigation."

"It doesn't matter if they're assholes if they're right. Theft is wrong. Abuse is wrong. Find out what's going on. If there's a crime take it to Lady Justice."

"As Your Majesty wishes."

***

"For today's flight I'm going for altitude," said Aster. She'd gone flying at least once a day in the week since the tree climbing exercise, usually just around the camp or down to the river. Goldenrod had started hinting that it would be good to stretch herself.

Her fellow mages cheered, Goldenrod loudest among them.

Aster focused. She rose into the air. In seconds she'd cleared the trees. She looked up, straight to the zenith, and kept going.

A glance down showed the camp as a spot on the bluff over the river valley. The river stretched far below her. She could see where it ran through a cleft in the mountains. A thrill of fear ran through her belly but Aster set it aside.

She looked up. Time to go higher.

It was a cloudless day. She could only gauge her height by the width of land below her. From here the mountains had a bit of curve to them.

Aster went higher.

There was movement in the corner of her eye. She turned to look.

The monstrous shape flung its wings wide to brake, like a hawk stooping on a mouse.

Before she could even think to evade a taloned foot wrapped around her torso. Aster grabbed a talon with both hands and yanked. No give at all.

A yellow eye, slit pupiled like a cat's, stared at her from a black head. Smoke trailed from the nostrils, eddying as the wings flapped to hold them in a hover.

It stank of sulfurous coal and rotting rhino flesh.

The dragon twisted its foot to look at Aster from different angles. The eye stared. Then blinked.

It flung Aster away. As she tumbled through the air she saw it flying off, so fast it was smaller each time she caught a glimpse.

Oh God I peed myself was the first thought Aster formed as she tried to pull her mind together. The ground was growing closer. She'd lost sight of the camp.

Focus, damn it. Three deep breaths. Then concentrating on flying.

It worked. Partially. She flew still tumbling, so she accelerated down and sideways as much as up. Which disoriented her enough to lose focus and fall again.

She could make out trees now.

Three breaths. Focus. And she was flying. Diving, pulling out of the dive, flying level. About a hundred feet up.

Aster spotted a gap between two trees. She dipped into it, went around the branches to the larger one's trunk. Knees bent as her feet planted hard on the ground.

Then she wrapped her arms around the solid, unmoving tree trunk and held on for a long time. *Why the hell didn't it eat me?* she wondered. Theories chased each other through her mind. Smelled bad, not enough meat, it was full after catching a rhino . . . none of which made any more sense than the others.

Thirst made her let go. She hadn't carried any water. She'd planned to be back at the meeting clearing in minutes. Hopefully she could find some water on the way home.

Which raised the question of how to get home. Well, she was on the far side of the river. Once she found that the camp would be easy. The afternoon sun was over there, so . . . she turned and started walking.

The woods should be safe. There'd been hardly any orc sightings since the big battle, and none in the past two weeks. As if they'd all fled the region. Fine with her.

After an hour of walking she still hadn't seen any orcs. She kept going.

Aster cursed. She was tired, thirsty, and the sun was going down. Walking was too slow. She'd have to fly.

Flying under the trees only worked at walking speed. If she wanted to move fast, and she did, going low would mean scraping her shoulder on tree trunks.

Rising above the trees she turned around slowly, scanning the horizon for anything in the air. Then a second scan for anything high up. No dragons.

She flew toward the river, staying just over the treetops. She accepted the occasional leaf in her face as proof she was staying low enough.

A stream gave her a chance to drink. She hoped it was clean water but by now she was so thirsty she'd accept sitting in a privy for two days as the price of water.

The forest went right to the edge of the river bluff. No sign of camp. She made her best guess and turned downstream. She kept to the edge of the bluff, where she could only be seen from one side.

Two minutes later she saw Goldenrod's weir. Almost home.

At House Applesmile the mood at the dinner table was grim. Rivet's injury was horrible, but losing Aster to a dragon made them feel all their efforts were doomed to fail. One mage crippled, another dead, and Goldenrod couldn't even cast any spells reliably.

Redinkle looked up from the table. A gap between tents gave a view of the river valley. "Look! Is that Aster?"

Goldenrod led the charge to the bluff edge. Aster landed, visibly exhausted, and was swept up in a hug.

"I thought we'd lost you!" cried Goldenrod.

"We thought you were dead!" Redinkle seized the next hug.

"No, the dragon just looked me over then threw me away," said Aster.

Pinecone whispered to Newman, "Good thing she's too skinny to be worth eating."

"Shut up," he shot back.

Aster spotted the men. "You!" She poked Newman in the chest. "How do you cure fear of dragons, asshole?"

He had the sense to not say anything.

***

Autocrat Sharpquill found Goldenrod weeding her vineroot patch. Redinkle was with her, passing along the gossip from the latest stitch and bitch. They were heads down in the plants and didn't notice him.

At the edge of the cultivated area he said, "Good morning, Your Excellency, milady."

They looked at him in mild surprise. "Good morning, my lord," they said together.

"I was hoping for a moment of the baroness's time."

"Of course," said Goldenrod.

Redinkle looked uncertainly from one to the other. The Autocrat jerked a thumb toward the bluff. Goldenrod nodded. Redinkle said, "Good day," and walked briskly off.

Goldenrod asked, "How can I help you, my lord Autocrat?"

She did not want to deal with him right now. She was in her worst dress, skirts hitched up, and her hands muddy to the wrists from checking the growth of the roots. She'd already been due for a bath. Having one would be her reward for finishing the gardening. If the Autocrat didn't screw up her day.

He sat cross-legged on a patch of grass. "There are some unpleasant rumors circulating about you and your council of mages."

Goldenrod grimaced. "We've been experimenting to learn the extent of our powers. Sometimes it goes badly."

"Hence the boy with the eyepatch?"

"I tried to get him to back off. Well, no. I didn't try. I just said a few feeble words. If I'd told him time out he would have stopped. Then we would have avoided him smashing the rock."

"Are any of the experiments successful?"

"Sure. Marjoram figured out which edible species her powers worked on so she's catching three or four waterfowl a day. Aster can fly reliably now. Sparrow can charge gadgets, light fires, and do tiny arc welds."

"I'm glad to hear it. Did someone get forced up a tree?"

"She wasn't forced. Aster wanted to overcome her acrophobia. We set up a safety line and she practiced climbing a tree to get more comfortable with heights."

"Did it work?"

"Um. More or less. She was climbing higher and higher on each attempt. Then she slipped and flew in panic. That put her higher in the tree and stuck out on a branch."

"Did you really cut off the branch?"

"That was Newman's idea. When he realized she was stuck and he couldn't get to her he just sawed it off. Dick move. It was still safe, she had the safety line. But he didn't give her a chance to get unstuck."

"Was she hurt?"

"No, Newman was. She started flying and beat him with the branch. He admits he totally had it coming. That got her to where she could fly on purpose. She had a close encounter with a dragon yesterday. I don't know if she's still up for it."

Master Sharpquill put the dragon aside for another time. "That may be very useful. I heard you visited the Green Stag."

"Oh, yes. I'm still working on that stuff. I meant to bring it to you when I'm done. Belladonna wrote up notes on how she cast the spell to bring us here. If we study it, do some brainstorming, and find someone with the right magic, we might be able to reverse it to go home."

"Really?" He leaned back, propping himself up with his arms. He hadn't let himself think of going home. Hadn't thought of home at all since Mistress Cinnamon had taken charge of him. To hear Goldenrod speak of it so casually staggered him.

"I don't know. But if we can go one way the other should be possible. And it was just sitting there. We should have investigated it from the beginning instead of just making it an open secret that all this is her fault and ostracizing her."

"Well, yes." Sharpquill tried to make his mind function again.

Goldenrod began to elaborate on Belladonna's notebook, the strange scroll, and her discoveries in them. The jargon blurred together for him. Sharpquill nodded in appropriate places.

At last he remembered why he'd come there. "You took the notebook from the Green Stag?"

"Yeah. I went through Belladonna's gear to find the magical stuff."

"You're being accused of theft."

Goldenrod's jaw dropped. "Theft? But I talked with Lady Yarrow. She was right there. She didn't object at all. She started a card game."

"Did you claim authority as a mage?"

"She asked why I wanted it so I said I was head of the council."

Autocrat Sharpquill frowned. "That's not a Royal council. It doesn't have any authority."

"I know. But it's not like Yarrow had any right to the stuff. Just because Belladonna was living in her tent doesn't make her Belladonna's heir."

"No, it would revert to the Crown. That's a very good point. Could be useful."

"So there's no theft. She saw I was taking them and didn't object."

"Part of the accusation is that you intimidated her."

"How? I didn't even touch her."

The Autocrat sighed. "Goldenrod, you can kill with a word. Talking to someone is threatening."

"But-but-" She couldn't form a coherent reply.

"This is going to wind up in front of Duchess Roseblossom whether there was a crime or not. You've given your enemies an opening and they're going to take it."

"Enemies? Why would I have enemies?"

"Christ give me strength." Sharpquill paused to gather his thoughts. "Did you know Duke Stonefist was a lawyer in mundane life?"

She blinked in surprise at the change of topic. "No. Doesn't surprise me. I knew he was a master armorer and a knight."

"He's the kind of guy who will succeed wherever he is. Roseblossom too. We have a bunch of people like that. Then there's those who wound up in the top layer by luck or a specific skill. The Kingdom gives high rank for fighting, medieval art, and keeping the outfit running."

Master Sharpquill looked around. There were many people working on the flood plain. Weir-tenders carrying fish. Water haulers with bottles. Farther off shit haulers going downstream.

"And then there's those who lucked into a position that gave them rank, through relationships or a skill that they can't keep up any more. They cling to it hardest because they can't climb to the top again if they have to start over."

He paused. Goldenrod nodded to show she was following.

"Now we're in a situation where respect and power go to those fighting starvation and orcs. It looks like magic is going to be a source of power now. So what's that mean for our current upper class?"

Goldenrod hadn't realized there would be a quiz. "Um . . . they have to share their power?"

"Maybe. Maybe the whole system collapses and our medieval fantasy is swept away in an anarcho-primitivist revolt. Or, and I'm taking a guess here, some of the upper class will try to slap down the upstarts and lock their current power in place."

"I'm an upstart?"

"You, Newman, the hunters and gatherers, the mages. The weir brought you nominations in both—sorry, I can't talk about that. The point is you're a threat to some people's status and they're pushing back. That's why you're only a baroness."

"Oh."

The Autocrat stood up and brushed dirt from his pants. "Find someone who can advocate for you at the theft trial. Watch your mouth. Someone will take the worst interpretation of anything you say. Touch base with your friends. Pass the word to your fellow upstarts."

A one inch weed was growing by Goldenrod's foot. She grabbed it at the base and yanked. "Dammit, why now? Things were going so well."

"That's why. We're not on the ragged edge. We have the energy for politics now."

***

"Let those who have business before Lady Justice come forward!" called the herald.

Lady Justice—Duchess Roseblossom when not presiding over a trial—sat in a large wooden chair under the Court pavilion. Her seat was ten feet before the thrones of King Ironhelm and Queen Dahlia. During the trial she ruled. The monarchs only reigned.

More than half the populace was gathered before the pavilion. Possibly as much as three quarters. The prospect of the popular Baroness being punished for a common crime brought out those who usually avoided Court.

Duke Mace came forward with Lady Yarrow. Stonefist had drawn on old English Common Law tradition. Anyone could prosecute a crime if they cared to. Mace had volunteered.

Goldenrod had Mistress Tightseam as her advocate. Newman followed them up, carrying the notebook, scroll, and ritual dagger.

Duke Mace spoke before the judge could. "Your Majesty, the defendant's advocate is a long-time friend and colleague of the judge. Should we not have someone impartial?"

King Ironhelm didn't hesitate. "Your Grace, there are less than two hundred people in this world. Anyone who doesn't know you or them is so lacking in social skills I would have no trust in him as a judge."

Lady Justice eyed the duke as he bowed and thanked the king. She kept the stare on him until Duke Mace gave her a bow as well. Then she said, "Your Grace, state your complaint."

"Lady Justice, we shall prove that five days ago, Baroness Goldenrod entered the House of the Green Stag, intimidated the head of the house into giving way, and removed several rare, valuable, and irreplaceable objects."

"Thank you, Duke Mace. Mistress Tightseam, your response?"

Tightseam squeezed Goldenrod's arm as a reminder to stay silent. "Lady Justice, we shall prove that there were no threats or intimidating actions, that the objects in question were not the property of Green Stag, that other property belonging to the late Belladonna had been taken without complaint, and that those objects are of no value other than to one investigating the magic that brought us here."

"Bring forth the items in question."

Newman walked up to the low table in front of Lady Justice's chair. He put down the notebook open to one of the complex diagrams. The scroll went flat overlapping one corner of the notebook. The blade crossed over them both to hold them in place. Lady Justice pointed him to a seat with the spectators.

"Where are the late Belladonna's other possessions?" asked the judge.

Yarrow whispered to Duke Mace. He said, "In storage at the Green Stag, your honor."

"Constable, escort Lady Yarrow to fetch them," ordered the judge.

Royal Court proceedings would fill a lull with minor business or bring up a bard for a story or song. Extroverted monarchs had been known to entertain the populace themselves. Lady Justice let them wait in silence.

Constable returned carrying a bundle. He unrolled it onto the table, careful not to disturb Newman's arrangement. A dress, two pairs of panties, and a bra were visible among the religious items.

"Did Belladonna leave a will?" asked Lady Justice.

No one answered.

"That's a no, then. Without an heir her property reverted to the Crown. That's certainly not enough clothes for a young woman to have for a three day weekend. I also don't see a sleeping bag or bedroll. Lady Yarrow, where are they?"

"I don't know, your honor."

"Very well." Lady Justice waved to Duke Mace to begin his case.

He said, "Lady Yarrow, please describe the intimidation you faced."

"She barged into my tent and got in my face and said she was head of the council of mages. She kills people by talking! She could've done anything to me."

Mistress Tightseam asked, "Did Baroness Goldenrod at any time make a threat of violence? Or use magic in your presence?"

"No, but she said being head of the council gave her the right to go through Belladonna's stuff."

"Did she ask permission to take any of the items?" asked Duke Mace.

"No, not at all," answered Yarrow. "She waved that weird thing about then picked up the others and left."

"Did you tell her to stop?" asked Tightseam.

"No, I was afraid of her. She's a witch."

"Did you report a theft to the Constable?"

Yarrow looked uneasily at Mace before answering. "I didn't think anyone would care, her being a baroness and all. But when a Duke asked me about it I thought it was safe to say."

Tightseam turned to Goldenrod. "Did you sense any objection when you took them?"

"No. Nobody cared. I tried asking them about the leather scroll but they blew me off. So I left. I didn't hide what I was carrying."

"Could you show us the items you took and describe them?"

Goldenrod went to the table. She picked up the blade first. "This is the ritual dagger Belladonna used while casting the spell that brought us here. I was there. I saw her cast the spell, though I didn't realize that's what happened until later."

She placed it gently down. "This is Belladonna's notebook. It starts out as a diary, but then she describes the research and experimentation she did to create the spell."

She exchanged it for the scroll. "She began that work when she found this. Belladonna never knew where it came from. I think it came from the world we've arrived on."

The populace had kept quiet until now. Lady Justice had not tolerated chatter during previous trials. Now a buzz sprang up, cries of shock followed by speculation or explanations to those who hadn't heard.

"Silence!" said Lady Justice.

Silence fell.

Mistress Tightseam resumed her questions after receiving a nod from the judge. "What have you been doing with them?"

"Studying them," said Goldenrod. "If I can understand the spell completely I could reverse it to bring us home."

A glare from Lady Justice stifled the crowd's reaction.

Duke Mace stepped in front of Yarrow. "You formed your mage council to research that?"

"I formed the council to help each other. We have these gifts and don't know how they work. Someone has to help us."

There was a twinge in Goldenrod's belly. She would have noticed it if her stomach wasn't so knotted up over the trial.

Goldenrod finished, "So we help each other."

The duke turned to Lady Justice. "A mutual help group wouldn't be maiming its members or providing a pretext for pretended authority. The council of mages should be disbanded."

The judge said, "Mistress Tightseam, do you have anything to add?"

"No, your honor."

"Then I am ready to render my verdict. Lady Yarrow failed to return royal property to the Crown. She allowed royal property in her possession to be stolen. I sentence her to two weeks of privy cleaning duty. My lord Autocrat, please schedule it. Constable, make sure the work is done to your satisfaction."

Lady Justice waved Yarrow away, then turned to Goldenrod.

"Baroness Goldenrod misrepresented herself as having authority not granted by the Crown. As punishment, her right to first choice of the fishing weir's catch is revoked."

That reduced the flavor and variety of House Applesmile's meals.

"This trial is concluded."

"What about the council?" demanded Duke Mace.

"The Council of Mages is not a subject of this trial. This trial is concluded."

Mistress Tightseam took Goldenrod for a long walk in the woods to work off her nerves. When they were far out enough to feel private she said, "That was as good an outcome as we could have hoped for."

"I can't believe she found me guilty," snarled Goldenrod.

"You went over the line so you got a slap. You were slapped in a way that reminded everyone you're responsible for all this fish they're eating. And I'll wager if you go down to the weir and ask for a favor the weir crew will let you pick something."

"Hmph."

"The important part is Yarrow being punished. The next time Duke Mace asks some commoner to be his judas goat they won't be so eager to help. Or at least they'll demand a bigger bribe."

"You think Yarrow was bribed?"

"She's been hinting around about how she deserves a senior service award for taking care of the newbies and strays for a couple of years now. Mace could have gotten her that."

"Gods. I hate politics."

"Yeah. But it's interested in you, so you should take an interest in it."

***

The next week's mage council meeting was at sunset. Not meeting while people could be doing other work was one of the suggestions Goldenrod had received for reducing friction.

The commotion over the trial had brought out more mages. Tonight's newcomers were a pair of women, one middle-aged, one older.

"Our tradition is for all the current members to introduce themselves and then people who are here for the first time." Goldenrod gave her practiced pitch and nudged Marjoram on her left.

When the circle was complete eyes turned to the newcomers. The shorter one had streaks of grey in her hair. Her knitting didn't falter as she started talking. "I'm Countess Fennel. I play with string in all its variations."

She lowered her hands to her lap. The knitting needles hung in the air, moving back and forth to twist the yarn into fabric. "This trick is new. Came in very useful when I had a rheumatism flare."

Fennel glanced at her neighbor. This one wore a richly embroidered gown, complementing her long, curly brown hair and elegant looks.

The woman raised a hand. One finger traced words in the air. Glowing gold letters floated in the air in its wake. I'M MISTRESS CINNAMON. She was in the shade of a tree, letting the letters stand out even more.

Soft oohs came from around the circle.

"I haven't found a real use for it," said Mistress Cinnamon. "But it is pretty."

"Finding practical uses for our abilities is what this group is for," said Goldenrod.

Tonight's experiments focused on Plane, an apprentice carpenter who could freeze water. He couldn't freeze more than a handful but it could be in any shape.

After he made a star Goldenrod encouraged him to "try something detailed." Plane plunged his hands into the bucket of water. Minutes went by as the young man concentrated. Then he pulled his hands out and opened them.

Murmurs of appreciation went around the circle. They pressed closer for a better look. Balanced on the palm of his hand stood an icy horse. The detail was fine. The eyes and nostrils and strands of the mane were well defined, though viewers needed to lean in to notice it.

"That's lovely," said Goldenrod.

"Thanks," said Plane. "Not very useful, though."

Countess Fennel was last in line to take a look. "If you packed it in clay you could make a lost-wax sculpture from it. If we need an intricate metal part you could make the template for us to cast one."

Plane brightened.

Goldenrod asked, "Do we have anyone who does lost wax casting?"

Mistress Cinnamon said, "Master Bronze, but he didn't come to this event. He's taught classes. We should be able to find someone who took one."

The two newcomers attended every meeting and experiment session for the next week. They regularly had helpful suggestions. Cinnamon had a look of calm expectation that would steady down mages nervous about the next experiment.

When Goldenrod grumbled about not being able to keep track of all the experiments she'd been running Countess Fennel took back the laptop she'd loaned to the Autocrat's staff. Over three days the countess interviewed all members of council about the experiments they'd performed or witnessed. The result was a spreadsheet listing everything they'd ever tried, and a much shorter report summarizing the useful abilities found so far.

She gave Sparrow an engraved bracelet in thanks for the effort he'd put into keeping the laptop charged up.

Mistress Cinnamon borrowed the laptop during meetings to take minutes and update the membership list. Goldenrod began to rely on her to keep track of the agenda.

As the latest meeting broke up Cinnamon asked Goldenrod, "Did you know Her Majesty is a weaver?"

"No, I don't know much about her. Did she bring a loom?"

"Oh, her regular loom is a floor one, much too heavy to bring to an out of state event. She's set up a hanging loom on the wall of their pavilion. Lovely work. Anyway, we were talking after the last crafters council and your troubles came up."

"Oh?" Goldenrod didn't think she wanted the queen talking about her troubles.

"It seemed to us that it would help things if there was a royal charter for the council of mages."

"That—huh. I never thought of asking for that."

"It certainly doesn't happen often. The last one in the Kingdom was the Pastyme Players, the theatre group."

"Would King Ironhelm be willing to give us a charter?"

"I feel he could be persuaded. The key would be collecting enough support among the Peers to let it go through without anyone making a fuss."

Goldenrod made a face. "I hate buttonholing people to ask for favors."

Cinnamon said, "Well, you have Mistress Tightseam and Master Sweetbread in your household. You could start with them. And I'd be happy to talk with my friends on your behalf."

"Oh, I'd really appreciate that."

"No trouble at all, my dear. Should we ask Fennel to help out?"

"Sure."

Tightseam and Sweetbread thought a charter would be useful and volunteered to lobby other Peers. Goldenrod left it to them and focused on the next set of experiments.

***

A week later Goldenrod received a hint she should attend Court that afternoon. She and Newman stood behind Tightseam and Sweetbread, sitting in their folding chairs.

After the usual opening ceremonies some people were called up for awards. Some hunters received the Order of the Arrow. A few gatherers were awarded the Order of the Basket. Newman nodded in approval as the hunters received theirs. He'd learned to do award recommendations to get his regular team the recognition they deserved.

More awards followed for senior crafters and organizers.

Then a courtier brought out an illuminated manuscript. With the paper supply exhausted, it had been calligraphed onto tree bark. One that grew along stream beds had bark that peeled off in wide sheets.

King Ironhelm stood and began reading.

"To the Peers and Populace of the Kingdom, be it known.

"Whereas the gift of magic has come to members of the Kingdom,

"Whereas these gifts may be crucial to our survival,

"Whereas those granted the gifts need encouragement and support to learn the full power of their gifts,

Goldenrod bounced on her feet and clutched Newman's arm. He patted her hand affectionately.

"Whereas these gifts must only be used for rightful purposes,

"Therefore do we Ironhelm and Dahlia establish a Royal Council of Mages, to sustain, aid, and discipline those with magical gifts. We hereby appoint Countess Fennel as Head of the Council, Mistress Cinnamon as Deputy Head for Membership and Discipline, and Baroness Goldenrod as Deputy Head for Research."

Newman felt the excitement drain out of Goldenrod as the names were read out. When her arms dropped down, he wrapped one of his around her. He turned to study her face. She'd kept her smile in place. The energy that filled it before was gone. But someone more than a few feet away wouldn't notice.

He missed the last couple paragraphs of the charter in his distraction. When the reading concluded, he followed Goldenrod's lead in cheering heartily.

The closing formalities were brief. When the populace was dismissed, the crowd turned into a churning mass as people tried to congratulate the head and deputies. Goldenrod smiled, shook hands, and said thank you dozens of times.

As the crowd thinned Countess Fennel offered her hand to

Goldenrod. "Thank you for all your hard work. I want to give you all the support you need. Noon tomorrow work for an officer meeting?"

"Yes, of course."

"My tent." Fennel turned to greet her next well-wisher.

Cinnamon said, "It's official!" with her handshake.

When a moment with no one demanding her attention came Goldenrod said, "Fish?" to Newman.

They headed down the bluff. Instead of walking to the fishing weir Goldenrod wandered upstream. Newman walked beside her. As they went farther from camp, he increased his alertness, watching all directions. He waited for her to start talking.

Goldenrod began, "If four weeks ago they'd come to me and said, 'We're starting a mage group, we want you to run the research part,' I would have been thrilled. Instead I busted my ass recruiting people and running meetings and then they just walked in and took it over."

"Did you know they're both master organizers?"

"No, they just said countess and mistress. Huh. Explains how they were so good at it."

Newman waited a moment. "I knew this captain who was really serious about tactics. Wanted to be working out how to deploy the company in different terrain, different threats, all that stuff. But what he actually spent his time doing was writing up privates for underage drinking and being late to formation."

"So you're saying I wouldn't like being head of the council?"

"Do you want to deal with it when Sparrow tasers somebody who doesn't deserve it?"

"Hey, he's a nice kid."

"He's a teenage boy."

Goldenrod maneuvered around a bush, trying to not let her feet get caught by the brambles. Newman watched for snakes and other bitey critters in the undergrowth.

"Anyway. It's not that I want to be in charge. Okay, I liked being in charge. But deputy's good. What pisses me off is that I let myself be completely blindsided. I should have seen it coming. I just delegated it to them and didn't follow up at all."

"So you could concentrate on the research."

"Yes. Okay, it makes sense. I'm still mad."

"At who?"

"Me. For being a fool."

Newman put his hand on her shoulder, stopping her and pivoting her to put them nose to nose. "I'm just glad you're my fool."

***

The vineroot patch was weedy again. In the week since Goldenrod last checked it some invading plants had sprouted to four inches high. She swung the hoe, chopping them down and kicking the debris out of her garden.

At one point she'd been stacking all the dead weeds into a compost pile but Goldenrod didn't have the time for that now. When she paused to catch her breath her mind wandered to the experiment schedule. Every new use someone thought of for a power needed experimenting to put into effect and practice to make useful. There were too many experiments and not enough people Countess Fennel trusted to oversee them. But delaying mages would lead to them doing unsupervised experiments. She thought of Rivet's eye and went back to killing weeds.

"Good afternoon, your excellency."

Goldenrod looked up. "Oh, hello, Mistress Seamchecker."

"May I give you a hand?"

"Certainly."

The head of the Crafters' Council sat at the edge of the patch. She yanked out weeds with hands calloused from months of gathering plants. "You're busy these days."

"I guess I am. The mage council has me hopping."

"I'm surprised you have time to keep up the garden."

"It's not that much time. I think it's important to grow our own food. I've been tracking the growth rate of the vineroots. The biggest ones we're gathering are years old."

"That we were gathering," said Seamchecker. "We're digging up smaller ones now. And going farther for them."

"I hadn't realized they were that scarce."

"Most of the gatherers are ferrying across the river every dawn. But the other side is going to be stripped as bare as this one soon. Then it'll be overnight trips. Walk out, gather, camp overnight, gather some more, and come back."

Goldenrod let the hoe rest for a moment. "That's—we're not going to last long term doing that."

"No. We need to be farmers if we're going to stay in one place."

"Or we start migrating."

Mistress Seamchecker shook her head. "We can't. Oh, a few would be up for it. But most of us have too much to haul around. Tools, furniture, cooking gear. And there's at least a dozen people too old or ill for that kind of hike."

"So we need a farm." Goldenrod could feel it coming now. A senior peer stealing her project out from under her. Just like the mage council and the fishing weir.

"Yes. We'd work it with the less productive hunters and gatherers. We're past the point of diminishing returns anyway."

"Making enough hoes for everyone will take Master Forge a couple of weeks."

"Yes. I also have him working on a different project. A plow."

"A plow? How are you going to pull it?"

"A harness for eight strong men."

"How are you going to get them to do that? They're still pissed over catching shit-hauling duty."

"We're making two plows. So we can make it a race."

That provoked a real laugh from Goldenrod. "Yeah, that'll make the boys do their best." She hoed a bit more. "What do you want from me?"

"Seed." Seamchecker's voice was firm now that they were past the dancing about. "We'd take all your plants, cut the eyes apart for new ones. Hopefully keep the roots intact. Then sow the fields with them."

It was the sensible approach.

"All right," said Goldenrod.

***

The stranger walked out of the forest. Though 'walk' did not capture the grace of his stride.

Two guards stood at the gate. They looked up into his face and flinched back from the look of disdain. He ducked under the lintel of the gate without breaking stride, seeming to just glance down.

People in the lane stopped and stared. The beauty astonished them more than the strangeness. It wasn't just the flawlessly sculpted face or the hair waving like a silk banner. The stranger's clothes were animal skins, fur still on, held together with a few stitches of sinew where they met.

Yet . . . the skins were symmetrical and curved around the stranger's shoulders without a wrinkle. The fur was a shade matching the brand new penny gleam of his skin, brushed and clean. The shorts were a darker fur than the vest, yet they went together.

Paris fashion designers lived whole lives without achieving such elegance.

The stranger looked side to side as he strolled down the lane. His haughty expression said it would be beneath him to acknowledge the hideousness or stench of what he surveyed.

No one challenged him. People stood aside to clear his path. Even those standing transfixed at the sight woke as he approached and scurried out of the way.

Merrybrew and Marjoram watched from their tent. "It's an elf," said Merrybrew in a low voice.

"Don't call it that," she whispered back. "We don't know anything about it. If you call it 'elf' just on its looks you're making assumptions about its culture, morals, everything. That could bite us."

"I'm not going by his looks."

"What then?"

"The arrogance."

The camp was quiet. No one dared shout at the stranger or even shout about him. Most watching were silent. The smithy and workshops stopped work as masters and apprentices gawked.

Goldenrod and Newman came around the Wolfhead tents to see what the lack of fuss was about. After a long stare Newman said, "The guards shouldn't have let him in. We should be talking to him."

"Likely no one dared," answered Goldenrod.

"God damn it." He handed his quiver and bow to her.

The stranger was coming down the lane toward them. Newman stepped into the middle and stood solid. As the stranger came into speaking range he waved an empty right hand and called out, "Hello! Welcome to the Kingdom. We're glad to meet you."

A few steps let the stranger stop in front of Newman as if that's where he'd always planned to be. A long hand reached out and settled on top of Newman's head.

Don't flinch, he thought. *This could be their handshake.*

A white glow flared under the palm.

Newman dropped to his knees, clutching his head.

The stranger looked at the crowd. "Who the fuck are you people and where the fuck did you come from?"

Newman put out a hand to brace himself as he pivoted from kneeling to sitting in the dirt of the lane. Then he put both hands to his forehead.

Goldenrod rushed to him. "Are you okay?"

"My head aches," mumbled Newman.

Encouraged by Newman's survival, others approached to answer the stranger's questions.

"We're the Kingdom." "We're humans, from Earth." "We were brought here by a spell." "Can you help us? We're barely surviving." "We're humans, what are you?"

More people came forward, shouting answers and questions over each other until no words could be made out.

The stranger said, "Stop! Where is your head man?"

Merrybrew had come closer to watch but hadn't joined in the babble. Now he called, "You want us to take you to our leader?"

A few humans laughed. The stranger replied, "Yes."

Another argument threatened to break out over whether to bring him to Their Majesties. It was averted by a curt, "Make a hole!"

As people gave way Autocrat Sharpquill came up to the stranger. He looked around and said, "Don't you people have work to do?"

The crowd melted away.

The Autocrat turned his attention to the newcomer. "Greetings. I'm Master Sharpquill. I manage this place on behalf of Their Majesties."

"Good day. I am Aelion, a wandering elf."

The name was more sung than spoken, moving up and down in pitch within each syllable.

Sharpquill didn't try to say the name. "Welcome, sir. What brings you here?"

"I am a wanderer. I was following the river to the rim. Then I saw you people. Such people I have never seen before."

"Yes, we came here from another world, brought by magic we don't understand. How do you know our language?"

"I learned it from him." Aelion pointed at Newman, who was staggering to his feet with Goldenrod's help.

"Happy to be of service," said Newman. "Headache totally worth it."

"Oh, is that still bothering you?" The elf laid a finger on the side of Newman's head.

Newman was too dazed from the pain to try to dodge. When the finger touched him the headache vanished. As did the soreness in his feet from the day's hunt and the twinge in his back from carrying a gutted near-deer three miles back.

"I'm sorry, how do you say your name again?" asked Goldenrod.

"Aelion," sang the elf, not hitting particular notes but making a glissando up and down in pitch, the kind of continuous change trombones could do.

"Ae-ael-ee-on," imitated Goldenrod, hitting the highest and lowest notes.

The elf flinched. "That's not right."

"Aelion," she sang.

He shook his head.

She sang the name twice more before the elf said, "Stop!"

Newman stepped forward. He said, "Aelion," in as flat a tone as he would use for any human name.

"Yes, call me that," said the elf. "Do not try to say my name."

Autocrat Sharpquill said, "Aelion, would you stay with us for a while? We have many questions about this land and about magic. You could be a great help to us."

"I am willing. Wandering is a lonely and hungry business."

Goldenrod looked over at House Applesmile. Master Sweetbread was putting the finishing touches on a haunch of venison. Some fish lay by to be smoked the next time Pernach went to the charcoal burning.

"If you're hungry, Aelion," Goldenrod said without inflection, "would you like to join us for dinner?"

He would.

A bit of rearranging found Aelion and the Autocrat at the Applesmile table. Pernach, Pinecone, and Shellbutton set up a folding table for themselves on the other side of the fire. Redinkle stayed at the big table because of her magic.

Autocrat Sharpquill steered the conversation. The elf cheerfully spouted information about his society, often talking with his mouth half-full as he shoveled in food. There was no kingdom or empire, just independent villages. They were self-sufficient. A century might go by between visitors. Several had been wiped out by the 'green vermin.'

Aelion was shocked that no one had magic before arriving here. "Never?" he asked. "There are elflings who have to wait a century before finding their power, but no adults lack magic."

"There are rumors of magical ability on Earth but no one's ever proved they have them," said Mistress Tightseam.

"Now we've been here for eight months and we're finding all sorts of magic." Redinkle lifted her hand. Red and yellow flames sprang from each fingertip.

Aelion swallowed. "A useful trick, one of the first elflings learn." He matched her then turned the flames green, blue, and purple. "Have you been taught control?" He shoved more vineroot into his mouth.

"I was taught nothing. I had to learn it by myself." She concentrated. The flame on her thumb turned green, then went out.

"How did you keep from burning yourself?"

Redinkle flushed and looked down.

Newman said, "She was burned so badly she might have lost her hands. It might be Goldenrod's magic that saved her."

Aelion looked to Goldenrod. "What's your trick? Healing?"

"Sometimes when I say things they come true."

The elf leaned back. Master Sweetbread placed a platter of grilled fish in front of him. For once Aelion didn't look at the food. "That— that's not magic, it's sorcery. Don't ask me about that."

Sweetbread sliced the last fish into the venison grease.

Goldenrod asked, "If you can't help me, can you help Redinkle?"

"Oh, of course. Simple tricks like that anyone knows."

Newman excused himself and walked to the Wolfhead encampment next door.

Foxglove was peeking around the corner. "So what's the elf like?" she demanded.

"Hungry," said Newman. "He's eight feet tall and it's all hollow. Can you spare us some cooked food? We're down to the last of what we've got."

"You can have the whole meal," said Wolfhead Alpha.

"What?" cried Husky, already standing in line with his plate waiting for the cooks to finish. He was only the loudest of the complainers.

"This is important. It's our first friendly contact on this world. If we need to skip a meal to make it go right we'll be hungry and glad of it."

Under the leader's glare Wolfheads picked up the waiting platters and carried them to House Applesmile. More waited for the last of the food to come off the fire.

"Thank you," said Newman.

"Don't worry about it," said Alpha. "They won't suffer. You six—" Alpha pointed at Husky and the other line standers. "Grab baskets and trot down to the weir. There should be a few fish there."

Husky and his friends stacked their plates and headed out.

"When they have those fish ready I'll check with you before I give them to my pups," said Wolfhead Alpha.

"Thank you," answered Newman, "but I hope it won't come to that. There should be other households willing to donate."

"There should. I don't know that they will. Don't ask Captain Spear's tent. The hungry time left them more protective than a dog with one bone."

"I'll remember that."

Newman went back to his table. Master Sweetbread was sitting now. Foxglove managed food distribution. She'd even given some portions to the small table. As he sat she placed some venison slices directly on the elf's plate.

They were still talking magic.

"No one is limited to a single form of magic," said Aelion. "There's no way to predict what an elfling's first spell will be. The others come later, a few every decade. In less than a century they'll know all the common spells."

"We usually live less than a century," said Redinkle.

"How sad for you. We'll see if healing magic can sustain you to a normal life."

Newman asked, "Do you have spells that cure aging?"

"What kind of disease is 'aging'?"

"It's when the body functions less well as we get older," said Mistress Tightseam. "Our skin is looser, some joints hurt when we use them. Muscles are weaker." She pointed to her chin and elbow to illustrate.

Aelion wrapped his hand around her elbow. "That sounds like damage. Damage can be fixed."

He removed his hand. "Try now."

She folded her arm double, then extended it straight. "Oh, my. That is better. One of us should learn that spell."

"It would be easy to teach to one who already knows some healing magic."

Tightseam looked at Goldenrod. "You'll introduce him to Lady Burnout, yes?"

"We already had a mage council meeting scheduled for tomorrow. I'll put out the word for full attendance."

Autocrat Sharpquill nodded approvingly.

"What's the difference between magic and sorcery?" asked Goldenrod. She was bothered by Aelion's aversion to discussing her talent.

"Magic is normal. Anyone can do it. Like carving wood. Anyone can take a knife and cut away splinters. You learn tricks from others and you get better with practice."

He'd let his mouth get empty. He forked a piece of venison, chewed and swallowed. No one else spoke. It was clear Goldenrod wanted a full answer to her question.

"Sorcery, now. I don't know much about it. I've heard rumors and guesses and apprentice's boasts. Not everyone can do it. It takes power, a special power. Not the same as being good at regular magic. Sorcery has words and chants and books. I've seen powerful mages passed over as apprentices."

Aelion seemed nervous. For the first time there were hesitations in his flowing speech.

"Sorcery is puzzles and mysteries. Blood is spilled for it. Apprentices die and their parents are never told how or why. The effects it produces casts all our petty magic in the shade. I don't know if there's any limits to it. I can't do sorcery. I'm glad I can't do sorcery."

For the next few minutes the only sound was chewing, utensils on plates, and Foxglove keeping the plates full.

Goldenrod finished a bit of fish and went into the pavilion. She emerged with Belladonna's leather scroll. She unrolled it and laid it before Aelion. "Have you seen anything like this?"

He laid down his fork and picked it up with both hands. "It's a scroll. I don't know most of these words."

He flipped it to the other side. "I can't remember seeing one scribed on both sides. That's a lot of extra work."

He turned it upside down and studied the diagrams before going back to the words. "Mostly I can see 'and' or 'then' between words I don't know. It's like—"

Aelion threw the scroll to the grass. "This is sorcery, isn't it?"

Goldenrod was back in her seat. "We don't know. The owner was killed by orcs. It might be part of the spell that brought us here."

"Sorcery. Don't talk to me about that. Talk to the sorcerer. Well, no. nobody should talk to the sorcerer if they don't have to. Talk to one of his apprentices."

Newman leaned over to pick up the scroll. He handed it to Goldenrod.

Redinkle asked questions about fire magic for cooking. The revelation that a fire could be held at constant intensity made Master Sweetbread sigh wistfully. Cooking over a campfire used only a fraction of his skills.

A few minutes after Aelion stopped eating he started yawning.

"Would you like a place to stay for the night?" asked the Autocrat.

The elf looked over the camp. A few trees had survived the demand for firewood and fencing timbers. He pointed at the nearest. "Is anyone using that one?"

"Well, no."

The elf walked gracefully to the tree and climbed to about thirty feet off the ground. He lay back on a branch, feet propped against the trunk, and lay still.

"I'd be amazed by someone balancing on a branch that narrow while awake," said Newman.

"I assume he knows what he's doing." Sharpquill ate his last bite of venison. "Lady Foxglove, if there's anything left it can go back to the Wolfheads. Please convey my thanks to the Alpha and Mistress Vixen."

***

Countess Fennel made no objection to Goldenrod replacing the meeting's agenda. Word of the elf brought out every mage. Even Lady Burnout was present, and she only came when an experiment was likely to draw blood.

"My fellow mages," began Goldenrod, "I present to you our guest Aelion, a wandering elf. He is volunteering to help us with our magic.

We're going to take turns showing him our abilities. He'll decide who he can help the most."

Sparrow was the biggest surprise to the elf.

Most powers were routine to Aelion. He declared Fennel and Rivet's abilities to be aspects of the same trick. He prescribed them exercises to broaden the objects they could move.

For each mage Aelion would demonstrate a new aspect of the talent. When Marjoram asked how he learned so many tricks he answered, "Five hundred years is plenty of time to learn them all."

Aster presented herself hovering three feet above the ground.

The elf grunted, "Sorcery," and waved her aside.

More mages received demonstrations and exercises.

Sparrow stepped forward. He held up his hands palm to palm six inches apart, and let sparks crackle between the fingertips.

Aelion sprang backwards off the tree stump he'd been sitting on, landing on his feet, knees bent to allow movement in any direction. "That's lightning!"

The imitation of Newman's Midwestern accent broke. 'Lightning' covered a full octave.

The teenage boy flinched back, shocked by the reaction.

Goldenrod intervened. "Yes, it's made of the same stuff as lightning. We use it to fuel some of our machines."

"Fuel? Like a cookfire?" asked the elf.

"Yes, in a sense. I'll have to show you some of our machines," said Goldenrod.

"Later." Aelion moved forward. "Show me that again, boy."

Sparrow gulped. He lifted his hands and created more sparks.

The elf reached for Sparrow, cupping his hands around the outside of the teenager's wrists.

Only the hiss and pop of the sparks was heard in the clearing.

"Enough." Aelion sat on the stump again.

Sparrow waited uncertainly.

"That is magic, not sorcery. Yet I've never seen such magic. It is a simple force but I have no ideas on how you can use it in other ways."

A smile appeared on Sparrow's face. "That's all right. I'm already working full time at what I can do. I don't need any more tricks."

"Very well. Is there anyone else?"

Lady Burnout had waited to go last. She drew a knife from her belt as she came forward. A quick slash left a four inch cut in her forearm. She sheathed the knife then waved her hand over the cut. It scabbed over instantly.

"A healer! That is a rare gift, to have healing as one's best talent."

"The medicines we came with are mostly gone," said Burnout. "Can you help me replace them?"

"There are many healing tricks."

"Then I demand you teach me first." The chiurgeon flashed a challenging look at the leaders of the mage council. None objected as she towed the elf toward camp.

***

Aelion was not impressed with Lady Burnout's surgical tools. Not that the elf ever looked other than politely disdainful at any human device. Medications drew an admission of "useful, if true" except for antibiotics.

"You feed poison to your children?"

Burnout defended her medicine. "They're not poison to people, just infections." She decided allergic reactions could wait to another day.

"I now know what your first lesson must be. Who in this camp do you trust the most?"

Elf and chiurgeon found Constable walking a round of the camp.

"We must touch you," was the visitor's greeting.

Burnout was more diplomatic. "Evening, Constable. We're hoping you could help with something he's trying to teach me."

"Well . . . touch away, then."

Aelion touched fingertips to Constable's chest. His other hand lay across Burnout's forehead. "Sense what I sense," he said to her.

One bit of magic let her feel the other. A sense she couldn't name conveyed Constable's *goodness*. It was a solid, warm, cheerful hum. She missed it when the elf dropped the spell.

"Now. Do it yourself." Aelion stepped back.

Lady Burnout placed her fingertips over Constable's heart. She carefully didn't use the first power she'd learned. Adding clots to a healthy body could give her friend a heart attack. She recalled the sensation the elf had shared and looked for it.

Body heat and heartbeat.

Aelion said, "Open your other mouth and breathe him in."

She tried to open an organ she didn't have. Legs took a wider stance. Elbows turned out. Fingers spread wide. A deep breath.

She felt it!

Goodness, flowing into her fingertips. As solid and dependable as any she'd ever felt.

"You're a good man," she said.

"I do my humble best, milady."

Aelion led her away. "Now we need his opposite," said the elf. He plucked a midge out of the air. "Sense this."

"It feels evil."

"Yes, it only sees you as a source of blood." He crushed the bug and wiped his fingers on his trousers. "Have you seen smaller creatures that will burrow into one's skin?"

"We had ticks where we came from."

"I must explain to you how disease works. What you call infections or colds are actually invasions by animals even smaller than ticks. Too small for you to see."

"Yes, we know that," said Lady Burnout impatiently. "We call them bacteria or viruses."

The elf snorted in disbelief. "How did you find them?"

"We looked." She fished a magnifying glass out of her belt pouch. Demonstrating it on her fingertip gave her the pleasure of seeing that Aelion could look surprised. She went on to describe microscopes and offered to give him a demonstration with the one in her tent.

"Yes, but later. Let us cure them before we look at them. Not all 'bacteria' are bad." He put a fingertip below her bellybutton. He lifted it to her eyes. "Sense this."

Burnout placed one fingertip against his. "It's good. One of my symbiotic gut bacteria."

"Yes. Let us find evil bacteria."

She led him to Daffodil's tent. The little girl's parents were awake. Merrybrew and Marjoram poured out an update on her symptoms. Burnout nodded. If the patient was an adult she would have declared the infection resistant and stopped giving any of the last handful of antibiotic pills. "We're going to try something new," she told them.

Aelion said, "She will need soap and water."

"We only have the lye soap," fretted Marjoram.

"That will be fine."

Daffodil was half-asleep on her cot. She didn't answer the chiurgeon's query. The scraped knee was red and swollen. She was sweating with fever.

Lady Burnout laid her hands gently on Daffodil's knee. She flinched at the feel of the swarming bacteria. Consumption, reproduction . . . nothing else.

Aelion said, "Now pull them to you. Command them to come."

As she thought it her magic forced the bacteria to move. Daffodil whimpered. Germs flowed out of the girl's flesh and stuck to her palms.

She held her hands up to look at them in the light from the tent flap. The layer of bacteria was too thin to have color. The slime glistened.

"Wash your hands."

Burnout obediently plunged her hands into the basin. The harsh soap made her skin feel tight. The bacteria died as it hit them. She could feel them die.

She could *feel* the bacteria die.

Her gleeful laughter alarmed Daffodil's parents. They stepped back, then began to slide around to their daughter's bedside.

The chiurgeon took control of herself before they could grab the girl and flee. "Sorry. The spell seems to be working."

"Get the rest," said Aelion.

Laying hands on the knee again brought out about a tenth as many germs. After scrubbing those off she went up and down Daffodil's leg to find ones in the bloodstream.

"Enough. Her body will defeat the rest," declared Aelion. He turned to the parents. "The knee should look better in the morning and be fine in two days. Feed her as much as she wishes."

Burnout giggled.

Aelion took Burnout by the elbow. "I must take her to rest."

The parents babbled thanks as the elf guided her out of the tent. He led her back to the chiurgeon tent.

Lady Burnout looked up at him. "What else can magic do?"

"Too many things."

***

No hunter had manifested magical powers. Nobody had a reasonable explanation for it. Aelion kept mentioning spells he used while hunting. Goldenrod decided to send him out with Newman's team to see if any of the magic would rub off on them.

On the walk to the hunting grounds they talked gear.

"I made this from two pieces of wood. Hickory for the back and yew for the belly," said Newman, holding out his bow.

Aelion touched it with his fingertips. "How do you hold the woods together?"

"There's fancy glue back home that makes a solid seal. We can't make that here."

The elf hefted his bow. "I took this from a *wolor* tree. Cut the wood from where the heart met the shell."

"How long did it take you to whittle down the piece to shape?"

"No time at all. One cut on each side." He mimed passing a blade over the surface of the bow.

"Yes, but this must have taken longer." Newman tapped the ridges where Aelion would grip the bow when shooting. They matched his fingers down to the wrinkles on the inside of each joint.

"Oh, those grew later."

"Grew?"

"It's a simple spell. Each time you use a tool, you make it fit your hand a little better. Wood fits quickly. This took ages to shape." Aelion pulled an obsidian knife from his belt. The blade was faceted as it had been chipped from the original rock. The grip matched the elf's hand to the lines on his palm.

Deadeye exchanged looks with Newman. This was magic they wanted.

After a couple of hours of hiking they left the rhino trails and cut into the woods. This was far enough from camp the deer were still present.

Aelion took the lead. He ghosted through the trees. Despite his size he made less sound than Newman at his stealthiest. The hunters followed, communicating by gestures if at all.

It didn't take long for the elf to find his prey. He pointed. Newman looked. He could see movement and glimpses of brown fur through the foliage.

Normally Newman would split his team at this point. They'd approach the deer from opposite sides, working closer until one spooked the herd. The other would ambush the fleeing prey, bringing down as many as they could.

Aelion nocked an arrow, drew, and loosed.

Newman watched in amazement. There wasn't a line of sight to the deer. He followed the arrow with his eyes.

The arrow curved around branches and shot through leaves. An agonized bleat sounded. Then the drumming hooves of the herd fleeing.

Well, one deer would be a better score than some days they'd had.

He followed Aelion through the woods, falling behind as the elf's long legs outdistanced him.

Aelion had recovered his arrow by the time Newman caught up. The wound was in the front of the ribs. Instantly lethal. The same magic that steered the arrow around obstructions must have guided it to the vulnerable point.

The obsidian blade was slicing open the deer's chest. Aelion pulled out the heart and a few other bits. "Take your share and let's go."

"We'll divvy it up in camp," said Newman.

The rest of the hunting party arrived. Deadeye tied a rope around the rear hooves. The others pulled it up to a branch and began gutting it.

"What are you doing?" demanded Aelion. "The smell will attract every scavenger for miles. Wolves. Orcs. A dragon if you spill enough blood."

"Wolves and orcs are scarcer than they used to be," answered Newman. "And the dragon hasn't paid any attention to us while we're on the ground."

The elf took another bite out of the deer's heart. "No wonder you had a hundred orcs attack your camp. I could smell this from ten miles away."

"Hey, if you're hungry for lunch we could build a campfire."

"So smoke can attract whatever the blood does not? Fires are for settlements, not wanderers."

Newman shook his head. *I'm figuring out why this guy was starving to death.*

***

Foxglove buttonholed Newman after dinner. "Did he not like the stew?"

She'd taken over supplying enough food to sate the elf. Tonight's main course had been a stew of venison and wild vegetables, served in a cooking pot.

Aelion normally cleared his plates completely. Foxglove put extra effort into making sure they were washed so they wouldn't accidentally go into the clean stack.

This pot had enough left in it to be a small serving for a human.

"He liked it fine," answered Newman. "I think he was just full."

"He's never been so full he left food on his plate before."

"Yeah. But we've been feeding him all he can eat for days. He had to catch up eventually."

Foxglove's brow wrinkled. "What do you mean, catch up?"

"Did you notice how the cords in his neck stand out?"

She flushed. "Yes."

"The flesh around them is filling in. I think Aelion was on the edge of starvation when he found us."

"But—I saw you at archery practice with him! He's a great marksman."

Newman shrugged. "Hitting the target isn't all there is to hunting. There has to be game out there. We and the orcs have thinned out the deer. Plus he had to keep away from the orcs. They were swarming this area until the battle. Aelion's made a few comments about being chased by them."

"I thought he could kick an orc's ass."

"One orc, sure. If he saw them at arrow range he could take down a dozen. In the woods, with how skinny he is, two orcs could kill him easy."

"Damn. And he's been out in the woods for a hundred years?"

"About. He says he wasn't counting."

***

Aelion didn't understand charcoal. "If you want a hotter fire, just burn the wood more," he said.

Arguing over how to do that took him and Redinkle to Pernach and Pinecone's clearing in the woods. A charcoal mound lay low, almost done with its burn. The boys studied its progress. Cut wood stood in stacks waiting for the next one.

A patch of dirt had been swept clean, ready for a new mound to be built. Aelion set a piece in the middle. "Ignite this," he said to Redinkle.

By now she had no need to touch something to start a fire. She stood four paces away as the whole length of wood sprouted red and orange flames.

Aelion watched it burn for several minutes. It seemed a very long time for him to be silent. The quiet infected Pernach and Pinecone as they stomped on the mound to settle it.

At last the elf took another split log from the pile. He laid it two feet from the other. Then he stood beside Redinkle.

"Watch with all your senses," he said.

The wood burst into white flame. The heat struck Redinkle as if she was before a bonfire. Pernach and Pinecone jumped off the mound, afraid it was flaring up.

Redinkle closed her eyes against the glare. When she felt the heat fade she opened them again. Purple afterimages blocked her vision. When they went away she saw a neat pile of grey ash where the second piece had been.

Her piece still burned. The side facing the ash was charred.

"Did you feel that?" asked the elf. "How all the wood wanted to burn? How it just needed encouragement?"

"I think so."

"Feel all the wood. Feel its readiness."

Redinkle closed her eyes. She'd learned to sense fire helping Pernach with the charcoal burns. Now she felt below the flames. Wood waiting to be hotter before it burned. Wood wanting more oxygen. Water soaking up heat that could have ignited wood.

She began to sort. Push water aside. Force heat into wood. Split the grain to let in air.

"Good. It's brightening. Don't spend yourself. Make the fire do the work."

Redinkle realized she could draw on the energy of the flame. That cooled the fire for an instant, but came back with a profit as split dry wood combusted.

Now she could feel the heat with her skin as well as her magic. Then it went away. The log was ash.

Redinkle opened her eyes. Her fire had been less neat. The ash spread wider and the color varied among multiple shades of grey. But the wood had burned up completely.

"Let us give this Master Forge his hot fire," said Aelion.

The blacksmith looked dubious as the elf dumped an armload of wood into the hearth box. The open-topped steel cube had been swept clean of ash by the apprentices.

"It's fire magic," explained Redinkle. "The wood can burn hotter than charcoal with the right spell."

"That wood hasn't even had time to season," said Master Forge. "It's as green as a growing tree. But I won't argue with you."

Forge's apprentices cleared away the practice pieces they'd been cold-working. Other projects waiting on the charcoal delivery were brought up.

Redinkle closed her eyes to focus on the wood. The rings laid down each year were like wrapped sheets of paper, ready to peel away from each other. The water was held like a sponge, saturating everywhere. Of the trinity of fuel and air and heat only fuel was present in quantity. Air was locked outside.

"Step back," she said.

She ignited the wood. The flames were only a cool red. All energy beyond that she shifted from the fire to the wood. Water needed to leave as water, not turned into steam. She squeezed the sponge, water moving down through the wood, droplets falling from the underside of the split logs.

The structure resisted the movement. She began peeling the layers apart. The logs expanded. As air came in the water flowed through the gaps. Redinkle realized she should have started with that.

"Mighty cool fire," muttered Master Forge.

Peeling layers burst into flame. Redinkle seized the energy to dry and shatter the rest of the wood. A puddle formed on the floor of the hearth box, unseen by everyone.

She released the flames. They flared up with their full energy. The fire spread through the wood, peeled layers allowing air everywhere.

"Holy mother of God!" cried the blacksmith.

Heat struck her skin. Redinkle took a step back. Fire spread through all the logs in the stack, consuming them.

"Douse it! Douse it! Stop it, girl, stop!"

The fire swelled, far hotter than what she'd done before. The flames were bright enough to hurt through closed eyelids.

Then the ground smacked her back and head. Her concentration shattered. Redinkle opened her eyes.

She saw Aelion slap Master Forge hard enough to lay him flat.

"How dare you strike my student!"

Sitting up she saw two apprentices pour buckets of water into the hearth box. A third plunged steam-scalded hands into the trough.

"Aelion, leave him be," she cried. "It's all right."

The elf set Redinkle back on her feet. The blacksmith stood more slowly. He looked at the ripples newly-formed in the side of the hearth box.

"My lady, I thank you for your efforts," said Master Forge. "I will call upon you if we plan to make cast iron. For wrought iron we'll stick to charcoal, if you please."

***

A summons to see the Autocrat privately did not seem to be good news to either Goldenrod or Newman. Arriving to find King Ironhelm as the other person in the tent made it worse.

The older men exerted themselves to put the couple at ease. Herbal tea and sweet berries were served. The king offered amusing anecdotes from his younger days, matched by Autocrat Sharpquill.

Newman shared a funny story of cultural misunderstanding from when he was deployed overseas and wondered what they wanted.

Master Sharpquill finally turned serious. "Our new friend has shared the local calendar with us. Winter starts in five months. It will last four. We're running a food surplus now but that's not much time to build up a stockpile."

"We still have some people below a healthy weight," put in King Ironhelm.

"The river will partially freeze over. So collecting fish will be dangerous. Same for hunting. Gathering will be impossible until the spring growth."

Newman and Goldenrod held hands. The constant fear for survival had faded. Now they felt it again.

"We also need to build shelters that can handle the winter." Sharpquill waved at the ridgepole of his tent. "This handles thunderstorms well enough but I don't want to endure a blizzard in it."

"Which means pulling people off of gathering and preserving food."

"As His Majesty says. So we will have to do something drastic to get enough food for the winter."

Goldenrod asked, "In addition to the vineroot farm?"

"That might serve. If everything goes as we hope. What we want to do is go outside the box. Trade for food."

"With the elves?" asked Newman.

"Exactly. We've surprised Aelion plenty of times. We need to find what we can offer his people. Tools, electronics, labor. Whatever it takes to get the food we need."

Newman stiffened. "Labor? Sell them slaves?"

King Ironhelm snapped, "Of course not."

"Doing a project for them, or having some volunteers work six month indentures, might be acceptable," said the Autocrat. "Whoever we send will have to make the best bargain possible."

"Who's getting sent?" asked Newman grimly.

"You two, of course," said Autocrat Sharpquill.

King Ironhelm leaned forward. "You've established a solid working relationship with Aelion." His eyes moved to Newman. "You were the first to talk to him. And you have experience dealing with different mindsets. You two might not be perfect for the job but we don't have anyone better."

"Counter-insurgency duty isn't diplomacy," said Newman.

"No. But everyone I've talked to in my life has been part of a Western industrialized society or an immigrant trying to adapt. You understand at gut-level there are other mindsets."

"Won't some people object to us getting the job?" asked Goldenrod.

Sharpquill answered, "We're describing it to them as a difficult and dangerous mission you might not come back from. Your enemies are just fine with that."

"When you return with the agreement we need," added the king, "there'll be no trouble getting you the honors you deserve."

Newman noted that returning without an agreement wasn't

considered. He met Goldenrod's eyes. They both nodded.

"We accept, Your Majesty," said Goldenrod.

"Then you are Our Royal Ambassadors," said King Ironhelm.

"Has anyone talked to Aelion about this expedition?" asked Newman.

"That," said the Autocrat, "will be your first task."

Aelion had developed the habit of dining with whichever mage he'd tutored that afternoon. Fortunately for the ambassadors he'd been showing bird tricks to Marjoram. She ate at the common pavilion, her family being too small to count as a 'household' for wood and food rations. Not being pleased with the commons fare he'd skipped it in favor of a visit to House Applesmile.

The rest of the household had been asked to make room for a private chat. Only Goldenrod and Newman sat down at the table with the elf.

"Good evening," he said.

They greeted him. Newman led off. "We'd like to visit your people."

"Why? It's nice here."

They'd discussed approaches earlier. Bluntness seemed safest. "We don't think we'll have enough food for the winter. We want to trade with them for more food."

"Oh. That makes sense."

"Would you be our guide to them?"

"Oh, no. I can't go back there."

The ambassadors exchanged a look. "Have you been exiled?" asked Goldenrod.

"Not an official exile. It's just that there's elves who'd kill me if I go back."

Goldenrod didn't seem up to tackling that one.

Newman asked, "Why?"

Aelion's normally haughty face turned to unprecedented dejection. "I don't like to tell the story."

"I can sympathize with that. There's a story I've never told anyone here. But we need more food to survive the winter."

The elf let out a long sigh.

Newman said nothing. When Goldenrod seemed about to say something he waved her to silence. At last the elf started talking.

"A visitor from another village taught my wife a new song. She liked it. She'd sing it every day. I liked it too. I liked it the first few hundred times she sang it.

"But she kept singing it. After two thousand times it irritated me. Another thousand and I hated it."

Newman said, "She kept singing it all the time?"

"No, no. Once or twice a day. But that adds up in a decade. I started interrupting her and yelling at her but she'd just sing louder. So . . ."

Aelion stared off into the distance. "So I told her if she sang it ten thousand more times I'd kill her. She believed me. Would only sing it twice a week. By then just the first four notes would make me clench my teeth. The second century of our marriage went by with me counting up. Half the village was making bets over whether I'd do it.

"Then she sang it the ten thousandth time. Staring at me the whole time with a smirk. Like she didn't think I'd have the guts. I grabbed her head in both hands and snapped her neck. No magic can fix that. Grabbed my pack and bow and ran. Been wandering ever since."

Goldenrod was horrified. Newman asked, "Did anyone try to arrest you?"

"Hold me? No. Her relatives would have killed me. My family said they'd kill anyone who hurt me, but no one wanted to spend time protecting me."

"How long has it been?"

"Century and a half. So they're all still around except maybe her grandpa."

Newman thought a moment. "So you can go back. You just need to be protected."

"Yeah. Don't really want to though."

"If you help us make a deal to get enough food for the winter then I promise you'll always be welcome here. All the food and shelter you need, forever. And we'll protect you against anyone who comes looking for you."

"Okay. I'll take you there."

***

"Why me?" asked Deadeye.

"My wife is going to be far from home, surrounded by strangers who might decide to hate us," said Newman. "If it hits the fan I want the most competent fighter I can find keeping her safe. No matter how much of an asshole he is."

"Dude, you're gonna make me blush."

"Are you in?"

"No way I'll pass up the first chance to see hot elf chicks. Who else do we have?"

"Me, Goldenrod, Aelion, and Verbena, who's one of Queen Dahlia's ladies in waiting. Don't know her but she's a new talent. Can heal small cuts. Also used to live in Indonesia so she can handle strange cultures."

"Useful. Hopefully Aelion can teach her to fix big ones on the trip. Or we can just not get cut."

"Let's pray for that."

"Who else have we got?"

"That's all. I want you to find three or four more. Volunteers. Good with a bow and a blade. I have to go listen to Master Sharpquill go on about trade possibilities." Newman rolled his eyes.

"I'll get them."

***

Two modern pop-up tents had been requisitioned for the expedition. Goldenrod and Verbena slept in the small one. The men not on watch took the other. Aelion, as usual, slept on a tree branch, looking as if he was about to fall but perfectly stable.

The first night Goldenrod resented being exempted from watchstanding. The second she collapsed into sleep when dinner was done. She was used to physical activity but the mile-eating pace the hunters used for hiking was something she'd only done for an hour or two at a time. Keeping it up for a whole day left her legs screaming.

Verbena was doing even worse. She'd done more gathering than most court ladies but the gatherers walked slowly out and back. Now at every rest break Verbena flopped down on the ground, only getting up to drink a little as they started the next march.

It didn't help that she was two inches shorter than Goldenrod. Aelion was exploring his borrowed English vocabulary for all the short leg jokes he could invent.

The men on the expedition were all tall, or at least taller than Goldenrod. They still didn't have a prayer of keeping up with Aelion. The elf would set the course than disappear into the forest. He'd reappear from a random direction, sometimes just making sure the humans were on course, other times bringing back berries or some other snack.

When the sun grew low Newman asked Aelion to guide them toward some deer. The elf did, but griped the humans would attract scavengers. Three arrows took down a medium-sized one. They gutted it in place. A sapling made a carrying pole to take the carcass along until they found a campsite.

A small fire let them cook slices on twigs. Once they were full extras were toasted for the morning. Goldenrod and Verbena collapsed in their tent, leaving clean-up for the boys.

"Setting up their tent and carrying their gear is going to get old," Deadeye muttered to Newman.

"They're not troops, they're payload," said Newman unsympathetically. "If we have to carry them on our backs to get them there, we do it."

"That's—"

"That's the mission. Do you want to sweet-talk a bunch of strange elves into giving us ten tons of food?"

"No." Deadeye looked away.

"When they're spending all day doing diplomacy you can spend your time sleeping and ogling elf chicks. Until then, shut up and soldier."

The next day's hike was easier. Goldenrod suspected the hunters were slacking a bit to make it easier on Verbena. Or she was just getting used to the exercise.

Whether she'd built up strength or wasn't having to work as hard, Verbena became chattier. Goldenrod was wary. It made sense to add someone with the lady in waiting's skills to the expedition but that didn't mean Goldenrod had to be friends with her.

Still, Verbena managed to turn Goldenrod's minimally polite responses into hooks for real conversations. By the fourth night Goldenrod found herself continuing to talk as they settled in for the night instead of going straight to sleep.

She was asleep when the watchman woke her with a cry of, "Wolves! Wolves!"

Goldenrod drew the Bowie knife Newman had commissioned for her as a wedding present. She looked out the mesh window of the tent. No wolves. The moonlight showed her the six-man tent, two hunters stretching its doorway wide as they tried to force their way out at the same time.

Newman's voice came from inside. "Take turns, dammit! Right side, then left side. Right side, left side."

The hunters squeezed out as a wolf was on the sentry. He screamed as jaws closed on his arm. Newman came out last, holding the lochaber axe low to the ground.

"Form line!" ordered Newman.

A wolf leapt at him and yipped as its nose met the blade of his axe. Another knocked down the man on Newman's left. The air filled with yells and growls. Newman brought the axe down on the spine of a wolf. The animal squealed and fell.

"Should we go help?" asked Verbena.

Goldenrod looked at her. The edges of a short dagger gleamed in the moonlight.

"No, they don't want us getting in the way. Just be ready in case one tries to force its way in."

The growls changed to squeals and yips. Then the remaining

wolves fled.

Newman cut through the cursing. "Sound off. Who's hurt?"

"Fine." "Okay." "Nothing." "My arm's bleeding. We got any antiseptic?"

"I could piss on it," said Deadeye.

"No thanks, I don't want the clap in my arm," said the casualty.

Goldenrod called, "We have soap."

She unzipped the tent door and crawled out holding a crock of lye soap. Newman was rinsing the blood off Crusher's arm. Both the top and bottom of the forearm had punctures.

Goldenrod dipped her fingertips into the crock. She smeared a bit onto a couple of punctures.

"Jesus fucking Christ!" Crusher yanked his arm away.

Goldenrod flinched. "Sorry, this stuff is rough."

"Yeah, sorry, I should've expected it. I'll hold still. Sorry. Go ahead, I don't want it infected."

Newman took hold of the arm at elbow and wrist to keep it steady. Goldenrod washed the wounds as quickly as she could.

Crusher hissed between clenched teeth.

"Done," she said.

Leadsmith stepped in with a jug of water. The arm was soon rinsed and dried.

"If it's clean I can help," said Verbena. Goldenrod made way for her.

Verbena squeezed the arm with her hands. When she took them away the punctures were just pink dots.

"Thank you," said Crusher.

"Sorry, I shouldn't have gotten in your way," said Goldenrod.

"No, it needed to be cleaned first. Lady Burnout got on me about that after I healed somebody and he got an infection from stuff caught in the wound."

Aelion's voice came from a few feet over their head. "I told you we'd get scavengers. Kill something, rip it open to spread the scent, then carry it bleeding to camp. I'm surprised it took this long."

"The wolves near camp are afraid of us," said Newman.

"Then we've gone far enough to find strangers."

"Thank you for shooting that wolf."

"I wanted quiet so I could go back to sleep." Soft scrapes told of the elf climbing back to his branch.

Newman took Goldenrod aside. "Are you okay?"

"I'm fine. We just sat in our tent with our knives out until it was over."

***

"Behold!" cried Aelion.

The view was worth beholding.

A wide waterfall poured over a sheer cliff made of blue and purple layers. A half circle of blue water sat beneath the waterfall in a basin of rock. The edges were bedrock, forcing the forest away from the lake. Sunlight reflecting off the rippling water made ever-changing patterns on the cliff face.

"Build a fire. I'll get some fish." The elf stripped off his clothes and dove into the water. They could see him clearly as he skimmed the bottom toward a school of fish.

Verbena muttered, "That was a memorable sight."

Goldenrod smiled. "Don't tell Foxglove. She'll be jealous."

"Really? I'd heard she was sweet on him. Did she . . . ?"

"She's sweet, but he's gotta be twenty times her age, so no."

A six pound fish landed on the rock beside them.

"Let's get some firewood," said Goldenrod.

The lake fish were tastier than the river ones they'd been eating.

Some of the hunters skinny dipped while waiting for their turn at the cooking fire. Goldenrod and Verbena considered plunging in but decided to avoid complications.

"I come here every three or five years," said Aelion. "It's one of my favorite places."

Goldenrod nibbled on some roasted fish. "I can see why. It's lovely."

"And that stream takes us straight to my village."

She followed the elf's pointing finger to the top of the waterfall.

"Newman?" she called.

He joined them.

"Aelion says we have to climb that cliff."

Newman looked up at the edge of the rock formation. Then back down at the elf. "Is there an easier way up?"

"It's not a hard climb. There's plenty of hand holds."

"I'm sure there are. But we don't climb as well as you do."

Newman walked over to the men at the fire. "Crusher, you're on the sick list, keep sitting. The rest of you go a couple of miles each direction along the cliff. We need to find an easier place to climb up it. Lanyard and Rasp go right, Deadeye and Pritchel left."

They were all back in two hours. Verbena had taken the chance to extract a leisurely magic lesson instead of a short session before sleep. Neither pair found a better place to ascend. From their descriptions the lake was one of the few stretches without an impossible to climb overhang.

"Well, that's why we brought rope," said Newman. "Let's set up camp. We'll tackle it in the morning. Tonight I'm going to teach harnesses and climbing 101."

The first step after breakfast was convincing Aelion to carry the rope up to the top of the cliff. He finally agreed saying, "Don't ask me to carry any of you up. This trip wasn't my idea."

The elf made a brisk free ascent. At a couple of points he sprang up to reach the next easy handhold. At the top he let the coiled rope go.

It was, thankfully, long enough to reach the ground. Newman tied the few extra feet into a harness. Then he started up.

He'd done some climbs on Earth where crumbly sedimentary rock threatened to give way under his fingers whenever he tightened his grip. That wasn't a problem here. The rock was solid, hard, and unforgiving.

Newman had to chin himself up some stretches. His fingers could fit into gaps his boot toes couldn't. Aelion's work on the rope was only barely a net benefit. The elf's tugs were as likely to jerk him off a hard-won handhold as pull him past a smooth patch.

"About time," said Aelion as Newman crawled over the edge. "Here's your rope. I'm going swimming." He dropped his clothes and gear on the stone, then slid into the waterfall.

Newman shook his head. He took a spike and hammer from his belt, drove the spike into the rock, then secured the end of the rope to it. He untied his harness and threw the rope down.

Bringing Deadeye up wasn't that hard. Newman found some gouges near the edge he could plant his heels into. Sitting down braced against the rock let him pull as hard as he could when Deadeye needed the help.

Two men pulling brought Lanyard up easily. Pritchel and Rasp came up with even less effort. When only Goldenrod, Crusher, and Verbena were at the bottom Newman went back down.

"Okay, this should be easy for you," he said. "We've got four strong guys up there to hold on to you. I'll do your harness so you're secure. So up you go. I'll follow with the rest of the gear."

Crusher could use his wolf-bitten arm. It just couldn't take his full weight. He ascended slowly without slipping.

Goldenrod had gone to a rock-climbing gym with Newman for their third date. He was confident in her abilities. Which didn't keep him from being nervous until her feet went over the edge.

"The bad news is you're the shortest," said Newman as he tied the harness onto Verbena, "so you won't be able to reach all the handholds we did. The good news is you're lightest so they can haul you past any place you have trouble with."

"Right." Verbena set her jaw and headed up the cliff. She made it twenty feet before needing a boost.

Newman had bundled all the tents and other gear into a single pack before breakfast. A few pounds of leftover broiled fish topped it off.

When the rope came back down he tied a harness on. The sling holding his lochaber axe went on over that. Then he put the pack on. He started up. Second ascents were always easier. You knew there was a handhold. You just had to find it again. He envied the climbers who could memorize an ascent on the first try.

The place he couldn't find a handhold he remembered. "I'm at the smooth patch," he called up.

"Pulling," replied Deadeye.

Everyone had needed to be pulled past this spot. The rope pressed hard against the rough granite edge as they pulled. Each time some fibers had frayed. With the gear Newman was the heaviest load the rope had borne.

This time it would snap.

Newman felt his harness taking up his weight. He held firmly on to his handholds until he started moving up. This time his feet almost lifted off their holds before the rope broke. They slammed back down, one foot slipping loose from the jolt.

Curses and yells came from above. Newman tuned them out. He held his weight with his hands until both feet were securely placed again.

The rope slithered past his chest as it fell. Then the ragged end went past and he felt nothing until the tug as it reached its full length below.

Newman thought, *Three deep breaths, then take stock.*

No point in going down. I'd just have to come back up again.

Straight up isn't an option.

I can go sideways until I find a way up.

I've done ascents this hard without slipping.

Newman looked left along the cliff. The straight expanse of rock was almost as scary as looking straight down. He spotted some hand and footholds in reach.

The view to the right had fewer holds. The bottom edge of the smooth patch sloped down to that side. If he went far enough to the right he would be able to land in the lake instead of on rock. But that was farther than he needed to go up.

A splash in the lake was probably the elf playing. No point in yelling for help. The waterfall would drown shouts out.

He'd rather get out of this mess on his own than ask the arrogant jackass for help anyway.

He went left.

His arm muscles complained. One ascent, part of another, hauling up the other men, and a descent was a serious workout. Newman moved slowly. When muscles quivered he held position until the spasm was over.

Carrying all this weight didn't help. Newman thought of his knife. He could draw it with one hand. Cutting loose the rope harness would be a lot of work and not save much weight.

The pack had two shoulder straps and a hip belt. They should cut easily enough. But when two were cut he'd get a nasty jolt as it flopped down to pivot off the third. Better to be safe.

Besides, they needed that gear. And Duchess Roseblossom would never forgive him if he lost the axe.

Newman kept climbing. He was working up and sideways now.

I owe Aster an apology. He chuckled at the thought. He was climbing in her style now. Only one hand or foot moving at a time. Sometimes he braced his torso against the rock for extra support while reaching for a new hold.

Newman glanced up. He was closer to the top now. Might make it all the way before his arms gave out. There was a head poking over the edge. He didn't look long enough to see who it was.

A disturbance made him freeze. It was a rope uncoiling past him.

Deadeye called from above. "We checked the whole thing. There's no more frayed spots. Grab hold and we'll bring you up."

After the break trusting a rope felt like insanity. But clinging on with his hands wasn't a good move.

Newman reached out and grabbed the rope. He flipped it to his other side. Then he let go of it and reached under his gripping arm to grab the rope again. Hooking his elbow over the length above him forced the rope into a loop under his shoulders. The loose end had been cut neatly and tied with some threads to keep it from fraying.

He couldn't tie a good knot one handed. But he managed an abomination that let him slide the loop tight against his chest. Then he grabbed hold, pulling the rope tight. He wrapped it around his forearm and pulled. As the rope took his weight he let go of the other handhold and took the rope with both hands.

Newman called, "Haul away!"

They pulled him up at a steady pace. He used his feet to keep from scraping against the rock. At the top hands reached over the edge to pull him over. Then everyone held him, carrying him inland from the cliff.

"Oh, your hands are bleeding," said Goldenrod.

"I'm not complaining," answered Newman.

Deadeye handled taking the pack off. Then Newman could rest while the others set up camp. He lay with his head on Goldenrod's lap, not quite asleep but certainly resting.

Verbena took Newman's hand. The abrasions faded to healthy skin. Even the cracked fingernails flowed together. She passed her hands over his arms and chest. "Some strained muscles here. I can fix that, I think."

Newman let out a contented sigh as his shoulders and pectorals stopped hurting.

"I didn't know you could do that," said Goldenrod.

"A week ago I couldn't."

"What's with tents?" asked Aelion, still dripping wet. "There's hours more sunlight."

Goldenrod answered for them. "We're camping here."

***

As they came closer to the elf village discussions on how to handle negotiations dominated campfire talk. Aelion objected when he found out he was expected to act as interpreter.

"Show up to meetings all day long? Somebody will kill me for sure."

"Well, how else are we going to talk to them?" asked Goldenrod.

The elf reached out and put his hand on top of her head. White light flared under his palm.

She bent over, singing out a string of words in an angry tone.

Aelion sang back apologetically. He touched the side of her head.

"You okay?" asked Newman.

"Yeah." Goldenrod rubbed the back of her neck. "He gave me a headache and took it away. But I can speak Elvish now."

"My village's Elvish. Others have their own tongue. That's why I learned the spell."

"Could you do that for me?" asked Verbena.

"Tomorrow."

***

"There it is. Home." Aelion's voice had no note of rejoicing. Some of the humans perked up, more from the end of a week of marching than the sight of the village.

The elvish village was a cluster of tall trees isolated from the rest of the forest. Platforms sprouted from the trunks in an organic fashion. Newman wondered if they were constructed or grown.

The platforms were wall-less but roofed over with half domes sprouting from the trunks in the same manner as their floors.

Most of the elves in sight weren't doing much of anything. They stood or sat or lay in pairs or small groups. Probably conversing, but from here he couldn't be sure.

The ground between the trees had some tables and benches holding more elves. Newman looked for storage sheds or piles of goods. He saw neither, which boded ill for their mission.

The space between the forest and the village was filled with garden patches, not plowed fields. He recognized many of the plants from what the gatherers had brought in.

No animals. So much for the hope of begging a herd of cattle. Crusher would be disappointed. He'd been hoping to work this world's first cattle drive. Too many cowboy movies.

The nearest elves were hoeing in the gardens. They were dressed much as Aelion was, wearing vests and shorts. Some had hats. One noticed the expedition, or at least Aelion, and waved.

Verbena waved back. Belatedly, so did Aelion.

Newman asked the elf, "Shall we go say hello?"

"Eh . . . better I follow you guys."

Newman shrugged. "Let's go, folks." He walked forward toward the elf who'd waved.

Goldenrod moved up to walk alongside him. Verbena walked on her other side.

Newman looked back. The escort was staying with them, spread out. They had bows accessible but no weapons drawn. They walked around the garden plots so they wouldn't step on growing plants. All as he'd discussed with them this morning.

The gardener stopped and leaned on his hoe as they approached. Newman was pretty sure about the 'his.'

"So you're back," he said. "Going to settle it with her family?"

Newman understood it. He'd been given the language this morning.

"What do you care?" answered Aelion.

"I can use the entertainment. We haven't had any excitement since you ran off."

"Too bad. I'm just here because my friends want to do some trading."

"Friends? Is that what they are. I thought you'd come up with some fancy wergild."

Newman studied the gardener. His skin was yellower than Aelion's, shiny as a new gold coin. The furs were precisely complementary shades. Gleaming bronze hair stretched four feet down to the elf's hips. The face—the face was staggeringly handsome. Aelion was pretty, but nothing compared to this Hollywood idol.

"Yes, they're friends," said Aelion. "Ophyol, meet the humans. This is Newman, Goldenrod—" He ran through everyone's names.

Ophyol nodded in acknowledgement. "You're short."

"We are," answered Newman. "We fit in small houses."

That provoked a laugh.

"Then let's get you to the village. I don't want to miss the show."

Ophyol led them toward the tree houses. Verbena struck up a conversation about the gardens. Just finding the elvish names for the plants the humans had been eating took them to the bare dirt under the trees.

An arrow from above flashed past Aelion's head and stuck in the dirt.

Deadeye nocked an arrow and sent it back. The other hunters readied their bows and drew arrows.

"Don't bother," said Aelion. "The peace enchantment won't let arrows hit here. That was just someone letting me know he's still mad."

A couple more gardeners had joined the procession. At the village more left their conversations to check out the newcomers—or the returnee.

All the elves had gleaming skin. Shades of silver, steel, or pewter were as common as the copper and gold they'd seen before. Hair was always long and perfect. The clothes were mostly furs but still looking elegant.

Newman realized how to spot the elf females. They wore skirts of overlapping vines or leaves or animal tails. That accentuated the size of their hips. Breasts were also larger on females than males, on average. But on a seven or eight foot frame the differences seemed so small as to be invisible at first glance.

One elf looked to be about nine feet tall. Newman wasn't sure. He was good at estimating human heights but once people were above six feet four he was fuzzier.

Goldenrod had found the headman, Lomlil. Now she was explaining where humans came from, how they arrived, and what they'd been doing here to most of the population of the village. She'd wound up standing on a table so more could see her.

The rest of the humans were clustered behind her. Aelion sat in the middle of them. Newman had spotted some of the elf's enemies. A knot of seven elves were sending death glares his way. More had given him friendly greetings, but none of those wanted to stand next to him.

Verbena said in English, "There's no metal, no cloth, no domesticated animals. These people aren't even Neolithic. They're Paleolithic."

"If we develop the level of magic they have our grandchildren might think metal tools were just a fad," said Crusher.

The elves broke into cheers. The ones standing around the humans knelt. One seized Crusher's hand and kissed it. Others began dancing.

"What the hell?" said Crusher as a second elf kissed his hand.

Verbena explained, "She just described the big fight with the orcs."

"Guess they don't like orcs."

Newman put out his hands in a calming gesture. Both wound up kissed.

A female elf forced her way through the crowd. She knelt and extended her basket to the humans.

Deadeye took a handful and swallowed. "Ooh. Those sweet red berries."

The others grabbed some as the smiling elf passed the basket around.

Goldenrod hopped off the table to get some. "I was going to tell them about learning magic next, but that's going to have to wait until they calm down."

The lowest platform shook as three drummers pounded out the dance beat. Some flutes joined in. The elves joined hands and danced in circles. When two circles drifted close together they let go their hands to let the circles interpenetrate. One circle moved across the other without any dancer bumping another.

The nine-foot elf came back with a waterskin. *"Lava!"* he said, holding it out.

Deadeye asked, "Goldenrod, what does *'lava'* mean?"

"Whiskey."

The hunter took the skin with a smile and nod. He put it to his lips and took a cautious sip. "Jesus!"

"Bad?" asked Crusher.

"No. Well, it's raw, but it's like rocket fuel. Pure booze." Deadeye took a mouthful. "Thank you, kind sir."

When he tried to hand it back the elf backed away, gesturing for it to be handed around.

Crusher took it next. "Whoo, you ain't lying."

When he went for a second drink Newman grabbed it. "No getting drunk. We just met them. We know some want to hurt Aelion. So stay alert."

"Okay, boss," said Crusher. He passed the skin on.

Goldenrod asked Newman, "Could you do that dance? It would be good if one of us joined in."

"Hell, no. I can barely follow the beat. They're doing two separate interleaved rhythms."

"I can't figure the dance out either. Haven't been able to tell if the footwork is repeating or if there's just phrases they include."

More treats were supplied. The same female elf held a basket of sweets out to each human, a wide smile on her face.

Newman nudged Deadeye. "Here's your chance to make your move."

When the elf came by Deadeye took a handful of sticky berries and said thanks without making eye contact. She completed her circle of the embassy before vanishing back into the dancers.

"So what happened to wanting a hot elf chick?" asked Newman.

Deadeye didn't answer immediately. "The paintings I remembered aren't like the real ones. They're pretty, but they don't do anything for me."

"Same for me," said Newman. "Too tall, too skinny."

"If they're too skinny what am I?" asked Goldenrod.

"Perfect," he answered.

Goldenrod kissed him.

***

Newman tried not to be jealous of the elves' gorgeous looks, or innate fashion sense, or their magical talents. Discovering they didn't suffer hangovers pissed him off.

One of the tree platforms had been detached and set on the ground for the non-arboreal guests. Most of the humans were asleep. Lanyard and Rasp were on watch when Newman awoke. He sent them to bed. He watched the elves go through their morning routines, all as cheerful and agile as they'd been before the party.

Baskets of fruit and cooked meat were waiting at the edge of the platform. He couldn't fault the elves' hospitality. A quick count showed everyone was here.

"Good morning, Newman," said Aelion. He sat cross-legged in the center of the platform.

"Good morning. Has anyone bothered you?"

"No. Having orc-killer bodyguards is keeping them away. How long are we going to stay here?"

"Shouldn't be long. Just need to come to an agreement on trade." Newman lifted a handful of red berries from a basket.

"Good. I don't like it here any more."

Goldenrod stretched without bothering to get out of her blanket. "Morning."

"Good morning." Newman knelt down and popped a berry between her lips.

"Ooh, breakfast in bed. I could get used to this."

He fed her more berries, but necessity forced her to get up anyway.

Soon everyone but the night guards were awake. The baskets emptied out quickly. They'd eaten lightly on the trip. They would have finished mediocre food. Having the best the forest offered in front of them made them gorge.

The leisurely debate over who deserved the last of the fig-like things was interrupted by the arrival of headman Lomlil. He introduced the female elf with him as Fordeen, the head gardener. Verbena promptly began interrogating them about the village's food production and storage.

Goldenrod sat back and listened until Fordeen described their food storage.

"Nothing placed in that cellar decays, but it was made by sorcery so we couldn't help you with that."

"Aelion thought some of the magic we did was sorcery," Goldenrod said. "Who can we talk to about that?"

Fordeen flinched and went silent.

Goldenrod looked at Lomlil. He stood and walked off the platform, waving for her to follow. Newman went with her.

The headman stopped on the far side of one of the great trees. "Sorcery is not something we speak of lightly."

"It's not a light subject for me," replied Goldenrod. "My own magic may be sorcery. I cast spells without intending it. I need guidance, teaching in how to use it."

"Do not ask the sorcerer for favors. The mere request may make him angry. He is capricious and proud."

"Was he at the party last night?" asked Newman.

Lomlil shivered. "No. He lives a mile from the village." His tone was grateful.

Goldenrod leaned into the headman's personal space. The effect was ruined by his being three feet taller than her. "What's this guy's name?"

"No one knows the sorcerer's name."

"He came from far away?"

"No, he was born here. He's the oldest person in the village."

"So why don't you know his name?" pressed Newman.

The head twitches of someone seeking a way to avoid answering an unpleasant question were the same on an elf and a human . . . yet on the elf it looked graceful.

"Twelve hundred years ago . . ." Lomlil sighed. "Twelve hundred years ago the sorcerer killed the last one who knew his name. Now none dare speculate, lest a lucky guess bring death."

"Oh," said Goldenrod.

"Is that someone you want to apprentice yourself to?" asked Lomlil.

Newman muttered an agreement with the headman.

"Not an apprenticeship. But I'd like to ask some advice. Or buy some teaching if we have anything he'd want to trade for."

Another sigh. "If I see any of his apprentices, I will send them to you. Perhaps then you will not need to bother the master."

***

"So these are the orc killers," pronounced the new arrival.

Newman looked her over. Brass skin, aluminum hair. Skirt made of strips of leather, more like Roman armor than the dress he'd seen on other elf females. The arms and legs bore rows of scars. Too neat to be from combat. Too ugly to be decorative.

She walked into their shelter, surveying the humans but ignoring Aelion. "I am Ymer. Where is the one who thinks she is a sorceress?"

Goldenrod stood. "I don't claim that title. I have abilities I don't understand. I want to speak to someone who knows higher magic."

"You are getting what you want. I am one of the senior apprentices." Ymer sat down before Goldenrod. "Speak."

"Since we've arrived on this world I've done things I can't explain. The first was the night we came through." Goldenrod described cursing Belladonna, finding vineroot, healing Redinkle, and then . . . killing orcs with a word.

Ymer opened her mouth, clapped a hand across it to silence herself, and waved for Goldenrod to go on.

She described the experiments she did with her powers. Then forming the mage council to help others.

"Oh, my," said Ymer when she finished. "The Master will want to see you. It's disappointing you didn't bring the one who could fly. How does she do it? Does she grow feathers?"

"No, Aster just wills herself to go up and she does."

"Interesting."

"So you're familiar with what I did?" asked Goldenrod.

"Nothing exactly like it. But you seem to have a form of *noroldwesru*."

"I don't understand that word."

The apprentice glanced at Aelion. "You wouldn't. It would be easier to understand in your own language. If you'll let me."

Goldenrod braced herself as the hand touched the top of her head. The pain wasn't nearly as sharp as when Aelion taught her Elvish, and it only lasted an instant.

"Let me . . . no, you don't have the word either." Ymer thought a moment. "Call it reality probability shaping. Hazardous stuff. I wouldn't dare attempt it."

"How would someone learn it?"

"Apprenticeship. Surviving apprenticeship long enough to attempt the higher magics. Surviving the trials of higher magic to attempt true sorcery. And if you survive that—then *noroldwesru*."

"How hard is it to survive apprenticeship?" demanded Goldenrod.

"An apprentice dies once or twice a century."

"And the rest?"

"That you'll have to ask the sorcerer."

"I will."

Ymer smirked. "I'll ask if he'll see you."

The apprentice stood and strode out, stepping over the seated guards as if they weren't there.

Goldenrod watched after her. She heard Newman's whisper in her ear. "Are you seriously thinking of dealing with that guy?"

"How else am I going to learn to use my magic?"

"He killed somebody for knowing his name. And he kills his apprentices."

"There's a lot of magical traditions where knowing someone's name gives you power over him. And she didn't say anything about him killing his apprentices. Magic is dangerous. Redinkle and Rivet nearly killed themselves with their own spells."

"We can't be sure of that."

Aelion interrupted. "He has killed an apprentice. I heard one was disrespectful to him. The sorcerer poured out all his blood."

"There!" said Newman.

"What? I can be respectful."

"Says the woman who pissed off half the Peers into organizing a conspiracy against her."

Verbena laughed.

"Look," said Goldenrod, "gathering information is part of our mission here. This guy can help us understand our powers. He might have a clue how we were brought here. If there's any way we can go back home it probably goes through him."

Verbena stepped into the conversation. "I agree. Dealing with the sorcerer is dangerous. But this whole trip is dangerous. We just need to be diplomatic. And make a full show of force. We should have everyone there."

***

"The master will see you now," said Ymer.

Her face was well lit by the late afternoon sun but it gave no indication of whether she liked or disliked the news.

"Thank you, we will come at once," said Goldenrod.

Newman snapped, "Get your gear. Like we talked about. Ready for action." He watched his men scurry to get ready. Not that physical weapons were likely to be any use in preventing the sorcerer from hurting Goldenrod. But if he could offer a credible threat of retaliation it might deter him.

Goldenrod and Verbena flanked Ymer as they walked out of the village. Newman walked behind them. The rest gaggled behind in a loose clump. He discarded the thought of trying to make them form a line.

"Do you really need the damn axe?" hissed Goldenrod.

"Yes. It looks good." Newman wore the axe in a harness that held it across his back, with the point of the blade peeking over his right shoulder.

Ymer didn't react to all the humans following her. She did notice Aelion in the middle of them. "Are you afraid to stay here alone, wanderer?"

"If you had as many threatening to cut your throat you wouldn't be alone either."

Newman thought the apprentice's laugh was musical but not pleasant.

The village was surrounded by garden patches except for here. The gap in the circle of cultivation was filled with shrubs, weeds, and bare dirt.

As they walked away from the village and into another grove of trees the ground became all dirt.

The trees weren't healthy either. The branches opposite the village had few leaves. Sometimes none.

Ahead they saw a tree with no leaves at all. Branches had broken off leaving holes in the bark. A wide hollow gaped at the base.

Ymer pointed at it. "The Master's Sanctuary."

"I can feel the power here," Verbena said as they approached the tree.

The opening of the hollow was wide enough for all the humans to stand in it, with room for Ymer and Aelion.

Newman studied the inside of the tree. It was lit by a glowing orb on the ceiling. The sorcerer was obvious. Not just by the rune-inscribed clothes, but the deference of everyone else. Two elves stood beside the sorcerer. Four kneeled at the edges of the room, faces down.

In the center of the beaten-earth floor was a circle showing an image of a forest from above. The sorcerer and his senior apprentices stood beside it.

All the elves had obsidian daggers. The sorcerer had a carved wood wand in his belt. No bows or other obvious weapons.

The walls were lined with shelves and cubbyholes. Some held books and scrolls, the first written material Newman had seen among the elves. Flasks and dried plants filled the rest.

"My wonderful vermin exterminators," said the sorcerer. "I'm delighted to see you at last."

Ymer bowed, "My Master, I present the short ones, who call themselves *humans*." She introduced everyone to the sorcerer. Aelion was mentioned only as "their guide."

The senior apprentices were Osdul and Ithuil. The latter was noticeably more deferential. The kneelers weren't introduced.

The sorcerer ignored everyone but Goldenrod. "Come here, child. The story of your gift fascinates me. The energies of your world and mine must have combined to create something new."

Newman tensed as she walked forward. The sorcerer waved his hands around Goldenrod's head, then her torso.

"Yes, something I've never seen before. The greatest surprise I've had in over a millennium. I thank you. This will take years to understand."

"The spells I've cast are more surprising than our arrival from another world?" asked Goldenrod.

"Oh, other worlds are no surprise. I've viewed many. No, you are different. A strange sensation, your magic."

The sorcerer looked at Aelion. "There's a touch of that feel on you. What spell did she cast on you?"

"She—she never cast a spell on me," sputtered the elf.

"Oh, she did. Perhaps she summoned you to be their guide?"

"There was no summons," protested Aelion. "I found them by accident."

The powerful gaze turned back to Goldenrod. "Around her, there are no accidents. I will need new words to describe this."

Ymer asked, "It's not *noroldwesru?*"

"This . . . gift the human has is like *noroldwesru* as the purest *lava* is to a fermented berry hanging on the vine."

The look on the sorcerer's face worried Newman. It was greed. Not a man looking at gold. The greed of a scientist looking at a new specimen to dissect. His right hand rose toward the axe. No. He forced it down. He didn't dare risk giving offense now.

Goldenrod looked up into the sorcerer's eyes. "Will you help me learn to use this gift?"

"Of course. Of course. But we must be careful. Mere fire can only burn. This could do anything."

"I know. That's why I want help with it."

"And you shall have it. But this will take thought. To begin we will need a day of storytelling. I must have every detail of what has happened before we tempt fate with this power again."

Newman relaxed. Talking wasn't a danger.

"Yes, sir. Oh, there's something I forgot to mention to Ymer." Goldenrod took the leather scroll out of her pocket. "The woman who cast the spell to bring us here had this. Have you seen anything like it?"

The sorcerer took the scroll, snapped its cord, and unrolled it. "The circle is complete at last. I've seen this. I wrote it."

"You wrote—how did Belladonna get it?"

"Oh, I've written hundreds of them. Then sent them forth on the currents of the universes like leaves floating down a stream. Each to a different world, seeking someone with the right gifts, right desires to use it."

He traced the lines of a diagram with his fingertip. A reminiscent smile crept across his face.

"For centuries every night I would cast the spell to match this one. And never did anyone perform the partner spell. Until at last one of you did. I felt such will in her as our spells met. Where is she? I would thank her."

"She was killed by orcs." This would be a bad moment for Goldenrod to mention her role in Belladonna's death.

"Inevitable I suppose. But you've killed so many orcs. It was a delight to see."

Newman's brain was frozen. That this elf was responsible for their kidnapping, their near starvation, all the deaths . . . He'd thought that responsibility was gone with Belladonna. Now the thoughts of blame and punishment were flooding back, too strong to handle at once. And as tempting as the thought of revenge was, justice must bow to survival. They needed help to make it through the winter. Picking a fight with the elves would doom them.

Goldenrod caught on the sorcerer's last word. "See? How did you see it?"

"Oh, the simplest of sorceries." He turned to the disk in the middle of the floor, waving the apprentices out of his way.

"A scrying pool. I can see where I wish." A few gestures changed the view to above the human camp. "There is your home."

Goldenrod's voice rose. "You knew we were here all this time and you did nothing?"

"Of course I knew you were here. I cast the spell that brought you. The scroll only let you leave your world. Both were needed for the journey."

"Then why didn't you help us?"

"I did help you. I cast a protection spell on all of you."

"But—we needed to find food, we needed warning of the dangers."

"You managed quite well."

Newman wanted to scream the names of those who'd died while

they'd 'managed quite well.' He saw Goldenrod struggling with the same temptation. He didn't know whether to hold her back or encourage her to blast the old bastard.

He looked left and right. Verbena was in shock. His men were looking to him for a cue. Newman pressed a palm down to signal *wait*.

In a surprisingly level tone Goldenrod asked, "Why did you bring us here?"

"The orcs."

"The orcs?"

The apprentices were shocked someone would treat their master with such disrespect. Newman watched their hands. If either raised one to Goldenrod his axe was coming out.

"Yes, they're becoming a greater threat every decade. They breed so fast. Every deer or *votha* or *dunu* is a host for their young. They've discouraged contact with the other villages. More than one has been wiped out. They keep attacking the apprentices I send out to gather rare herbs. If one comes back full of worms that's easily fixed but there's nothing I can do for the ones who are eaten."

Newman's palm itched for the haft of his axe.

"We elves don't have a gift for violence. So we needed you to bring the orcs under control."

"As mercenaries." Goldenrod's voice was low and cold.

"No, simple exterminators. This isn't a war. It's vermin control."

"Fine. We've slaughtered hundreds of them. We're done. Send us home."

"How can I send you home without someone there to receive you? And there's plenty more orcs to kill."

"No there aren't. We haven't seen an orc in weeks. The ones who survived the battle ran and didn't come back."

"Yes, they ran." The sorcerer manipulated the scrying pool again. The viewpoint rose into the air. The last rays of the sun glinted off the river. It kept rising. A spot of light came into view.

"That's where we are."

The view kept spreading. A few other villages came into sight. As the view widened they saw the mountains Newman had visited south of the camp . . . and then the whole ring they were part of, marking the rim of a crater.

"And now we see all the land within the Blasted Ring. There are orc bands everywhere but where you killed them."

Flecks of green light, the bright green of orc skin, appeared. The area around the human camp stayed black.

"The surviving orcs fled and joined other bands. They told of your violence and the slaughter you wrought. When orcs hear of such a threat they have only two reactions. Flee to seek a safer hunting range. Or attack the threat to destroy it. I've used a persuasion to convince them to attack. They've spread the word of humans to the other bands. Now all the orcs inside the Blasted Ring are on their way to you."

"How many?" demanded Newman.

"A hand of hands of hands of hands of hands."

Newman was still in too much shock to do the multiplication. Verbena, who'd been handling the trade negotiation, translated. "Over three thousand."

"There's no way we could survive an attack like that," said Goldenrod. "And if we're all fighting we'll starve this winter."

"Of course you'll defeat them. You killed ten or twenty for every one you lost before. And now you have magic."

"We're not all fighters. There's old people. Children. Cripples."

The sorcerer shrugged. "If you cannot handle the task I will summon others to succeed where you failed."

"No. You will cast another persuasion. Convince the orcs to avoid us."

Now he was amused. "I will not."

"You will," declared Goldenrod. "Or we will force you to do it."

The elves laughed. The sorcerer and senior apprentices openly. The junior apprentices without lifting their heads. Even Aelion chuckled.

"You are brave, in an endearing way. But you know attempting that will result in your destruction."

Goldenrod pulled her Bowie knife from its sheath. She stabbed up at his belly.

Before the thrust landed the sorcerer shoved his palm into her face, knocking her flat.

"Leave the pale-haired one. Kill the rest."

Newman reached behind him to grab the haft of his axe. Pulling it forward brought it across his body in a prime parry. Then he had both hands on it, pulling it out of the harness, and readied it for a swing as he rushed at the sorcerer.

His first swing was deflected before it even reached the elf's body. The sorcerer stood still, only watching him. Newman braced his feet to put the whole power of his body into the next blow, swinging at shoulder height for maximum force. The axe bounced back in mid-air. The recoil knocked Newman into the shelves. He fell to the floor.

One of the embassy guards rushed at the sorcerer, sword high. The elf clasped his hands together. Rasp was smashed against the ceiling of the hollow, wooden spikes tearing his flesh.

Ymer drew her obsidian blade and struck at Verbena in a single motion. Blood splashed the healer's face as Crusher blocked the blow with his left arm. The arm fell limp. He swung his sword at Ymer, cutting her arm. As he pulled the sword back for the next blow the cut closed up, leaving only a few drops of blood as evidence it happened.

Verbena touched Crusher's arm. She closed up the wound, knitting muscles and tendons without scars. She felt the signs of shock beginning and cured that too.

Fighter and elf traded blows. He could block her short knife, but the wounds he left healed instantly. Then Ymer went limp. Her head cocked to the side as Aelion pulled his knife out of the back of her neck. "I always hated her," said the elf.

Osdul flung a fireball into the face of the nearest human. Lanyard's hair and clothes went up in flames. The apprentice flung another at Deadeye, who had an arrow nocked and aimed at him.

Deadeye dropped to the floor, letting the fireball pass over him. He loosed the arrow into Osdul's belly.

The elf pulled out the arrow with a momentary spurt of blood. Another arrow pierced his chest. As Osdul pulled it out a third impaled his eye. The elf crumpled to the ground.

As Newman tried to climb to his feet one of the junior apprentices jumped on him, wildly swinging a knife. He used the haft of his axe to deflect the knife arm but felt a sting where his scalp was cut.

Verbena caught up to the burning man as he rolled across the ground to put the flames out. "Lanyard, stop! Let me help." She put her hands on his blistered face.

"Ow. Okay. Better. Ow." Lanyard stood and drew his knife.

Ithuil flung an icicle into Pritchel. The man went down on his face. He sent another icicle into Crusher's chest. That man stumbled but kept his grip on his sword.

Aelion came next. Ithuil sent an icicle straight at his heart, but the wanderer waved his hand and it shattered into harmless bits of ice.

Then Crusher stabbed the apprentice in the throat. He kept twisting the sword in the wound as the elf fell.

Aelion looked at the icicle sticking out of Crusher's chest. "Doesn't that hurt?"

"Yes. The trick. Is not minding. The pain," panted Crusher.

Wrestling with the axe wasn't getting Newman anything but more superficial cuts. He let go with one hand and drew his Ka-bar. He stabbed the elf in the belly.

"Hurts, but I can heal, human," hissed the elf.

Newman pulled the knife through the elf's gut. Instead of leaving a gash the knife moved through the elf, wound healing as the metal moved on. A hand locked on Newman's knife arm, pulling it back.

Pulling weakly. Elves didn't have more muscle. They had a longer moment arm from their long limbs. Crushed together like this the elf couldn't use his leverage.

Newman hooked his other arm around the elf's neck and pulled. He kept cutting. The elf flailed and squealed. The Ka-bar cut the elf's heart in half. Pink blood sprayed over Newman's torso. The elf went limp.

He rolled to his feet, flipping the lochaber axe to the ready.

Verbena was bent over a kneeling Crusher, pulling something from his chest. Another elf rushed toward her, knife outstretched.

The axe cut through the elf's arm and into its chest. Newman twisted the handle to pull it loose. He looked around.

Two elves kneeled in the pose he'd first seen them in. Deadeye and Pritchel, both bleeding, stood over them. The rest of the apprentices were dead. Verbena moved to Pritchel and lifted his shoulder, searching for his wound.

Elf blood wasn't really pink, decided Newman. It was just paler than human blood so it seemed pink by comparison.

The tree hollow was full of comparison.

The sorcerer hadn't moved. "This ferocity is why you will defeat the orcs."

Goldenrod stood before him, poking at the invisible bubble with a finger. "You will persuade the orcs to avoid us."

"No. You've ruined centuries of my labor. But you can't harm me. You can't make me cast against my will. As I need new apprentices, you will become one. In time you will learn my magic. Then you may persuade orcs as you wish."

The sorcerer looked around the bloody room. "The rest of you may atone for this atrocity by going home and killing many, many orcs."

No one had a response to this.

Newman stood beside Goldenrod and leaned his axe in. When he felt the barrier he kept it there.

Goldenrod took a deep breath. "Your magic is now mine."

White light flowed from the sorcerer to Goldenrod, pouring into her eyes, her mouth, her hands, her heart. As the flow stopped she screamed in pain, clutching her chest. She fell to her knees and bent over.

"What? What?" The sorcerer waved his hands.

When he felt the barrier gave way Newman pulled the lochaber axe back and swung hard, pivoting his hips to put the weight of his body into the blow.

The blade cut into the sorcerer at the base of his neck. The blow went at an angle, coming out under the shoulder. The sorcerer's head and arm hit the ground still connected.

The body toppled into the scrying pool. As it hit the spell shattered leaving only a puddle of blood.

Goldenrod's scream faded to moans. Newman turned and knelt down to embrace her. "Honey? What's wrong?" He searched her torso for wounds.

The wooden spikes holding Rasp to the ceiling vanished. He fell to the ground. Verbena rushed to him. She pressed her hands on his wounds, stopping the bleeding and sealing the holes in his flesh.

Aelion was panicking. "You killed him? The whole village will want to kill us!"

"We'd already killed the apprentices," said Deadeye.

"No one cares about the apprentices. He cast the peace enchantment. He cast the protection that kept orcs out of the village. It's going to be overrun, just like the others."

Goldenrod vomited blood. Not the coffee-grounds vomit of partially digested blood. This blood was bright red, completely fresh. She vomited more into the puddle under her.

Newman cried, "Verbena! Help!" Combat he could handle. This terrified him.

"Give me a moment." The healer squeezed the last of Rasp's wounds shut. Then she crawled the ten feet to Goldenrod, too rushed to stand.

Verbena ran her hands over Goldenrod's back. "Stomach and esophagus are ruptured. Multiple tears. I'm reconnecting as best I can . . ." She went silent, eyes closed, face intent.

Newman held Goldenrod's hand. He stayed still, not wanting to interrupt the magic. The blood coming out of her scared him more than all the blood he'd ever lost.

"Okay. Bleeding's stopped. But it's a weak seal. Her magic is fighting me. Goldenrod, can you hear me?"

She nodded.

"Good. Don't talk. No eating, no drinking. We'll see if you're healed enough to drink tomorrow. If not, Lady Burnout taught me a way to rehydrate someone. We'll need a stretcher for you."

"We're on it," said Deadeye.

Aelion finished closing Deadeye's wounds and said, "We must flee."

"We will," said Newman. "But we need to get ready."

"What about our gear?" asked Crusher.

"Is there anyone here without elf blood on him?" asked Newman.

Rough chuckles answered him.

"We're not walking into the village like this. We'll improvise lean-tos on the way back. Lanyard, what the hell happened to you?"

The burn victim's heavily tanned face was now pink and hairless. Blisters covered the top and sides of his head and his chest.

"I caught a fireball in the face. I'm not blind any more. And not complaining."

"I was in a hurry, all right?" said Verbena. "Let me recharge and I'll work on him some more."

"I thought it took you overnight to recover your magic?" asked Newman.

"Not here. This place is just overflowing with magical energy."

Goldenrod sat up and pointed at the shelves.

Newman followed the gesture. "The books?" Nod. "You want to take the books?" Nod nod nod.

He walked over to the shelves. "This is what I get for marrying a Ravenclaw," he muttered. Louder: "I don't think we can take them all. They're heavy."

He brought one over to her. The pages were thick leather. Runes were burned into both sides. A thick piece had been stitched in to hold an elaborate diagram.

Goldenrod nodded. Newman went back for more. As he picked one up she shook her head. He moved to the other side of the gap where he'd taken the one from. Nod.

"You want the newest ones?"

Nod.

The age of the books showed on their bindings. Scruffs, stains, cracks were absent on the ones he grabbed. He put them down on the nearest piece of dry floor. Holding them before Goldenrod and flipping through the pages brought nods.

"Stretcher's ready," said Deadeye.

"I think everyone's as healed as I can get them tonight," said

Verbena.

Newman ordered, "Let's head out."

Loading Goldenrod onto the stretcher without straining her took his full attention. The fighters lifted it smoothly.

A gasp caught his attention. He turned to see Aelion wiping blood off his knife with some leaves. The two captive apprentices lay bleeding from cut throats. "Can't have them telling people which way we went."

Newman put that aside for later and picked up the books.

***

Aelion could make his hands glow. They used that to hike through the woods when there wasn't enough moonlight to let them travel safely. Newman insisted on a ten minute rest break every hour, as well as he could time them by the stars.

This break was early. A stream gave them a chance to drink their fill. Goldenrod had stayed asleep when they set the stretcher down, so they didn't have to worry about rubbing it in.

When the star he was measuring by disappeared behind a leaf Newman said, "Are you ready for another march or do we need to camp here?"

Crusher answered, "That whole horde of vengeful elves thing keeps me from feeling sleepy."

Several laughed in agreement.

"I've cast some spells to obscure our track," said Aelion.

"Does that prevent them from following us?" asked Deadeye.

"Depends how many spells they cast to track us."

Everyone began standing. The stretcher bearers lifted Goldenrod as gently as they could but she woke up."

"Hey. Where are we?"

"In the woods," said Newman. "Marching home. Go back to sleep."

"No. I figured something out. Help me stand up."

Verbena said, "Try not to talk so much."

"It's all right. Help me stand."

Goldenrod swung her legs off the side of the stretcher. Newman let go of his corner of it to catch her.

"Good," she said. "Now, everybody, group hug."

Verbena burst out, "Don't try any magic! It could kill you in your condition."

"This isn't *my* magic. It's *his*. Now. Group hug."

The men looked to Newman. He said, "Huddle up. Do it."

"Tighter. Close together," ordered Goldenrod. "Aelion, lean over and touch your head to mine."

When the elf complied she began chanting Elvish words. A sudden blackness seized them.

Then the stream and trees were gone. Campfires lit the night.

Newman looked around. They were in the Kingdom's encampment. It looked like a normal night. Someone was singing a Scottish folk tune. Goldenrod sagged into his arms as she passed out.

He swept her up and headed for the Chiurgeon's tent.

"Hey, they're back!"

The normal routine vanished. People surged forward to greet the returnees. "Hello!" "Welcome back!" "Did you find the elves?" "How did you get into camp?" "Will the elves feed us?"

Newman called, "Lady Burnout!" as he approached the tent.

The flap opened. Burnout held it as he went in and laid Goldenrod on the examining table. Verbena followed him in.

"What's wrong with her?" asked Lady Burnout.

Newman didn't know how to answer that.

"Magic," said Verbena. "Two different kinds. She used her power and it ripped her stomach and esophagus apart. Then she cast a spell with stolen magic. She fainted."

"With this much damage I'm not surprised." Lady Burnout looked up at Newman. "You have anything you need to do?"

In other words, 'Stop hovering over me.' Newman said, "I should report in."

"We'll take good care of her," said Verbena. "She'll be fine."

Newman walked back to the clearing between the Court pavilion and the common pavilion where they'd arrived. It was practically a party there. Every member of the expedition was surrounded by at least half a dozen people asking what happened.

Everyone looked so short.

Newman looked around for an authority figure. King Ironhelm was watching the commotion from by his tent, flanked by a squire and herald. He walked up to them, turning a reflexive salute into a bow.

"Good evening, Your Majesty."

"Welcome home, your excellency. How did it go?"

"Terribly. We did fine with the common elves, but meeting their top magic user turned into a bloodbath."

Lord Joyeuse held his torch closer to Newman. "Literally," said the squire.

Newman tugged at his tunic. It was stiff with dried blood, some of it his own. "He brought us to this world. There's three thousand orcs on their way here."

"Three thousand?" asked King Ironhelm quietly.

"Yes, Your Majesty."

The king turned to his herald. "Count Dirk, Master Sharpquill, and anyone they need for a war council to my tent at once."

The herald nodded and ran.

Ironhelm said, "Let's get you a drink. It's going to be a long night."

***

Newman felt more uncomfortable sitting down as the King's tent filled to standing room only. When Ironhelm ordered his chairs taken out to make more room he started to stand only to be waved back down.

"Drink your tea, your excellency," said Ironhelm. "You've had a long day."

The pavilion was stuffed full with dukes, knights, counts, and even non-Peers who led warbands. Wolfhead Alpha stood in a corner, looking as uncomfortable as Newman felt. The royal bed held all six dukes sitting on the edges.

Lord Joyeuse, Ironhelm's squire, offered to top off Newman's tea.

"No thanks, it's finally cool enough to drink."

"All right. Water? Another sandwich?"

"Sandwich would be good." Newman wasn't hungry. His stomach was tight around the first sandwich. But the squire wanted something to do.

The king stepped away from his conversation with Count Dirk. "Is there anyone else we *need* to wait for?"

The headshakes and mutters were all negative.

"Then we'll get started. If anybody's wondering why we're here, the embassy to the elves returned with word of a massive orc attack impending. Baron Newman will brief us on the situation. Then we'll figure out what to do about it. Your excellency?"

Newman swallowed the last of his tea and put the cup down on the chair as he stood. He'd spent the wait mentally organizing what happened in the format that Battalion made him use to brief reconnaissance patrols back in the Sandbox.

"Key points: we made friendly initial contact with the elf village. Contact with the master magic user became violent. Three thousand orcs are on their way to attack us."

That sent a stir through the crowd. The expressions said "I'd hoped that rumor was false" more than "Oh my God."

The king made it clear he wanted all the details of the encounter with the sorcerer. Newman summarized the negotiations in the village then went blow by blow with the sorcerer. Count Dirk shushed anyone who tried to interrupt.

The count took notes on a laptop, typing fast enough to keep up with Newman's report.

"Then Goldenrod woke up and teleported us here with one of the spells she'd stolen."

Count Dirk claimed the first question. "How solid is that three thousand number?"

"Not at all. It's a round number in base five."

"How long will it take them to get here?"

"At least a week, if they move at our own speed. Most were farther from us than the village. They're spread out enough the first wave will be a few days before the last."

"Will the elf villagers act against us immediately?"

"I don't know." Newman rubbed his head to make his tired brain function. "I don't think so. They're not very organized, they're not warriors, and they don't have a trail to follow."

Dirk hit Newman with several more tactically focused questions before letting anyone else have a turn.

"Couldn't you have taken the sorcerer prisoner?" asked Duke Mace. "We'd know more if we could interrogate him."

Before Newman could reply King Ironhelm snapped, "There is no time for backbiting or recrimination. We need to focus on survival."

He felt guilty as he realized he could have tried to knock the sorcerer out. He'd been so focused on chopping the guy the moment he could that he'd never even thought the sorcerer might be less of a threat after Goldenrod stole his magic. On the other hand—the guy was about two thousand years old and had a magic wand. One smack from Goldenrod probably didn't get all his tricks.

After a few more questions King Ironhelm stopped the interrogation. "That's all the useful data we can get. Now we're going to brainstorm possible plans. When we have all the possibilities we'll pick one. Then we'll work out how to implement it. It's going to be a long night, gentlemen. Don't be shy about asking for more tea."

That produced a few chuckles.

"Plans for survival. Go."

Captain Spear offered, "Let's just beef up the fence. Close up the gate, fence the river bluff, build fighting platforms behind it."

"Would have to build it taller," said someone. "Reinforce it with stone," said another.

A couple of others spoke at once, but the king cut them off. "Details later. New ideas now."

"They're spread out," said Duke Mace. "Let's hit them first before they concentrate. Start on a flank and march across their front.

Dirk typed it in. Several looked like they wanted to object but held their peace.

"We need better ground," said Joyeuse. "We could retreat to the mountains. Or better yet to the island we saw off the coast. It's already shaped like a castle."

"There's all the magic users," said Sir Flint. "Can't they find a way to get us out of this?"

Count Dirk looked up from the laptop. "Miracles don't require logistical planning. Let's focus on what we can do."

"But Baroness Goldenrod teleported a dozen people!"

Newman snarled, "That effort left her unconscious in the chirugeon's tent. And it was less than a dozen. Two dozen would kill her."

"Magic is not part of this discussion," declared the king.

"We could hide. Natural caves or maybe dig a tunnel," said a knight Newman didn't know.

Dirk typed it in.

Somebody else asked, "You said the village had a spell protecting it from orcs. Could we go there?"

King Ironhelm looked inquiringly at Newman.

"I don't think they'd want to help us. And the sorcerer cast that spell so it might be broken now."

"Right. Other ideas?" said the king.

"We could train all the non-fighters to use pikes," said Wolfhead Alpha.

"That's an option whichever plan we go with."

Nobody else said anything.

"All right," said the king. "Defend, attack, retreat, hide. That's our options. Which do we choose?"

"Best defense is a strong offense," said Duke Mace. "Fifty of us together could smash all the orcs we meet."

Sir Flint scoffed. "And when a couple of bands slip past and slaughter our families?"

"There'd be the hunters and militia to guard the camp."

"Then we're dividing our forces in the face of the enemy," said Wolfhead Alpha.

Mace kept arguing for an offensive without much support until the king moved the discussion to defending the camp.

"We built the fence in a day. We've got a week to strengthen it," said Spear. "It can stand up to them."

"The fence is already rotting in places," said Wolfhead Alpha. "We'd need to replace the whole thing."

"So do it. Reinforce it with stone while we're at it. We've got that kid who can make stone fly."

"There's not much easy stone around here. Hell, the forest has been cut back so far for firewood we'd spend more time hauling wood than cutting it."

Sir Flint jumped in. "I don't think wooden walls will stand up to a full attack. Those things throw spears. They climbed over the current fence. I think they're smart enough to make a battering ram out of a log. It might take them days but they'll make a hole in it."

"Why'd we build the thing then?" muttered a duke.

"To keep out animals," replied another one sitting next to him on the bed.

The one on the other side said, "And you didn't do any of the work?"

More arguing didn't come up with a way to build a sturdy enough fence. Packed earth was more vulnerable to orcish spears than wood.

"This place is indefensible without building a stone castle," said Lord Joyeuse. "We need to go someplace else. Castle Island."

People looked from the squire to his master to check if he was speaking on his own or for the king. Ironhelm stayed impassive.

Duke Mace said, "Has anyone else seen this island?"

"I have," said Newman. "It's bare rock. Maybe a hundred yards off the coast. Squarish. The sides have a steep slope, maybe a fifty or a hundred feet high. One corner rises higher, like a keep. No battlements. But it's the closest thing we've got to a castle."

Lord Joyeuse described the path to it.

Sir Flint shook his head. "The mountains are nasty. But the distance worries me the most. We have a lot of people who can't walk that far."

"So we carry them," said Wolfhead Alpha. "Travois. Carts. It's not hard."

"Anybody carrying a little old lady can't carry a tent. Or food. Sounds like we'll have to bring all our food there. How much do we have to bring?"

Autocrat Sharpquill spoke up. "We have six weeks' food stockpiled for the winter. Subtracting vineroot and other food that has to be cooked there's four weeks' worth we can bring to a siege."

"Great. A week there, a week back. If the siege lasts over two weeks, we starve."

"Orcs have to eat, too," said Captain Spear. "I doubt they could sustain a siege for one week, let alone two. It'll be a big assault then the survivors fleeing. Just like last time."

"Your lips to God's ears," came from the middle of the crowd.

"What about hiding?" asked Count Dirk.

"Has anyone found any natural caves?" asked the knight who'd suggested it.

The non-peers standing along the walls shook their heads.

Lord Falchion said, "There's no limestone here. It's just soil over igneous rock. It appears to be an impact formation, so no lava tubes."

"Then I don't think we can hide. We could dig a big hole, but it would be obvious. Hiding won't work."

"Fine," said King Ironhelm. "Fortify or retreat?"

Count Dirk leaned back from the laptop. "Retreat has lots of problems but I think we can solve them. We can't solve making an unbreakable wall."

"We shall retreat to Castle Island," declared the King. "Start working out the plan."

Count Dirk began issuing orders. The first was to make announcements to the populace before the rumors went out of control. The second was to summon Master Chisel and his best carpenters.

Ironhelm leaned close to Joyeuse. "Get him into bed."

The squire took this literally. He led Newman back to House Applesmile and wouldn't leave until he was in bed. Newman didn't resist. Facing the war council had him as stressed as a lethal fight. As the adrenaline ebbed he almost fell asleep on his feet.

***

The herald dismissed the populace to their duties. Lady Buttercup thought the announcement had gone well. No one panicked. Not even her. Maybe they were all used to massive disasters now.

In front of the Court pavilion the populace was dispersing. They were anxious but not panicked. Knots of crafters discussed how to build carts, wheelbarrows, or sledges in a day.

Buttercup waited for the crowd to thin. She'd arrived early to be in front of the seats. There were still people blocking the straight path back to her tent. She didn't want to zigzag around them.

Finally enough left to clear the way. Buttercup pivoted her wheelchair to face home. Her hands gripped the rails and pulled hard. Yank after yank had her arms aching but left her moving briskly past the people still chatting.

Then an idiot stepped right into her path. Buttercup gripped the brakes, burning off all her hard-won momentum. It was Master Chisel. Probably wanted one of his apprentices to push her as a lesson in 'chivalry'. She wouldn't need the help if he hadn't stopped her.

"Good day, my lady," said Chisel. "How do you fare?"

"Busy, lad. I have lots of work to do."

"I hope you won't have to—"

Buttercup snapped, "Look, Chisel. I knew you when you were wandering around wearing a Latin motto t-shirt with a sappy grin on your face. Don't waste my time."

Chisel braced himself. "I want your wheels."

She gripped the arms of her wheelchair. "Volunteering me for the heroic rear guard?"

"No, no. I want to build a cart. You can ride in the cart. But we'll have supplies and such in there. And it'll be easier than trying to wheel yourself."

That . . . made sense. Buttercup knew she couldn't go nearly as fast through the forest as she could in camp, and she'd need two or three men to help her across a stream. But still . . .

"Can you put the chair back together when we're all done?"

"I don't know. I'll try. If I can't fix it I'll build you a new one. And put decorative knotwork all over it."

A medieval tech all wood chair would weigh four times as much as her current one. But Chisel was a good lad, he'd work with her to improve it.

"All right. Take me home and you can have the wheels."

"Thank you, my lady."

An apprentice came around and grasped the handles behind her.

***

"Good morning, Newman. Did you sleep well?"

Newman almost dropped his fork. He'd been so focused in his first good breakfast in a dozen days that he hadn't noticed Count Dirk's approach. "Yes, Your Excellency. Very well."

"Good. I'd like to speak with you. When you're done." Dirk dropped into a relaxed parade rest, radiating patience.

Newman thought the subtext of this was 'If your breakfast is more important than my valuable time'. He swallowed the bit on his fork, wiped his hands and face, and joined the count.

Dirk didn't waste any time on pleasantries. His eyes had deep bags from a sleepless night. "We figured out a way to buy more time for the evacuation. A strike force to distract and harass the orcs. Some hit and run attacks would get them moving in the wrong direction."

The older man's eyes looked past Newman, through the fence, fixed on the horizon. "Then they'll have to outrun the orcs to rejoin the rest of us. So this will have to be our most physically fit archers."

Newman nodded. "Yes, sir. I volunteer."

"Good. I want you to command it."

Newman normally stood with his weight on the balls of his feet. Now his heels sank down as his weight landed on them. "Oh, no, I'm sure there's someone more qualified."

The count jerked a thumb toward the front gate, pivoted, and started walking. Newman followed.

This felt like times when the sergeant major felt his feedback was too much for the tender ears of Newman's squad. Though the sergeant major didn't have to go far to find a private spot. Dirk led him through the crafting shops, past the Court pavilion, and out the gate. They crossed the bare swath where trees had been taken for lumber and firewood. They kept going into the woods until no lumberjacks or plant gatherers or hunters could be heard.

This was more privacy than Newman and Goldenrod had on their wedding night.

Count Dirk pivoted to face Newman. "You have real leadership ability. But you won't use it unless you're forced. Either you're ordered into it by royal decree, or things hit the fan so badly you have to step up. After you've passed up a few chances to prevent it becoming a disaster. You need to take initiative as a leader."

Newman looked aside, staring at a flowering bush. "I am not a good leader."

"I saw you in the battle at the gate. You rallied untrained men, made them an effective unit. Might have tipped the battle. Probably saved my life."

"Maybe I have some good moments. But I screw it up if I do it too long. You're talking about a long-term mission. I can't do that."

"I'm going to need an explanation of that." The count's eyes were locked on Newman, a bright blue presence in his peripheral vision.

"You wouldn't understand. It's stuff that happened in some Iraqi town you never heard of."

Dirk leaned against a tree. "Try me."

The movement caught Newman's eye as Dirk lifted his right foot above his knee. Knuckles rapped on the calf with a clacking sound. He pulled up the leg of his trews to show a plastic cup holding the stump of his leg. A metal rod vanished into his leather shoe.

"So talk," said Dirk.

"It's . . . I can't. . ." said Newman.

"Fine, I'll talk. I went over three times. First tour I just did the minimum number of stupid lieutenant tricks. When I went back I commanded an infantry company and did a damn good job swaying the tribe in my sector to our side. Until an IED blew up my humvee.

My first sergeant had to get me out with a saw while the engine burned and bullets flew by."

Dirk was staring at the horizon again. "I put him in for a DSC but those sons of bitches at Brigade knocked it—anyway. Third tour I was a major. Hardly ever got outside the wire. Realized I was wasting the time of everyone doing the real work. When I got home I hung it up."

His gaze went back to Newman. "So maybe, just maybe, I'll understand."

Then Dirk shut up. The bird-things were cough-coughing in the branches. Wind shook the tops of the trees, making the spots of sunlight flicker and dance.

Newman took a deep breath. "My first tour was nothing special. Second I was a squad leader. We were going house to house. Breaching walls because the streets were too hot. We blew a hole, Ramirez went in on point, I followed."

"It was a big foyer with a balcony. Two hajis jumped down onto Ramirez. There were a bunch more on the balcony. I ordered my squad back to the rally point. Then I tried to grab Ramirez and drag him out. More hajis jumped me. I don't know why they didn't just shoot me."

"Wanted prisoners?" said Count Dirk.

"Or hostages. Whatever. The town had been cut off so long the hajis were half-starved. They didn't have any body armor. And our CSM really liked teaching knife moves. So two minutes later we were standing, barely, and eight hajis were on the floor."

Dirk watched as Newman's eyes flicked side to side looking for threats.

"We went back through the breach. There'd been a command detonated mine in the house. My guys were all over the walls. None of them made it."

He locked his eyes on Dirk's. "I ordered them back. If I'd ordered them forward Ramirez would still have both hands and my guys would be alive. That's why I shouldn't be a leader."

"You made the best decision you could with the information you had."

"Shit, is that something they teach in officer school? That's the exact fucking words my battalion commander said to me."

"It shows up in after action reports, yeah. One bad call doesn't make you a bad leader. Everybody makes some bad calls."

"Everybody doesn't get all their men killed."

The birds screeched and flew off. Newman realized he'd shouted.

"No. But that's war. I need you."

"I don't want to ever be responsible for getting men killed again."

Dirk was still leaning on the tree. Bark flaked away as his grip tightened. "Too bad. If I had a dozen West Pointers and twenty NCO Academy grads I'd let you sulk in your tent. But I don't. I have you and a bunch of amateurs. I love amateurs, they never do the minimum to get their paycheck, but they don't have your training or experience."

"Why are you badgering me? Just get the king to order me."

"The last time the king put you in command you dumped it all on Deadeye and didn't step up until it went to hell. I need you to do the job willingly."

"Even if I get them all killed?"

"Yes. This mission has to buy us enough time to get everyone to the mountains. Otherwise we all die. I will sacrifice some men to keep the rest of us alive. If you bring some back, great. I'll be thrilled. But diverting the orcs comes first."

Dirk paused.

"It's your best shot at keeping your wife alive."

"That's low," snapped Newman.

"I have a job. So do you."

"Fine." Through gritted teeth. "I'll do it."

***

The grass in front of House Applesmiles' tent was trampled to death from months of constant walking. The ladies of the house had woven straw mats to keep the dirt from coming inside or becoming a quagmire.

Goldenrod lay on one mat, her back propped up by a haybale, a book in her lap. She looked up as Redinkle flopped down on the neighboring mat.

"Good Lord. Are they still making charcoal?"

The fire mage groaned. "No. This is from helping Master Forge."

"I thought he didn't want you melting his firebox."

"That was three thousand orcs ago. Plus he figured out that if I only burn a little wood at a time it won't get as hot."

Goldenrod could smell woodsmoke from her on top of the soot smudges on her face, neck, and hands. Cooks spending the whole day over a campfire didn't smell that much of smoke.

"What's he working on? Wagon parts?"

"Pikeaxes. Those dozens and dozens of hoes Mistress Seamchecker wanted for the farm? Turn the blade ninety degrees and it's a war axe on a long pole. Hammer the neck into a spearpoint. Pikeaxe. Count Dirk wants all the fighters to have one. When they ran out of hoes they confiscated tent poles with steel spikes."

Goldenrod looked at their pavilion. The banner with a pig smiling around the apple in its mouth hung from a pole. "I'm surprised they didn't come after ours."

"There's two peers living here. Four, with you and Newman, sorry."

Goldenrod waved the apology away. Being a baroness didn't feel quite real to her either.

"Anyway," continued Redinkle, "they would have come for ours if Lady Burnout hadn't shut down the forge when one of the apprentices went down from the heat."

Goldenrod set the book aside and put a hand on the bale to brace herself. "Heatstroke? Why aren't you drinking?"

"No, no, no, don't you dare," Redinkle sprang to her feet. "Burnout would take a switch to me if she saw you standing and me lying down."

Goldenrod sank back down. "I'll be walking all day tomorrow."

"All the more reason to heal as much as you can today." Redinkle poured water into her goblet and emptied it at once. A second goblet-full went down nearly as fast.

When she offered a drink to Goldenrod the answer was, "You have one more first."

Then the water pitcher was empty. Redinkle started the campfire and put a pot of river water on to boil. Then she sat next to Goldenrod. "Seriously, the way Burnout and Verbena were talking your insides were shredded."

Goldenrod shrugged. "Strong magic has a price." She turned the page.

"What are you reading?"

"Books we looted from the sorcerer. His notes on magic, I hope."

The page was covered with the slashes and Xs of Elvish runes and a diagram that could be a football play.

"You can read that?"

"Aelion's spell and what I stole from the sorcerer gave me grammar and the basic words. Connotations and technical jargon are the hard part."

She turned the page. These two were all rows of runes.

"Want me to get Aelion to help you?"

Goldenrod shook her head. "He doesn't know any of this stuff. We killed all the ones who did."

"So what are you going to do?" Redinkle added another piece of wood to the campfire.

"Context clues. Finding usages in different contexts. If all else fails a spell asking for translation."

Redinkle raised a hand. "If I catch you trying to cast a spell I'll slap your face. Don't think I won't. Burnout would write me a thank you note."

Irritation crossed Goldenrod's face. "What good is a thank you note to a frog?"

"Depends. Do I stay a frog after you bleed out?" Redinkle crossed her arms and stared down. "Newman wouldn't want you casting spells now either."

"Fine. I'll behave."

***

"I hear you're a marathoner," said Newman.

Lord Joyeuse looked up from the breastplate he was polishing. "I ran three half marathons. Mediocre times."

"Orcs are built like weight-lifters. They're going to suck at long distance." Newman slid a helmet aside to make room to sit down.

"This is for your long range patrol?"

"Yes." Newman said it calmly. He was willing to own it now.

"I'm a sucky archer."

"The mission isn't to shoot them to death. It's to lead them the wrong way. If missing them pisses the orcs off it's as good as a hit. What we need is to break contact so we don't get eaten. That means runners."

Joyeuse put down the polishing rag. "I'm in."

"Do you need to get permission?"

"He can't say no to this."

Newman picked up the helmet. "You have to pack light."

"I only dug all this out because the evacuation has a lot of people who are going to walk slower than a man in armor. One of the militia can have it."

"Good. Meet for gear inspection by House Applesmile at sunset. We head out at dawn."

***

Someone gave Aelion a fish for his lunch. The elf was shaving it with his obsidian blade. Paper-thin sheets of flesh curled into tight rolls, which he popped into his mouth.

While sitting on a tree branch twenty five feet off the ground.

Newman looked up at this. A persuasive chat worked better face to face than shouting uphill. But this wasn't the easiest tree to climb. He un-knotted his belt and left it at the bottom of the tree. None of his gear would be needed for the talk.

He backed up some yards then ran at the tree. Planting a boot on the trunk he converted horizontal to vertical momentum and leapt up, hands outstretched.

One hand caught the lowest branch. Swinging back, his other hand grabbed on. Then he braced a foot on the trunk to stop his swaying. Some contortions brought his feet up and twisted him around to on top of the branch.

When he was standing on the branch, he spoke in Elvish. "Greetings, Aelion."

"Greetings, friend Newman," replied the elf.

The next branch was in reach, if he didn't mind his feet falling off his current perch. Then it was the same series of contortions.

"I apologize for interrupting your lunch."

"Friends and food go well together. Would you like some of my fish?"

"Thank you, but I've already eaten." True, and the venison and vineroot were threatening to leap out of his mouth to escape further gymnastics.

Aelion shaved some more flesh off the fish.

Now Newman was on the closest branch just below the elf's. He sat on it and wrapped an arm around the trunk for stability.

"We've made our plan for escaping the orcs," he began.

"Good. I was afraid you'd want to make a stand here."

"No." Newman summarized the evacuation to the island and his mission to divert the orcs.

Aelion stopped eating. "You're bringing the old and sick with you?"

"Of course."

"They'll slow you down. The orcs would catch you."

Newman suppressed the sharp words that leapt to his lips. "That's why my patrol is going to divert the orcs. To give the evacuation more time."

"Foolishness. You're throwing away strong bodies to protect the weak ones. Keep that up and you'll have a tribe of weaklings, soon exterminated."

"I'd like you to join the patrol. You have more speed and accuracy than any of us."

Aelion laughed. "If I wanted my asshole stretched wide and

orclings crawling out of it I'd join your stupid expedition. I don't and won't."

"Fine. You can go with the evacuation."

"With the weaklings? What of your promise to protect me?"

"We promised to protect you in our camp. The camp is moving. Your protection goes with it."

"But you will not be there." The fish was forgotten now, idly clutched in one hand as Aelion leaned over to stare into Newman's face.

"I will protect you by diverting orcs away from the camp."

"Nonsense. You'll be eaten. Then the rest of the humans will be caught and eaten. What you must do is take the healthiest humans and flee across the river. Stay ahead of the orcs. Cross the Rim into the Outer Lands if we must to escape them."

Now holding onto his temper wasn't a way to achieve his goals. It was just professionalism. "And leave the rest here to be eaten?"

"It would slow the orcs down more than your patrol."

"No." That was the politest way Newman could say it.

"Then I will go by myself."

Newman shrugged. It wasn't an elvish gesture, but Aelion had learned human body language along with their words.

The elf took his bow and other gear from a fork in the tree. Newman watched his neck. It was healthy and smooth, shining like a new copper pipe. He remembered how it looked when he'd first seen the elf—shrunken, tight, cords and tendons stretching the skin as if they might break it.

As the elf slid down the tree Newman called, "Come find us when you get hungry again."

***

Count Dirk authorized a dozen for this patrol. Newman settled on eight, including himself. More wouldn't be a bigger diversion. And a larger group would be easier for the orcs to track when it was time to leave. Besides, there weren't that many good candidates for the mission.

Inspection started with introductions. Joyeuse didn't know many people outside court. Whippet was a Wolfhead who'd been hauling wood and water, enlisted on Borzhoi's recommendation. Pliers was a woodcutter who'd kept up his jogging routine.

Newman ordered new knives for Whippet and Pliers. He allowed Borzhoi and Joyeuse to keep their metal swords. No one had packed non-essentials.

"We're going to carry a lot of arrows on this patrol. Only half of us are good archers—sorry, Crusher—so the other half will be arrow caddies. Caddies, stick close to your archer. Keep him fed. Whippet, you're Borzhoi's caddy."

The two Wolfheads nodded to each other.

"Crusher, you're with Deadeye." The heavy fighter was tough enough to deal with Deadeye's shit.

"Pliers, Leadsmith. And Joyeuse, you're with me."

The squire looked relieved to not be paired with a stranger.

"The weapons and arrows can stay here. We're getting a bunch of the smoked venison and fish so leave room in your packs. Fill in the gaps in your gear and get a good night's sleep. See you in the morning."

***

Enough well-wishers wanted to see the Long Range Patrol off that Count Dirk deployed a few guards to urge them back. Lord Pulpit moved them out of his way, saying "I am invited."

Borzhoi turned to greet the pastor. "Thank you for coming, my lord."

"It's no trouble." Lord Pulpit took a worn Bible from his pocket.

Borzhoi and Whippet knelt down before him. Newman realized what was happening and knelt on Borzhoi's other side. Joyeuse joined him. Then the rest of the patrol. The crowd fell silent.

Lord Pulpit read, "When he came to Lehi, the Philistines shouted as they met him. And the Spirit of the Lord came upon him mightily so that the ropes that were on his arms were as flax that is burned with fire, and his bonds dropped from his hands. He found a fresh jawbone of a donkey, so he reached out and took it and killed a thousand men with it."

He continued with other tales of Old Testament violence.

Good choices, thought Newman. *This is no day for turning the other cheek.*

After the last inspirational tale Pulpit closed the Bible. "My friends, we are gathered to bid farewell to our champions. Let us pray. Almighty God, these young men have volunteered to place themselves between our people and the desolation threatening us. We give them our thanks and our prayers. Lord, we beg Your blessing on their feet that they be swift. We beg Your blessing for their hearts that they not tire or fail. In Jesus' name we pray. Amen."

The crowd echoed the "amen".

Newman walked back to Goldenrod.

"I didn't know you were religious," she said.

"It's—sometimes," he answered. "I'm a metatheist. I don't believe in God, but I believe I should."

That forced a chuckle out of her. The tension was visible in her face. "You're coming back, right?"

"Of course I am."

"Promise me."

"I promise I will come back to you."

Goldenrod wrapped her arms around him and squeezed.

He returned the hug, his strength gentle, not frantic.

Newman whispered in her ear. "I've fought trained terrorists. I've hunted all through these woods. I'll be fine. Worry about the other guys."

"Damnit. I should—"

"No. You're too weak now. You've done plenty. Rest. Heal."

Goldenrod buried her face in his neck. He felt the tears she'd held back until now.

He stroked her back, whispered endearments, and held her. Then he had to step back. "I have to get to work now. I'm sorry. I love you."

Goldenrod gave him a quick kiss and ducked into the tent.

Newman looked at his men. They were all finishing their goodbyes.

Karl K. Gallagher

Even Deadeye had someone seeing him off. She was a lanky blond in a shapeless tunic. "I don't mind if you lose an arm or leg, but you bring that dick back, you hear?" she said.

"Got it," answered Deadeye.

Newman shook his head. Some people he'd never understand.

The backpack of food went on first. Then four quivers, all full of arrows. Last he picked up his bow.

The others noticed Newman donning his gear and broke off their embraces to prepare for departure. He walked among them to make sure the straps were on right.

Then there was nothing left to do. Newman tried to think of something eloquent. He failed.

"Okay, let's go."

The guards walked ahead, waving people aside to clear a way to the gate. The lane was lined with people waving, cheering, calling out, "Good luck!" "Knock 'em dead!" "We'll be praying for you!"

All the bards were gathered in front of the common pavilion. As the Long Range Patrol came into view they struck up a vigorous march. The song was taken up by some of the crowd. The whole populace shouted the chorus, "How many of them can we make die!"

Newman grinned. His pack felt lighter. This was the way to go to war. He went through the gate and turned north.

***

Mistress Filigree made a point of being at the front of the crowd as the evacuation began heading south. Not with the scouts, she wasn't even going to try to keep up with them. She wanted to be in the lead of the main body.

For the first hour she kept up. Then her will couldn't overcome the stiffness in her joints any more. Younger people moved ahead of her. And some not so young. But she was staying ahead of everyone her own age.

When the rest break was called she kept walking, regaining the ground she'd lost. Most people had flopped down on the ground to let their legs recover. Some sat, drinking water or nibbling on some jerky.

At the front Filigree considered lying down herself. Her legs wanted the rest. Needed the rest. There was still some of the break left.

Her knees twinged as she knelt. Stretching out on her belly let her relax without the additional burden of turning over.

Three blasts on a whistle marked the end of the break. Everyone started getting up.

Filigree braced her hands. A shove brought her to hands and knees. Then she brought up her right knee to put a foot on the ground. The knee still pressed in the dirt complained.

"Want a hand, milady?" A young man held out his hands.

"Thank you."

She raised both hands. He seized them and pulled Filigree to her feet. Her right ankle screamed in pain as it bore the pressure of her whole body.

"No trouble," he assured her. He lifted a hefty backpack and strapped it on. Then he picked up a sack in each hand and started off.

Filigree put one foot in front of the other.

On the lunch break she just collapsed where she was. Hips, knees, and ankles were screaming. When the pain faded enough she took some roasted vineroot from her pocket.

A herald called out a five minute warning for the end of the lunch break. Filigree stood with the help of a tree and walked. She reached the front when the whistle blew.

The lunch rest didn't make up for all the walking she'd already done. More and more people passed her.

Most were good about going around her. The teams of men pulling the wagons likely would have been politer about asking her to move out of the way if they weren't so short of breath.

The wake of the wagons was a nice empty stretch to trudge along in. Her friend Buttercup was in the last wagon. They traded waves.

Buttercup's wagon pulled ahead. That wasn't usual for them. Normally Filigree had to slow down for Buttercup.

The next vehicle Filigree had to move aside for was a travois pulled by two of the royal guards. Countess Ribbon was strapped to it.

Filigree waved in reply to Ribbon's "Good day."

Break time meant lying down now. When they started up again a teenage girl with a water bottle offered Filigree a drink. She declined. This trip was enough of a pain without having to pee in the woods. When the girl kept insisting Filigree took a sip just to make her go away.

Walking behind the travois made Filigree glad she was walking. The contraption was two pikeaxes with a harness holding them together. If orcs attacked Countess Ribbon would be left on the ground while the guards took their weapons and charged off.

Watching the grimace on the countess' face as the travois bumped over a tree root motivated her to keep walking.

As the travois pulled ahead Filigree found herself walking with the rear guard. Heavy fighters shouldering pikeaxes. She'd heard their banter as they came up. The usual coarse language of young men. They quieted as they came closer to her.

A pair of royal guards came up beside her. "Are you tired, Mistress?"

Filigree looked them over. Pikeaxes. Backpacks. A tangle of ropes and boards looking like the pieces of a travois.

"I'm fine, lads. Just getting used to all this walking."

They didn't bother her with conversation but stayed with her. Even as the rest of their squad of fighters moved ahead.

Filigree pushed her legs harder. If she fell behind the rear guard she'd wind up on a travois whether she liked it or not. Her hips and knees shrieked with pain as she swung her legs harder. She focused her eyes on the ground ahead of her to make sure she didn't trip.

"Make room, boys," said a new voice.

Filigree looked up. "Hello, dear," she said to Lady Verbena.

The apprentice healer watched Filigree's walk for half a minute.

"May I touch you?" she asked.

Filigree nodded. She didn't stop.

Verbena put a hand on each side of her hips.

Warmth flowed in from the hands. The pain in the hip joints faded. Her thighs moved smoothly in the sockets, not sticking as they had for the past decade. The knees screamed as she swung the legs harder. Her face twisted with the pain.

"Hold up a moment." Verbena squatted, touching the knees and ankles. "Try now."

Filigree stepped out. None of the joints hurt. Not the big joints. Some foot bones twinged, but that was nothing compared to what she'd been dealing with all day.

She tripped over a root and laughed. She'd seen it, but not lifted her foot because it was far away.

"Better?" asked Verbena.

"Oh, God, yes." She gave the healer a hug. Not a firm one, her elbows and shoulders would complain about that if she did. She walked briskly away. Over her shoulder she said, "Come on, boys. I'm not waiting for you."

***

Crusher and Newman boosted Pliers up to catch the bottom branch of the tree. He pulled himself up and climbed to thirty feet off the ground.

"That'll do," said Newman. "Drop the rope."

"There's room for more in here," said Whippet, holding up the canvas bag with the package of jerky.

"No, we just want the ones in plastic. That way scavengers won't smell them. Put those bundles of arrows in."

The cache was hauled into the tree. Pliers looped the rope around it to hold it firmly to a branch.

When he returned to the ground Newman led the patrol to the bluff edge. They had a full view of the river and its far bank.

"Take a good look. Spot some landmarks. Memorize them. Look upstream and downstream. Memorize the bends."

Newman let them look until a couple let their attention wander.

"The next time we come through here there will be a thousand orcs chasing us. We'll be out of food and low on arrows. We'll need to grab the cache and get across the river as fast as we can. So whoever's on point, could be any one of you, has to say 'turn left' or 'turn right' the moment you reach the bluff."

He paused. They were all paying attention now. To him, not the river.

"A wrong turn then will get us all killed. So study that damn view until you're sure you can make the right call."

They turned back to the river.

After a moment Whippet said, "Best landmark I see is those two fallen trees making a vee at the base of the bluff."

"Can you point it out?" asked Crusher. "I was looking at that big boulder on the river bank."

"There."

"Oh, yeah. That's pretty close to the boulder. We can look for them together."

Joyeuse said, "I see them too. That's a good downstream landmark. We need one we can spot if we're upstream."

The discussion continued without intervention from Newman. He listened, feeling the bonds of the team forming, and hid a smile.

***

Her patched-together guts made lying down and standing up painful for Goldenrod. Once she was vertical she was fine. Walking didn't bother her at all. She strolled in the center of the crowd with a book open in her hands.

Peripheral vision was enough to keep her from running into trees. After a few painful stumbles she adopted a high-stepping gait that cleared roots and deadfalls.

No one walked near her. Killing with a word already had most people wary of her. The tale of what she did in the fight with the elves circulated in hushed whispers and versions of varying accuracy. Her husband was on a suicide mission. And her friends were all busy with keeping the evacuation moving.

That bubble of privacy kept anyone else from hearing her muttered comments as she read through the book. "Oh, that's what *ulathu* means." "This doesn't make sense." "Bastard had no morals at all."

Goldenrod didn't notice the call for lunch until she almost walked into some people sharing a picnic blanket.

"Are you all right, Your Excellency?" one asked.

"Yes, sorry, just distracted." She turned to the right and walked a few yards to an empty spot. A tree had a three way fork in a branch. She shoved the book she'd been reading into the fork, spine-up.

Her backpack went next to the tree with a thump. She knelt down, bracing both hands on the trunk to hold her torso vertical as she lowered herself down. Then she turned around to sit on the ground, stifling a moan of pain.

Mostly stifled. The two on the picnic blanket cast her worried looks. Goldenrod ignored them. She took a book and a slice of fish jerky from the backpack.

As she read she took a bite of jerky and a sip of water. Then she chewed. And chewed. And chewed. She'd been lectured by Burnout and Verbena in chorus on the fragility of her esophagus. She kept chewing until the food felt liquid.

She wasn't surprised when the 5 minute warning came before she finished the chunk of jerky. She put the remainder in the backpack. One hand held the book as she pushed against the tree to painfully lever herself back to her feet.

Bending down to pick up the backpack hurt almost as much as standing. Another jolt of pain hit as the pack swung around and landed on her back. Getting the other arm through the straps didn't hurt, she just had to juggle the book from hand to hand without dropping it.

Then everyone was walking again. Goldenrod started moving with them, waiting for the positions to shake out before starting to read again.

"Your Excellency? You forgot your book." It was one of the picnic blanket couple, pointing at the volume lodged in the tree branch.

Goldenrod glanced back. "Oh, I don't need that one. There's nothing useful in it for our situation."

"You're just throwing it away?" Picnic guy was shocked by this sacrilege.

She shrugged. "It's too heavy to carry as a luxury. You can have it if you want."

Picnic guy wore an over-stuffed backpack, had a bundle wrapped in the picnic blanket under one arm, and dangled a heavy bag from the other. He looked at the book, sighed, and trudged after his partner.

Goldenrod walked on. There wasn't anyone next to her so she opened her current book and resumed reading.

***

The first orc band they found wasn't trying to be stealthy. They tromped along, breaking branches in their way, and discussing something in their grunting language.

"How they hell do they catch deer?" whispered Borzhoi.

"They're probably quieter when they're hungry," replied Newman.

Leadsmith quipped, "Or horny."

Newman's glare kept the chuckle silent. He said, "Drill Alpha."

The rest of the patrol faded back to set up the ambush. Newman and Leadsmith advanced toward the orcs, hiding from view as best they could.

Leadsmith chose a bramble bush as his firing position. He loosed an arrow into an orc as the band passed by.

A screech and answering grunts said he'd hit.

Newman held his nocked arrow in case an orc sprinter came close enough to be a threat. The duo faded through the woods to rejoin the patrol.

The ambush was well set up. Newman only spotted half of the patrollers as he moved through to take his spot at the rear.

He located the rest in a few minutes of listening as he kept still. Breathing, scratching, a rustle as a leg moved. But they were doing a damn good job.

Pliers and Whippet were loudest. They had no hunting experience so they were learning stealth from the other patrollers. Joyeuse could be very quiet, but he couldn't hold it. Every few minutes he'd have some audible twitch.

Deadeye said, "They're not coming."

"Not on the direct path," agreed Newman. "They might be circling around."

"Either way we don't want to stay here."

"We'll go back to the contact site, see if we can spot them."

The contact point was easy to spot. The orcs had milled about, trampling a circle in the undergrowth. Then the trail continued in the direction they had been going.

Newman made a circle gesture as he followed the footprints. The patrol spread out, looking in every direction.

About a hundred yards along a bloody arrow lay on some moss. Leadsmith wiped it off with some leaves and put it back in his quiver.

A blood trail started there, ending fifty yards later at the body of an orc. The arrow hole in the chest was the only wound.

Orcs didn't go into shock. If an arrow didn't hit anything critical one could run around for hours before dying of internal bleeding. Pulling the arrow out accelerated the bleeding.

"I don't think this bunch heard how arrows work," said Newman.

***

"Good morning, Lady Aster."

"Your Majesty!" The young woman bowed hastily, almost losing her balance as the basket on her back shifted.

King Ironhelm put a steadying hand on her shoulder. "My lady, we need your help."

She flinched, then stood tall. "You need me to fly somewhere?"

"Yes. We have scouts looking for the best path for us to take. Best for the wagons. But they're worried about the mountains. We could go through a pass and find it takes us down to a sheer cliff. Scouting that out on foot would take too long. We need you to find the best way."

Aster took a deep breath. "I'll have to talk to the scouts to know what to look for."

"Falchion is head scout. He'll give you everything you need."

The king reached out and lifted the basket from her back. He swung it onto one shoulder. The straps were too tight to fit over both.

Aster bowed. "Thank you, Your Majesty." Then she lifted a foot into the air and moved away.

The scouts were older than she expected. Falchion gathered them in for her briefing.

"Gentle slopes," said a leathery woman. "It's worth going miles out of our way to avoid steep terrain."

A man with a little salt in his dark beard added, "It would be great if you found a path the wagons can go over. We're expecting to leave them at the mountains and hand carry everything from there."

The others grew more detailed. When they started to repeat themselves Aster tried to end the conversation. Then she realized she didn't need to.

"Thanks for the help. I'll let you know what I find." She rose straight up into the forest canopy, knocking a shower of leaves onto the scouts. Aster stopped as her head poked out of the tree.

"Anybody out there?" she muttered as she pivoted through a full circle. No dragons in the sky. She went up a dozen feet, high enough to see over the trees to the horizon, and turned again.

Just birds.

The knot in her belly relaxed. She tilted forward and skimmed south over the trees, leaves brushing her feet. The forest she left to the scouts. She looked to the mountains past them.

The planned route for the evacuation followed the river bluff and then the shore of the lake puddled against the mountains. She followed it until the trees petered out into scrub at the base of the ridge.

Past the lake she could see the river disappearing into the cleft in the mountains. The rumble of the waterfall on the far side was audible from here. It drowned out the soft sounds of the wind and leaves. She could still hear the birds coughing at each other.

After another check of the sky, Aster flew through the pass right above the edge of the lake. This one wouldn't do. A wall of rock blocked the middle. Strong men would have some trouble climbing it. The sick and weak wouldn't be able to get through at all.

The other side curved down into the mountain slopes. Aster landed and walked to where she could see the ocean.

It stretched out to the horizon, vast and empty. She smelled salt on the crisp breeze. No ships or whales in sight, just rolling waves turning white-capped near shore. The islands sticking out of the water looked like they'd been made in the same explosion that produced the rim mountains, irregular chunks of black or grey rock.

She spotted their destination easily. It didn't look like a castle. More a sand castle that had been rained on. But it felt safer than any other place she'd seen.

Hopping down the slope let her see the seaward side of the mountains. No dragons perched on them.

Several deep breaths gave Aster the nerve to lift up over the slope. Seen from above, the crater wall rippled as it descended to the ocean. Sheer cliffs alternated with gentler slopes. A few spots even had sandy beaches.

The ripples crossed and bent enough to let someone zig zag from pass to water without having to descend a cliff.

Aster dropped down and approached the castle island. Seaweed and barnacles along the shoreline marked the high tide lines. The waves hit a cliff about ten feet below the line.

Was this low tide? Or would the ocean ebb more?

Aster paused to scan the sky and horizon. She wished someone else would learn to fly. This would be less scary with a partner.

Spray struck her face as she flew over the waves. This would be rough water to swim through. The waves were two feet high, sometimes more.

The surf would be loud if the waterfall wasn't drowning out all other sound. Aster was getting used to the background roar. When she tuned it out the whole scene seemed eerily silent.

She reached the beach across from the castle inland. Aster laughed. A narrow stretch of rock connected the island to the beach. The middle was still underwater.

Aster found a boulder to sit on. The tide kept going out. The isthmus appeared. It was wide enough for a cart—if they could figure out how to get one to this side of the mountains.

We're going to have to figure out the tide table, Aster thought. *That's going to be tough with three moons.*

She lifted a couple of feet off the boulder, her legs falling straight under her. Turning to face the slope she followed a ripple to the right, trying to match the path people would take down from the pass.

Seaweed and barnacles changed to lichen and then bare rock. The ripples of rock had a liquid appearance, like a mound of melted candle wax scaled up. At the top of the slope a solitary fern sprouted from a crack. It was the last spot of green for a mile left or right.

Time for another scan of the sky. Nothing except a few birds.

The waterfall demanded her attention. Aster flew closer for a look at it.

The scouts mentioned a theory that something had blasted a notch in the crater rim. That fit what she saw. The water fell straight down, landing on a pile of rough boulders that would fill a major league stadium. Water foamed and sprayed into the air as it forced its way through the sharp rocks.

A barrel wouldn't be enough to survive that.

Aster turned to the passes. She dreaded this part. If she couldn't find a usable pass everyone would be trapped between the lake and the mountains trying to fight off the orcs on a level playing field. With three thousand orcs and less than two hundred humans that wouldn't last long.

The pass closest to the river was a relief. It was rough. They'd never get the carts through it. But a normal person could climb all the slopes. She checked by landing and scrambling up with hands and feet.

The second pass might be better. The oceanside slopes were easier than the previous one's. It connected better to the network of ripples. The only problem was a step about fifteen feet high, almost vertical. She tried climbing it. Maybe an athlete such as Joyeuse could scale it. Not her.

Then again—it wouldn't take much of a ladder to get over it. The rest of the crossing would be easy. Not her decision. She'd report to the King and let him decide.

Half a dozen more passes, back to the one she'd first crossed through, weren't any better Several were completely impossible on foot.

That was what Aster needed to know. She looked around at the sky and started flying back. It was late. They'd be making camp.

***

This band had caught a deer. They weren't hungry.

"Oh, that poor critter," said Borzhoi. "Can I put it out of its misery?"

Newman said, "No. We want them furious, not irked."

There was already some fury among the orcs. A pair were squabbling, possibly over who had the next turn with the deer. Shouts became head butts. Then they were rolling on the ground gouging each other.

Orcs not otherwise engaged sat around the wrestlers and hooted.

"I don't think one arrow will be enough to get their attention," mused Newman.

"Oh, if you want attention," said Whippet. He moved toward the orcs. On the way he broke off a length of vine clinging to a tree.

"Hey, what are you doing?" demanded Newman.

Whippet kept going.

Dammit, thought Newman. *Shouting at him could alert the orcs.* "Alpha," he snarled.

As the rest prepared an ambush he and Leadsmith followed Whippet.

"Are we going to rescue him?" asked Leadsmith.

"Probably not."

Whippet moved quietly through the trees. It was wasted effort. Between the anguished bleats of the deer and the grunts of the wrestlers and the cheering sections, Whippet could have been singing without any orcs noticing.

He stepped around a tree to behind some of the seated spectators. The vine whipped across an orc's face, raising a dark green welt.

"I count coup!"

The next stroke caught another orc in the eye, producing a howl of pain.

"I count coup!"

Whippet's next swing left a welt on an orc's cheek.

"I count coup!" He sprinted into the woods. Orcs leapt to their feet to chase him. The deer galloped off.

Newman pivoted away from the fracas. "Let's go."

When Leadsmith caught up he panted, "We aren't going to wait for him?"

"He's faster than we are. Or dead."

The howls and snarls of the orcs drowned out running feet. Newman didn't realize Whippet was with them until he said, "Hi, guys"

"Hi," said Leadsmith.

Newman just kept running.

"So, they're mad now," said Whippet.

"If you trip I'm letting them eat you," said Newman.

The ambush worked perfectly. The three runners raced between the two lines of the trap. In this close-quarters fight the caddies were allowed to use their bows.

The orcs had formed into a narrow column in the chase. The front rank went down to shots in eye and heart. The bodies tripped the next wave. When they fought their way clear Crusher and Joyeuse drew their swords.

Orcs trying to parry swords with a spear lost their fingers. Ones trying to outflank caught arrows to the chest or head.

Then only a handful of orcs were left, crashing through the woods as they fled.

Deadeye lined up a shot on an orc's back.

Newman knocked his bow aside.

"He's getting away," snarled the archer.

"Yes. He's going to tell all the other orcs there's a hundred ten foot tall humans here. That's exactly what we want."

Newman looked at the rest of them. "Get your packs on. We're going to head northeast and find a new target."

***

The heralds announced the day's march was done. Goldenrod flopped to the ground. The quicker she lay down the faster the pain was over.

The faster the intense pain was over. The chronic pain stayed with her. Goldenrod could hear the sound of people getting their dinners out all around her. She should eat. After resting a bit. She closed her eyes.

"Are you sleeping or in a coma?"

Goldenrod opened her eyes to find Verbena kneeling over her.

"I'm okay. Just aching."

The healer slowly trailed her fingertips from Goldenrod's throat to her bellybutton. "A couple of tears have partially reopened. Have you been chewing your food thoroughly?"

"Oh, God. Yes, I'm chewing. I'm probably burning more calories chewing than I'm getting out of the food."

"Something's straining the wounds."

"Yeah. Standing up and lying down. It hurts every time."

"Damn. I'll have to reseal the tears." Verbena sat back on her heels.

Goldenrod waited a minute before saying, "Going to let me suffer some more first?"

"Burnout needs to practice it. I've been teaching her but the real thing is different."

"Fine. Oh, I figured out how I did the teleport."

"Oh?" said Verbena.

"Yeah. Current book has the whole spell. I can go to any place I know well by concentrating."

"Any place? Back to Earth?"

"No, this spell is just crossing physical distance. The interdimensional magic is scattered through the books. I don't think the sorcerer really knew how it worked."

"So we're trapped here."

Goldenrod laughed. "Not forever. I want to make scrolls like he did. We can scatter them on the universe streams. If one can make it to

Earth somebody can cast an anchor spell for us to follow back."

"That would take . . . years." Verbena didn't sound hopeful.

"Maybe. If I heal up enough to use my wish-magic I might be able to speed it up."

Lady Burnout appeared above them. "Don't you dare cast anything until I clear you."

Goldenrod nodded. She stayed silent as the healers applied magic to her insides.

***

They'd split into pairs to search a wider arc for orcs. This was Newman and Joyeuse's first private moment since the patrol formed up.

"What's the chain of command for this outfit?" asked the squire.

"Weeell . . . Pliers takes orders from anyone. This is his first time any distance out of camp so he's a bit intimidated. Whippet will obey Borzhoi and anyone Borzhoi obeys. Crusher doesn't have much hunting experience so he'll follow the hunters."

Newman pulled a branch aside for them both to pass then eased it gently back. Even when they were chatting he moved quietly by habit. "That's Deadeye, Leadsmith, and Borzhoi. They've spent a lot of time together in nasty situations. They trust each other. Deadeye would lead them because he's hard over on the competent/asshole quadrant. Borzhoi is next—he's more tactical."

They paused to listen for orcs. No grunts, breaking branches, or unhappy deer were in earshot. Newman started moving through the woods again.

"What about me?" said Joyeuse.

"Nobody knows you except Borzhoi and me. You never hunted. Your combat experience is all up close hack and slash, which is a good way to get killed on this mission. So that's three reasons to not take orders from you. Four if you count the mission and staying alive separately."

The two men kept walking. Newman quietly, Joyeuse rustled leaves and sometimes let go of a branch too early, producing an audible snap.

Finally Newman answered Joyeuse's silence.

"Yes, you're a squire and you have the Order of This and you're a Companion of That. You think that should make you second in command after the baron. Right?"

"Yes."

"If we were operating where the king could see us it would, and Deadeye would become an unofficial sergeant and the guys would look to him to 'interpret' your orders."

Newman waved at the thick trees.

"Out here your rank doesn't mean shit. A second's hesitation could be the difference between life and death. The guys will follow whoever they think has the best shot at keeping them alive. That's not you."

The squire stared straight ahead. "Thank you for your honesty."

"If I didn't think you could handle truth I wouldn't have brought you. Watch where you're putting your feet," Newman said as a twig cracked under the squire's foot.

"So I'm going to spend this whole mission as an arrow caddy for you or some other hunter."

"Maybe. If everything goes exactly as planned. Which it won't. Then you'll have a chance to use all your talents. You've already proved you're not an effete courtier who needs a page to hold his dick while he pees."

"They did not think that."

"Deadeye said it, but that was probably him being an asshole again."

Joyeuse shook his head.

***

Mistress Filigree could keep up with the parade easily now. She walked with the wagons and travois anyway. This way she was near her friends. They would chat during the breaks. Lady Buttercup enjoyed sharing her opinions on the musculature of the young men taking their turn at wagon-pulling.

Between breaks she had no breath to spare for chatter.

Countess Ribbon's travois was alongside Buttercup's cart. Filigree followed the travois. This pair of pullers were doing a good job of going around roots and other obstacles.

A whistle blew, long and loud. Travois and cart stopped as the men looked back.

Tweet! With the second signal the cart pullers threw off their harnesses. They dashed back to the wagon, pulling pikeaxes from its sides. The travois crew lowered Countess Ribbon to the ground then undid the ropes of the travois to slide out their pikeaxes. They dashed off in the wake of the cart crew.

Filigree stood still. The men were running past her so fast she'd be knocked flat if she guessed wrong trying to get out of their way.

Ribbon started twisting in the remnants of the travois.

"Want me to unstrap you, Your Excellency?" asked Filigree.

"No, they'll be back soon. They just laid me on a pinecone or something. If you could?"

Filigree knelt smoothly beside the countess. Then she reached less smoothly under her. Her back hadn't had the magical healing her legs had.

The seed pod was as hard as a pinecone, but shaped more like a bunch of grapes. Filigree tossed it aside.

"Oh, that's better," said Countess Ribbon.

"Hey, Filly," called Lady Buttercup. "Go see what the boys are up to. If we don't have a witness they'll pass off all sorts of tall tales."

The others on the cart agreed.

Mistress Filigree grinned. She'd been fighting curiosity, but if she had someone else to blame for being where she shouldn't, why not?

There weren't any fighting men in sight. A line of backpacks marked where the rear guard had been walking. Sounds of clanging and shouting came through the trees. She followed them.

She found them as everyone moved to their proper place and shut up. The fighters were lined up in a clearing.

The men, ranging from teenagers to ones only a decade younger than Filigree, were in a long line with a couple of gaps to split them into three even pieces.

A line of women, all in their twenties, stood behind the center line of men. Count Dirk marched between them. He'd been doing most of the shouting.

A scout dashed out of the woods on the far side. He didn't bother shouting anything. A band of orcs was right behind him.

The center squad parted ranks to let the scout through, and closed up again. The orcs attacked them, spears thrusting.

"Cannae!" ordered Count Dirk. "Cannae!"

The female squad obediently backed up. The men retreated more slowly, drawing orange blood when the orcs pressed too hard. One man had his pikeaxe yanked from his hands. He fled. The men on his left and right sidestepped to fill the gap.

The orcs had red blood on their spearpoints but hadn't taken anyone down. They kept attacking, following as closely as the swinging blades let them.

Filigree looked at the side squads, wondering why they weren't doing anything. Then she saw them start to wheel, closing behind the orcs like a double door.

Most of the orcs didn't notice the trap in time. Two dashed out through the gap as it closed. The next two fell from axe blades to leg and belly.

"Archers, get those two!" ordered Count Dirk. The archers who'd stood on the left and right ends of the line dashed into the woods.

The surrounded orcs went down fast. A few flung themselves on the humans, taking lethal wounds to inflict some pain before they died.

When the last one fell Dirk called, "Captain Spear, take your men to back up the archers."

Men peeled out of the mob and trotted off.

Lady Verbena and Lady Burnout walked past Filigree. Burnout gave her a harsh look.

Filigree returned to her friends to recount the battle. "He must have sent twenty or thirty men against those two orcs. I guess he's pissed enough to want no survivors."

"He doesn't want them telling the rest where we are, dear," said

Countess Ribbon.

***

Rhino trails were great for chases. No chance of tripping over the underbrush. An easy straight run without weaving around the trees. A clear view of the pursuing orcs. And nothing in the way of an arrow shot.

Their lead had grown enough to keep them clear of aimed spears. "Time to needle them," said Newman.

The patrol slowed to a walk. Newman and Deadeye stopped, turned around, and nocked arrows.

"I got the mouth-breather on the left," said Deadeye.

Newman studied the orcish front rank. He didn't want to discourage the chase. He passed over the eager orcs. One was panting and stumbling. Probably about to give up. It might make the others follow its example.

"Take 'em." Newman loosed his arrow into the stumbler's gut. Deadeye put his into another orc's mouth.

The war cries had faded as orcs saved their breath for running—well, jogging—after the humans. Now they roared out again.

Whippet yelled, "Get off the trail! Get off the trail!"

That was suicide. Going through the dense woods would slow the patrol enough to let orcs on the trail catch them.

But for all Whippet's faults he didn't panic easily. There had to be a good reason for his call. Newman turned and plunged into the woods, Deadeye at his heels.

Ten yards into the trees was enough to muffle the noise of the orcs. Then Newman felt Whippet's reason.

The footsteps were felt more than heard, a vibration through the ground. Then they could see the crash. A bull rhino led his cows and calves down the trail.

"I wonder if they hunt rhinos," said Deadeye.

"We may be about to find out."

They rejoined the rest of the patrol, all well clear of the occupied trail.

The bull let out a noise like an eighteen-wheeler blowing its horn.

Instead of war cries the orcs were making a lot of grunts and hoots. Borzhoi asked, "Is this good for our mission or bad?"

"I don't know," said Newman. "Let's get the hell out of here and find a different bunch of orcs to piss off."

***

King Ironhelm, or maybe the Autocrat, had gone with Aster's recommended pass. Travois had been broken down to make three ladders. That was the bottleneck now.

Three lines of people stretched down the bare rock before the pass. The ladders weren't sturdy. No more than one person at a time could be on each. Some people couldn't climb quickly.

Those with the skill—and arm length—to climb using the cracks in the rock face bypassed the ladders. But that wasn't enough people to speed up the lines.

Aster helped with luggage. She took everyone's backpack or basket or dufflebag at the bottom and flew up to leave it at the top. The original plan had been for three men to haul stuff up with ropes, but she could do it faster with less chance of spilling. And without fraying the ropes. They'd given up and been reassigned to unloading carts.

Mistress Filigree wasn't worried about the ladder. If it had survived some of the people she'd seen ahead of her there was no danger of it collapsing under her skin and bones.

Putting a foot on the first rung and pushing up was no trouble. Then her arms pulled on the ladder to keep her balanced on the vertical ascent. Her elbows flared with pain. Her shoulders screamed.

After the second rung she stepped back down. Staggering to the side she waved the next one in line to the ladder.

"Milady? Are you all right?" asked Aster. She spoke just loud enough to be heard over the waterfall.

"Just resting," said Filigree. "My arthritis didn't like trying to pull myself up the ladder."

"Ah. I'm sorry. I know they're planning a rope chair for people who can't climb."

Filigree shifted her hips on the rock. "Oh, that'll be fun."

"Or. . ." Aster studied the older woman.

"Yes?"

"Do you think you have enough strength to hold on to me? You don't look much heavier than some of the baskets I've been carrying up."

"If I can wrap my legs around you, yes."

Aster dropped to hands and knees besides Filigree. "Let's try it."

Climbing onto the girl's back was embarrassing but Filigree would rather be helped by her than another bunch of rough young men. When her legs were wrapped around Aster's hips she said, "I'm ready."

They rose straight into the air. Filigree squeezed her legs tighter and grabbed Aster's shoulders hard enough to hurt her elbows again.

Once over the ledge Aster drifted on a dozen yards to a clear spot. "Here you go, milady."

"Thank you."

Aster looked thoughtful. "That's interesting. Carrying you didn't tire me at all. Carrying cargo does. That might just be my arms getting tired from picking stuff up. My magic is stronger than I thought."

***

Goldenrod sat on the slope below the pass. It was covered with people except for a gap directly under the pass. No one wanted an out of control cart rolling over them.

The cart was under control. A dozen men had their hands on its rear to shove it up the slope. Ropes tied to the front were pulled by a score. The wagon's load was stacked at the bottom of the slope, waiting to be hand carried through the pass.

Goldenrod only looked up from her book when the cursing grew loud enough to make her wonder if the cart had broken loose. No, they'd reached the vertical bit. Once the rope crew climbed up the ladders were moved aside.

She looked down and picked up a pebble. It went in the center of a diagram on the left page.

"Talun fethun banthu." The words were sung in the elvish manner, sliding through notes instead of hitting them. The people sitting around Goldenrod gave her wary looks.

The pebble sitting on the book disappeared. It reappeared two feet away, stationary in the air. It fell down and rolled down the slope.

Goldenrod put another pebble on the diagram. She sang a similar phrase. This pebble reappeared two feet above the book. It bounced off the spot it had rested on then rattled downhill.

People sitting next to Goldenrod found other places to wait.

A cheer brought her attention to the wagon again. It scraped over the edge of the ledge as the pushers shouted and clapped. When the rope crew hauled it out of sight the ladders went back in place.

The pushers climbed up and started shoving on the wagon. A minute later an argument broke out. From what Goldenrod could make out the pass was too narrow to roll it through. After some shouting there were grunts of men lifting something heavy. Then people began climbing the ladder.

Goldenrod went back to her book. She'd need to take the ladder slowly. There'd be a gap in the line eventually.

"You've been casting spells." Lady Burnout stood in front of her, arms crossed.

"Not wish magic. Just sorcery. That doesn't hurt me."

"It's powered by blood. You have no idea how it works. And you think it won't hurt you?"

Goldenrod hefted the book. "I'm learning the theory. None of the spells I've tried use blood."

"That puts considerable faith in the competence of an insane slaver."

"It's the best we have."

Burnout switched from stern to pleading. "Can you let it wait a few days? Heal, heal completely. Then do your research."

Goldenrod met Burnout's eyes firmly. "In a few days we're going to have orcs here. Maybe hundreds. Maybe thousands."

Thousands assumed her husband had failed, and probably died in the attempt.

"We'll need all the magic we can get," she finished.

***

Buttercup had a good seat for watching the men unload the wagons. The fallen tree wasn't exactly comfortable, but it wasn't bump-bump-bumping along. That made it 'good' by her current standards.

The flying chick zoomed by again. Or she would have if she hadn't landed right in front of Buttercup.

"Would you like a lift, milady?"

"Sure." It wasn't like Buttercup had anything better to do. In camp she'd spent hours on end in the kitchen but her help wasn't wanted with field cooking.

A minute's work had a belt holding Buttercup to Aster's back. The older woman's arms went under the other's shoulders, palms on the collarbones. That could become a full Nelson if the ride grew too rough.

Lifting into the air was disappointingly free of magical sounds or auras. If she'd had her eyes closed she'd think Aster had just stood up.

"Do you mind if we go through the other pass?" asked Aster. "I hate flying over a crowd."

Not wanting to be the focus of attention was something Buttercup completely understood. But if they were taking a detour. . .

"Could we fly over the river? I've never gotten a clear look at it."

She could have. All she'd needed was a couple of volunteers to push her back up the bluff. Not a favor she wanted to owe.

Aster banked away from the mountain's slope. "Sure."

She approached the river over the edge of the lake. Dipping down from the foothills to skimming over the water filled their nostrils with rotting plants and stagnant air. Flashes of overwhelming sweetness from clusters of flowers didn't make it better.

Reaching the river was a relief. Clear air blew the swampy scents away. Deep blue water rushed under them. Aster turned into the gap.

The sound of the waterfall hurt this close up. Aster shouted something. Buttercup could feel her chest squeezing out the words but couldn't hear them.

They went past the end of the river. The water dropped away below them. Aster dove to follow it.

Below them was a cloud of mist. They flew into it. Cold water slapped Buttercup's face and arms, making her squeeze her ride involuntarily.

Aster pulled out of the cloud. Past it the water seethed through a pile of gravel. If a jagged rock six feet across counted as gravel.

Then they were passing over the shore. The evacuation's destination was obvious. The island stood out, a solid block with the ocean as moat. Getting to it would be a nasty swim. Buttercup was good with that. Everyone said orcs couldn't swim worth a damn.

They landed next to a flat-topped boulder. Aster grunted as her magic let Buttercup's weight drop onto her legs.

"This spot is above the high tide line," said Aster. "It's a safe place to wait for everyone."

Buttercup eyed the incoming waves. If true, this was high tide. The rock didn't have any seaweed or water stain on it so probably true.

"Fine. Set me down on it."

Once the belt was undone Buttercup settled onto the boulder. She'd have a good view of the whole Kingdom filing past. Possibly stripped down for swimming.

***

Finding the supply cache was no problem. Carrying it was. The orcs were too close for them to divide the supplies among the patrollers.

Crusher and Joyeuse handed their bows off and grabbed the sides of the big canvas bag. They started down the river bluff. Their free hands grabbed at roots and vines to steady them as dirt slid away under their feet.

Behind them an orc let out the grunt-grunt-hoot that seemed to mean "I see them!"

Bowstrings twanged as patrollers tried to discourage the orcs. Then dirt sprayed over Crusher and Joyeuse as the rest came down the slope after them. A spear flew over their heads.

"Find some driftwood," ordered Newman.

The patrollers spread out as they skidded down the buff. A sprained ankle meant death here. But so did being out run.

The supply bag reached the bottom first. Crusher trusted a foothold that gave way like sand. As he fell he kept his grip on the bag, but that pulled it out of Joyeuse' hand. Then he rolled over and lost the bag anyway.

It rolled down the slope and met the flood plain with a crack of breaking arrows.

Crusher didn't bother standing. He slid to the bottom on his muddy rear.

There was no breath for recriminations when Joyeuse caught up to him. They grabbed the bag again. The river bank was two hundred yards away.

A spear landed to their right, quivering as it stuck out of the ground. Neither dodged. Orcs were only accurate with their spears out to twenty yards. They had the strength to hurl them much farther but hitting was a matter of luck.

As the bag carriers lumbered up Pliers tied a last knot on a conglomeration of driftwood and rope. "Dump it on, guys, it should hold."

They heaved the supply bag on. Pliers tied the bag on so they wouldn't lose it if the makeshift raft flipped over.

Newman panted up with a couple of dry tree branches. "Get in the water. They're gaining."

A glance back showed orcs were almost to the bottom of the bluff.

All four shoved the raft into the water. It held the bag almost completely out of the water. Pliers slung his bow, jumped in, and started kicking. The rest followed, using branches to hold them up.

"Wish I'd had time to get my boots off," muttered Joyeuse.

"Shut up and swim," retorted Newman.

The patrol spread out as they moved into the swift flowing center. A few spears splashed into the water.

No one tried to fight the current. They let it carry them as they struggled to reach the far side.

The orcs' war cries had been fading. Now they swelled again as the monsters followed them down the river.

Whippet was first to reach the bank. He left his log in the water. He took a moment to squeeze water from his hair and shirt. Then he took the coil of rope hung over his shoulder and unwound it.

The first toss landed short of the raft with the supply cache. He hadn't allowed for the extra weight of the wet rope.

The next attempt was close enough for Pliers to grab it.

"Swim over and I'll haul you all in," called Whippet.

Joyeuse had been alternating pushing on the raft and swimming on his own. He was too far away to reach Whippet's rope. He reached for the raft and wrapped his hand around one of the ropes holding it together.

Newman looked at the rope, well out of his reach. "Just bring the raft in. We'll catch up."

A minute later Whippet was helping Pliers and Joyeuse onto the bank. All three grabbed the bag to haul it a few yards inland. Pliers started untying the raft to recover its rope.

Whippet picked up his rope and scanned the river to choose his next rescue. "Hey, Crusher! You okay?"

The fighter was lagging well behind the rest. A spear splashed into the river ahead of him.

"This damn log barely floats," grunted Crusher. He had it tucked under one arm while the other stroked through the water and his feet kicked. Much of the effort went into keeping his face above water, slowing his progress.

Whippet sent the rope his way, uncoiling through the air. "Crap! It's not long enough."

Joyeuse started undressing.

"Let me get this untangled and we can tie them together," said Pliers, as he wrestled with the knots holding the raft together.

The next throw landed by Leadsmith. He thrashed his feet to get to it. Whippet hauled him to shore.

Joyeuse's white tush flashed in the air as he dove into the river. Free of boots, belt, and clothes he stroked through the water like a dolphin.

Crusher started as the squire popped up out of the water.

"Keep the log. I'm going to tow you."

"Right."

Joyeuse flipped to his back, hooked his left arm around Crusher's, and started stroking vigorously.

More orcs were massing on the far bank. War chants filled the air. A spear landed in the water almost to the patrol.

The second rope still had some knots in it as Whippet pulled Borzhoi to shore. In a minute everyone was on land except Crusher and Joyeuse. They held onto the rope as three men hauled them in.

"Taunt them," said Newman. "We need to make them cross."

Leadsmith started capering on the bank. "Na na na na na!" He had the old playground rhythm. Waving his arms over his head he repeated, "Na na na na na!"

When the last two climbed up the bank they all started taunting the orcs. Joyeuse did take a minute to get dressed first.

The orcs didn't have clothes weighing them down but their muscled bodies were too dense to let them swim well. One orc was angry enough to run into the river but he was back on the bank coughing up water in a minute.

Smarter orcs were gathering driftwood. One band hauled a fallen tree to the bank.

"Guys, stop," said Leadsmith. "We're a jumble. We need to synchronize."

Everyone looked at him.

"Keep it simple. Everyone do na na na. On me," Leadsmith waved his hand to conduct them. "Na na na-na na!"

They repeated the chant over and over.

Leadsmith was right. The orcs responded to the chorus with intensified war cries. Some began a dance with provocative hip thrusts.

He sang louder, encouraging the rest of the patrol to match him. When he was sure they had the rhythm down he waved his arms in the air with the chant. The rest followed him.

A spear hissed across the river. It impaled Leadsmith on the left side of his chest. He fell, held off the ground by the foot and a half of spear sticking out of his back.

Borzhoi dropped to his knees beside him, lifting Leadsmith into his arms to take the man's weight off the spear.

On the other side Newman unfolded the saw blade from his multitool and started cutting the spear where it stuck out of the chest.

Leadsmith grunted in pain as the sawing jerked the spear around in the wound. His face was pale. His mouth moved but no words came out.

The orcs were holding one of their number up on the others' shoulders. The war cries changed pitch, mocking the sudden silence of the patrol.

"Grab all the gear. We are leaving," ordered Newman. He shifted to Leadsmith's back to cut off the other end of the spear.

Joyeuse found the first aid kit. He laid a thick gauze pad over the stump of the spear and taped it into place. Blood soaked through the gauze.

When Newman finished the second cut Joyeuse applied another bandage. This one soaked through even faster. "I'll have to cut up a shirt for a pad," said the squire.

"They're crossing," said Newman. "Let's go."

Orcs were visible on the river. They were being swept downstream but they were crossing.

Four men carrying Leadsmith and two with the supply bag left Whippet to break trail. He scouted the bluff, finding gentle slopes where they could climb without going single-file.

At the top Newman looked back. Two trees were coming across the river, each propelled by two dozen orcs hanging on. More orcs were crossing on driftwood, sometimes two or three to a piece.

A leaning tree on the far bluff ripped free from its roots and slid down, the orcs who'd been jumping on it leaping clear as it fell.

"Into the woods," ordered Newman. "We need to get some distance and find a way to break our trail before we head for the sea."

Pliers protested, "We have to stop his bleeding first."

"No time."

Deadeye countered, "A blood trail will lead the orcs straight to us."

"I think it's too late," said Joyeuse. He held a hand over Leadsmith's nose, then applied fingers to his throat. "No breathing, no pulse."

They lowered him down.

"CPR?" asked Pliers.

Joyeuse shook his head. "That only helps when there's an ambulance on the way."

"Right," said Newman. "Get his arrows and food."

Pliers whirled on him. "Loot the body? You fucking ghoul."

"We need the arrows. And food. Plus I don't want to leave any for the orcs." Newman emphasized his words by stepping into Pliers' personal space.

The younger man took a step back and looked down.

"He is food for the orcs," said Deadeye. "We going to bury him?"

"They can dig him up faster than we can bury him. And we don't have the time."

"Hmph." Deadeye knelt down and transferred Leadsmith's arrows to his own quiver.

Joyeuse opened the belt pouch. Some jerky went into his own pouch. The man's wallet he passed to Newman. "For next of kin."

Last he took the sheath with Leadsmith's Damascus blade and offered it to Pliers, who'd been the archer's arrow caddy.

He accepted it.

"Let's go," said Newman. "They're coming."

"I'm taking his bow," said Deadeye. "I don't want the orcs getting ideas."

Seven men headed into the woods.

***

"Make way," called Countess Ribbon's thin voice. "Make way!" She sat atop a wagon, holding the rope tied over its load.

Filigree hastily moved off the track, climbing uphill until it was too steep.

The wagon rolled backward down the slope, slowed by over a dozen men pulling on ropes. One fell and was dragged until he let go of the rope. He sprang to his feet and ran to catch up.

It was loaded to overflowing with food, blankets, and other gear. Ribbon waved as she passed under Filigree. "Don't dawdle," she said. "They can see the main body from the pass."

Then the wagon and its line of men were past. Shouting broke out as the leader demanded they stop at a corner. Ribbon whooped as the wagon ran up on a ledge.

Filigree stepped into the empty path left by the wagon and resumed her walk. She watched the island waiting in the ocean. Seeing the end of the long walk made her step out a little stronger.

When she reached the beach the wagon was already crossing the causeway. Ribbon was still on top.

A marshal standing at the water's edge said, "The tide's coming in. Don't start unless you can make it across."

She looked over the causeway. The middle was underwater. People were walking through it. She could see their knees.

"I'll be fine," Filigree told the boy.

The causeway had lousy traction. The slopes were all bare rock, solidified lava from whatever cataclysm created the mountains.

No plants grew on the slope. Even lichens hid in the dips in the terrain providing shelter from the ocean storms.

The start of the causeway, only under water a few hours a day, was just a damp version of the slope. High tide was long ago. The rock had dried. Filigree strode firmly along. The rest of the crossers were well ahead of her.

She skidded as she stepped on a slimy patch. Something was growing on the deeper portion of the causeway. Not thick enough to be called moss. Just a bit of green tint to the rock and slipperiness under her sandals.

Filigree weaved among the patches, wanting to keep to bare rock. Falling would lead to a fuss as people ran back to pick her up. She wanted no part of that.

That wasn't an option in the middle. The water was turbid enough to keep her from looking through it for gaps in the growth. It grabbed her feet, demanding even more effort to keep moving forward.

Her back twinged as she put more strength into wading. The other crossers were widening their lead. They were out of the water and walking freely.

Filigree glanced back at the shore. No one else was crossing. A dozen figures waited on the beach. Wimps.

The water was rising. The underwater stretch was longer than when she'd stepped onto the causeway. But she was close to the middle.

Good thing. The water was climbing up her thighs. Then her hips were covered. That made her a bit more comfortable physically. Swinging her legs underwater saved her from the slosh, slosh, slosh of wading.

The water was closer to the island now. The tide was rising. But she was catching up.

Slosh, slosh, slosh was even worse with her clothes soaked. She worried more about falling in the shallow water. Slipping in the middle would just mean a moment of floating. Here she could get hurt.

When Filigree's foot skidded in a patch of moss, pain went through her. Not from falling. She pivoted fast enough to save her balance. Her spine screamed in protest at the twist.

"I need Verbena to fix the rest of me," she muttered.

A wave slapped against her thigh. The tide was still coming in. She stomped forward, forcing her way through the water.

A middle-aged man came down the causeway from the island. "Would you like a hand, mistress?"

Filigree repressed an answer unbecoming to a Peer. "Thank you, but I'm quite all right."

The traction improved as she walked through the shallow water. There wasn't much growth on this stretch.

He wouldn't leave but at least the guy didn't keep pressing her.

When Filigree stepped onto the damp rock he politely offered his arm without a word. She rested a hand in his elbow, not putting any weight on him. They walked up to the island together as if arriving at a ball.

He bowed to her. "I'd best get back to work, Mistress."

Her helper joined the people unloading the wagon.

The island didn't have a beach. A shelf of basalt sloped gently from the water to the wall of the island's core. The wall wasn't vertical. It tilted in enough some men were going straight up it with a bag under one arm. Most stuck to a diagonal ripple in the wall. That was filled with a line of porters, bunching up as they went through the trickier bits.

Anyone wanting to carry a second load had to slide down the steep parts. A gentler bit had several men gathered above it waiting their turn.

"Oh! Ants," said Filigree, realizing what the sight reminded her of. While the majority followed the swarm some wandered off to explore new routes.

She waited for her clothes to stop dripping before attempting the wall. She took a moment to empty out her shoes as well. Slipping was scarier twenty feet up than three feet under.

When she was just damp and sticky Filigree slipped into a gap in the line going up the ripple. It was narrow. Experimentally putting her feet beside each other left a toe hanging in the air.

She matched the pace of the porters. A guilty part of her wondered if she should have carried up a bedroll or something. Arthritis pain in her wrist and elbow cured that. She had to brace one arm on the wall for stability. Her balance wasn't good enough to keep her on the trail without it.

The first clog left her standing still for a couple of minutes. Then the line moved again. When Filigree reached the obstacle she understood.

The ripple smoothed out for a couple of feet leaving a gap. The tall man in front of her hopped over, swayed and put his shoulder against the wall to steady himself without dropping either bundle under his arms.

Hopping wouldn't work for her. She'd already resorted to keeping her left foot always in front of the right because the ripple was too narrow to let her move one foot past the other. To get past this. . .

Filigree rested her left toes on the end of the ripple, holding up the foot to let the other slide under it. She braced her hands on the wall.

Pushing off with right foot and both hands sent her across the gap. The left foot landed on the far side. Her hands slid across the rock. One hand caught an irregularity and pulled. Hard. The other grabbed on. Her shoulders flared with pain as they took her weight.

Her arms pulled her across the gap. The left foot held her while the right waved around, unable to find a toehold. She hopped a few inches ahead to create one.

Then she held still a moment to let the spasms of her abused spine calm down.

"Are you all right, mistress?" came a voice from the other side of the gap.

Filigree answered, "Yes, fine," and started scooting forward again.

The next bottleneck wasn't a problem for her. Irregularities in the ripple left it too narrow in spots for the porters' feet. Hers were already smaller than most so a few long strides took her past.

Once on the edge of the wall the top of the island spread out before her. Again she thought of ants, but this was the chaos of a kicked anthill, not marching lines.

Filigree walked forward to make room for the porters behind her. At the edge Count Dirk and Captain Spear pointed down and muttered in low voices. Piles of supplies were added to by the porters and pulled apart by women on the other side. Everyone was moving in different directions.

She kept moving, seeking a place to lie down where she wouldn't be trampled.

Moving around the outside of the mob, she reached the far side of the island. Some people were lying down with Burnout and Verbena moving around them. A seated figure waved.

Walking closer, Filigree saw the waver was Lady Buttercup sitting with her back against a rock outcropping. The skinny legs stretched out straight before her.

"Welcome to paradise," said Buttercup.

The outcrop had plenty of room. Filigree levered herself down to sit next to Buttercup. "Thanks for saving me a spot."

The other woman nodded. Her eyes drifted across the plateau.

Filigree muttered, "What a clusterfuck."

"It's not that bad," countered Buttercup. "There's islands of organization. Look at Burnout. She's been booting out helpers as she stabilizes the patients. Then they wander around looking for something to do. Most of the organizers have all the people they need right now. If they need more volunteers, bam, somebody's right there. Rest of the time all the others wander around looking for work because everyone's too excited to sit down and rest."

"I'm not too excited." Filigree took out her canteen. There was still a mouthful of water in it. She swirled it around her mouth to restore her dry cheeks and tongue, careful not to let any drops escape. "Crap, I'm dry."

"Relax. We have plenty of water."

She glared at Buttercup. "We can't drink seawater."

"Don't have to. One of our magical girls can purify water. She's working on the puddles up here. If you see someone standing sentry in the middle of the plateau she's guarding a clean puddle. Some of them are ten feet deep."

"Good." Irregularities in the rock dug into her back as Filigree relaxed enough to rest her weight on it.

Buttercup passed the time by commenting on developments among the mob in front of them. Most exciting was when a new team began putting up lean-tos. She was satisfied with Filigree's grunts as acknowledgements.

As the sun drifted lower a new subject arose.

"Buttercup . . . where's the privy?"

She pointed a thumb over her shoulder. "The whole seaward edge."

"Hell. I'm going to fall off the cliff."

"There's a cleft you can stand over. Can't miss it. Even with your eyes closed."

***

After a day's march with no sign of orcs the patrol was certain they'd broken contact. They moved along the top of the river bluff, just far enough into the woods to stay hidden.

Every hour or two Whippet and a partner who didn't want a rest break would peek out at the river valley. It had been delightfully free of orcs all morning.

This time Whippet was excited, running up with a grin on his face.

"What is it?" demanded Newman.

"Trees!"

The patrollers looked around. This patch of forest only let a few bits of sunlight through. The gold coins jittered over the seated men as the wind blew on the tree tops. Anywhere they looked there were trees.

"Dead trees," clarified Whippet. "They're on the flood plain. Three of them, close together. If the orcs can make a raft with a tree so can we."

Everyone started getting to their feet.

Newman wanted to take a look at the dead trees. He didn't mind everyone else coming along. Which was good, because ordering them not to wouldn't go over well.

Yes there were three trees, ranging from fifty to a hundred yards from the riverbank. They discussed rafting on their way down the bluff.

"My biggest worry is the falls at the mouth of the river," said Newman. "There's no way we'd survive going over."

Joyeuse was unconcerned. "If we can paddle well enough to stay off the banks we can steer into that lake by the rim. Then we just go over a pass the orcs aren't using and we're back with everyone."

Newman saw some holes in that plan but he didn't have anything better.

"Can we even ride on one of them with all the branches?" asked Borzhoi.

"Let's see how hard they are to break off," said Whippet.

Up close they were the kind with heart-shaped leaves. A bit soft for good firewood. Hopefully they'd be better as rafts. The bark was smooth, which their asses would appreciate.

Rolling the trees to the bank snapped off most of the branches. Some of the stumps were sharp spikes.

Crusher poked at one and winced. "Don't walk on the raft. You don't want to fall on this."

There wasn't enough rope to tie the whole length together. They shoved the logs together. Stumps of branches locked them into place. Then each end was tied together.

Joyeuse sorted through the snapped off branches to find paddles. Most candidates needed to be broken further or roughly trimmed with a knife.

"You have nine. Lose count?" snarked Deadeye.

The squire kept working. "We'll need spares."

When the raft was ready an argument broke out over whether to launch it immediately.

Newman vetoed it. "It's late afternoon. We're exhausted. I don't want to be paddling in the dark when we haven't learned how yet."

He pointed back to the bluff. "We'll sleep in the woods, out of sight. Then we head out at first light."

The prospect of getting home—meaning their people—made them all light sleepers. They were at the raft before dawn, finding paddles by starlight.

The sun wasn't over the bluff when they launched. Newman waited until they could see if there were orcs on the far side. Then he gave the word.

Shoving the raft didn't work. They had to take the paddles, bows, and supply bag off the raft and flip it over twice. Then half the patrol stood in hip deep water to keep it from escaping while the rest piled stuff on.

They managed to all board without flipping again. Despite a few "ows" the broken branches didn't draw any blood.

Just as they reached the center of the river Pliers cried, "Crap!"

Deadeye pulled the dropped paddle out of the water. "Stop that. You're making his lordship look smart."

The first orc sighting was greeted with, "I hear banjos."

They paddled fast enough not one bothered throwing a spear.

Once around the bend they rested, letting the current carry them along.

"My arms are killing me," moaned Whippet.

Crusher laughed. "This whole trip has been one long leg day. I'm fine with giving my arms a workout."

They drifted a bit longer.

The pressure of survival kept Newman from appreciating how beautiful this place was. The dark green of the forest leaves faded into the bushes and flowers of the valley. The river was a deep blue, sometimes brown at the banks. No trash, no smoke, no obnoxious salesmen.

Newman had to admit the neighbors here were obnoxious in other ways.

"Hey! Something's got my foot!" cried Pliers in the bow. He flailed at the water with his paddle.

Crusher reached over from the other side of the raft and grabbed Pliers' backpack. He yanked on the younger man, hauling him onto the middle tree.

Two pale tentacles wrapped around his right leg. More came out of the water and slithered over the side trunk.

"Cuttlefish," snarled Deadeye. He slid into the water, pulling himself forward along the raft. His paddle pointed ahead of him like a spear.

"Damn, I've got one too," said Borzhoi. His feet came out of the water bound together by a tentacle around his ankles.

"Watch the balance!" shouted Newman. He leaned away from the raft as it tipped toward Borzhoi and Crusher on the left.

More tentacles appeared around the middle log. They poked at the piled backpacks. Joyeuse drew his knife and crawled toward them on left hand and knees. A hard cut took the tip off one member. The others whipped around and entwined his arm. He covered his right hand with his left, keeping the knife from falling, but the cuttlefish pulled him off balance. He fell against the raft, a broken branch digging painfully into his belly.

Deadeye shoved hard against the raft, rocking it. He disappeared under the water. Twelve seconds later his head popped up. "One down!" A cuttlefish wriggled on the end of his paddle.

The tentacles holding Pliers went limp.

Whippet had cut Borzhoi loose but had his own arm entangled. The older Wolfhead stabbed down with his paddle. He didn't kill the cuttlefish but it released Whippet and descended into the murky water.

The critter wrestling with Joyeuse also gave up. Its tentacles slithered out of sight.

"Any casualties?" asked Newman.

"No." "No." "No."

Joyeuse rubbed the sore spot on his belly and stayed quiet.

Pliers unwound the severed tentacle from his leg. The clammy flesh gave him goosebumps.

Crusher held out a hand for it.

He handed the tentacle over with a dubious look.

A few knife cuts produced some inch-wide slices. Crusher popped one into his mouth.

"Are you nuts?" said Deadeye.

Swallow. "Nope." Another slice went in.

"That stuff tastes vile."

"Ain't about the taste." Crusher swallowed a third piece. "Not so bad if you don't chew."

He lifted a fourth piece. Paused. Tossed it into the river. Then Crusher bent over and vomited into the water. Cuttlefish slices, his fish jerky breakfast, all the water he'd drunk. He kept spasming until the heaves were dry.

When the spasms stopped Crusher took a few deep breaths. Then still facing the water he yelled, "Welcome to the middle of the food chain, assholes!"

The whole patrol laughed. All the tension of the dangerous mission drained out as they laughed until their bellies hurt. The noise echoed off the river bluffs.

When they calmed down Newman said, "Paddles up. Let's get down the river before something else fucks with us."

***

Count Dirk studied the orcs on the shore through his binoculars. Their behavior was different since the last few bands arrived. Yesterday they'd sat on the beach while a few hurled inaudible insults toward the humans. Spears were poked into the sand.

Now the orcs danced in circles waving their spears in the air. The mass chanting could be heard clearly on the island even over the waterfall.

Dirk wondered if a leader had arrived or they'd reached a critical mass. He glanced up at the moons. Low tide would start soon.

The orcs kept dancing as the causeway emerged from the sea. Then as the water lowered more, some circles broke up. The orcs walked on to the causeway, stopping short of the water in the middle. More circles broke up and followed them.

"Fighters into armor," he said to his herald.

The trained voice sounded over the island. "All fighters, all fighters. Armor up. Armor up. Stand ready under arms. All fighters, armor up."

After a moment the herald whispered, "Your Excellency, many of them are heading for the privy."

"Good. They're taking it seriously."

Dirk lifted the binoculars again. Two days ago he'd met a band of orcs at the end of the causeway. A line of pikeaxes held them there. Archers on the flanks picked off orcs waiting their turn to fight, and later trying to escape. None of his men were wounded enough to need more than a brief touch from the healers.

There were too many orcs to do that again. If they all came through at once they could stack up bodies and break through the line. He'd ordered everyone to defend at the edge of the plateau.

But if only some of the orcs attacked . . . he focused the binoculars on the beach. More circles were breaking up. No, this wouldn't be another small attack.

Count Dirk shifted his gaze to the middle of the causeway. The submerged portion was shrinking. A few orcs were brave enough to advance ankle deep into the water. It wouldn't be long now.

The fighters were in their gear. Heavy armor for the first line. Jackets and helmets for the second line. The third line wore their clothes and held whatever weapons they could find.

Some veterans were using the waiting time to instruct the newbies in their fighting drill. Nothing that would win a tournament, just a few moves that would cripple a naked orc or force it back until better fighters were free to finish the job.

Dirk checked the causeway again. The wading orcs were splashing ahead as the tide receded. Then they reached the midpoint. The lead orc broke into a run, reaching the exposed rock on the island side. The rest trotted after.

"Drummer boy," snapped Dirk. "Sound alert!"

The boy lifted his bodhran and beat a rapped tattoo with the tipper. The fighters surged toward the edge of the plateau. The first line lay prone, lifting their heads to peek over the edge at the incoming horde. The reserves lay or knelt behind them.

Dirk handed the binoculars to his herald. "Secure these. Then report to the medics." The young man trotted off.

He picked up his helmet and squeezed it onto his head. The chin strap fastened snugly. He checked his sword came easily out of the scabbard. Then he picked up his shield.

He walked the line, looking at the deployment. Some of his squad leaders had arranged their men oddly. Count Dirk made no comment. Delegating meant putting up with how the guy chose to do it.

A few spears flew over the edge and bounced off rock. The civilians who'd edged closer to see the action scooted back a few dozen yards.

A boy ran up and gave Dirk a Cub Scout salute. He gave an Army one in return.

"Sir, Lord Bodkin requests permission to fire back."

"Denied. Arrows are for emergencies only."

The messenger boy repeated what he'd said and ran back.

Dirk looked over his reserves. Rapier fighters holding polearms and hoping for a chance to use their blades. A line of new fighters with pikeaxes and spears they barely knew how to use. The archers and their limited supply of arrows. King Ironhelm, his squires, and some dukes past their prime.

Behind them all the mages. Willing, powerful, and of totally unknown effectiveness. He'd told them they'd be saved for when the shock of their magic would have the greatest impact. He hadn't told them that was when he'd be desperate. The magic he'd seen was too fickle for him to build a plan around it.

When all the plans failed Dirk would add magic to the chaos.

Crawling up to the plateau edge let Dirk see the oncoming orcs. No chaos here. They were as smooth and predictable as water poured from a bucket. The wave spread out from the causeway. Some were already climbing up the center of the wall. Hoots and war cries filled the air. The few orcs still doing group chants were drowned out by the rest.

A spear hissed over his head as Dirk ducked back. He looked back to check for casualties. The troops were staying low enough to be safe. Two civilians cried as they were carried to the healers. Hopefully the rest would learn.

"At 'em!" ordered a squad leader. Fighters in the center rose to their knees and swung their pikeaxes. Dirk couldn't see the targets. They were below the edge. But the blades came back up orange with orc blood.

Screeches and screams came from the orcs on the wall. Angry ones. More orcs surged up. More fighters stood to meet them.

Dirk assessed the initial results. His veterans were knocking the orcs back down the wall and drawing blood as they did it. A couple of fighters went down from thrown spears. They were hauled to the healers as second line fighters stepped up to replace them.

Three orcs leapt over the edge, parrying pikeaxes with their spears. The fighters facing them were bodyslammed to the rock.

Count Dirk was in position to face them. He charged the right hand orc, shield held before him. The orc dodged, sending his spear at

Dirk's leg. The other two moved to flank him and Dirk gave way. A swing at his target's head was blocked by the spear, held two-handed.

Second line men were pressing the other orcs. More green-skins were climbing over the ledge.

Dirk swung again, this time cutting off some fingers as they moved the spear into his way. The sword carried past on momentum. Then he pulled it into a low backswing, ripping open the orc's gut.

It stumbled. Then a second-line pikeaxe caught the back of its leg. Dirk sliced its neck as it fell. Then he raised his shield to block a spear thrust from the next set of orcs. As the point scraped off the shield he sliced into the orc's arm just below the shoulder.

It flinched and stepped back.

Dirk rammed his shield into the orc's face, pushing it over onto another orc clambering over the edge. Both fell down the wall.

Beside him a line of pikeaxes forced the other orcs off the flat. They screeched as they fell.

Sharpedge took charge of sorting the reinforcements into first line, second line, and casualty haulers. Dirk stepped back to leave him to it.

A walk along the line showed him they were holding well. Not as many casualties as he'd feared. The king was keeping the reserves calm. It was a whack a mole battle. Orcs popped up then were knocked down.

One fighter knelt to reach an orc further down the wall. He let out an exultant "Ha!" as his pikeaxe connected. Then he tugged at the shaft. It pulled him down flat onto the rock.

Dirk opened his mouth but before he could utter the words "Let go" the fighter was pulled over the edge.

A flurry of cheerful hoots sounded.

Count Dirk ground his teeth. Damn it, he shouldn't have to teach people not to play tug of war with monsters.

Squad leaders were swapping in second-stringers for tired fighters. Water bearers moved among them.

The war cries were higher in pitch now. The orcs were stressed and desperate. In humans this would predict a rout. Orcs just threw themselves away even faster.

Troops on the flanks were standing easy, just watching the fight. The orcs had run out of spare spears to throw.

Dirk waved some aside to gain a spot on the edge. He took his first look at the whole battle.

Orcs climbing the wall were scattered enough to be met at the top by two or three fighters at once. Many climbers didn't make the top. They'd grip rock covered in fresh blood and slide down.

The diagonal path was full of orcs. Some had arm wounds keeping them from climbing. They calmly walked up the path to the top.

Maximus had appointed himself the reception party. He swung his pikeaxe at the orc's neck as it came into range. "Nine!" chanted his squadmates. The body fell straight down. Another orc tried to parry and took the point in its belly. "Ten!"

Dirk shook his head. He didn't understand orcs. If they stayed on the beach they'd inflict more casualties as the humans came down to finish them. Or at least they'd force him to use up irreplaceable arrows.

"Eleven!"

Some orcs had sense. He could see them wade back across the causeway as the rising tide covered it.

The rest . . . well, he shouldn't complain. Their stupidity was saving his men's lives.

"Twelve!"

The next orc forced Maximus back with rapid thrusts. It took two steps over the edge before a swarm of fighters brought it down. The one behind it died as it stepped over the edge.

Then someone took up the executioner post again.

When no more orcs came up the path Dirk sent men down to finish off the wounded. He followed the second squad.

Poking the bodies with spears found a few orcs playing possum. Most were as dead as they looked. Once everyone was convinced no live orcs remained the fighters laid down their weapons and picked up the bodies.

In groups of three or four they carried dead orcs to the water and tossed them in. Some didn't disappear under the waves. They lay half submerged on top of corpses from the causeway fight.

The troops didn't grumble much. The island smelled bad enough already without adding rotting bodies to the spilled blood and open air privies.

Lord Pulpit took charge of the tug-o-war player's bones.

The loudest complaint was from Lord Badelaire. "I hauled all my fishing gear here and there's so much blood in the water the fish won't come near the island."

***

Goldenrod missed Newman. Her dreams featured awful things happening to him. Her stomach was too tense to handle jerky without complaint. And it was harder to concentrate on her reading.

To keep concentrating she needed privacy. The flat, smooth parts of the island were crowded with people resting or gossiping. Whenever she opened one of the books people moved away, barging into already crowded groups.

And then they *whispered*.

Ordinary gossip Goldenrod could filter out. "Martha said Beth said Joey is sweet on Angie," just blurred like the sound of rushing water. Current gossip focused on who was recovering from wounds or being demoted from first line for freezing during a battle but she could still ignore it.

Not the whispers. Those made her paranoid. What were they saying? Were they talking about her? Eavesdropping would consume her attention.

So now she walked away from the crowd to read.

One of the seaward corners of the island was taller than the other. Unanimously nicknamed "the Keep," it was too jagged for most uses. Goldenrod found a relatively smooth outcrop to sit on. Up there no one minded her reading. Or singing. Or experimenting with what she'd learned.

Today's experiment used a chip of stone the size of the nail on her pinkie finger. She cupped her hands around it and sang a few syllables of elvish.

Nothing happened.

Goldenrod looked at the book lying open beside her. She sang again, concentrating on sliding smoothly between the notes. The third time she was smooth enough. The stone chip vanished.

The next experiment was on a stone the size of her head. Placing her hands on each side of it and singing perfectly produced a quiver, not a disappearance.

Goldenrod flipped back a few pages and re-read them. Then she left the book and walked down to the crowd. House Applesmile's bedrolls were abandoned. Searching the crowd was fruitless. She finally found Redinkle watching her husband at drill.

"I thought they knew how to use pikeaxes already," said Goldenrod.

Redinkle answered, "They keep working at whatever somebody screwed up in the last battle."

"Okay. Can he do it without your help?"

"Yes. Why?"

"I need a hand with something. Come up to the keep with me?"

Once they were past the crowd Redinkle said, "You know, we shouldn't call it the keep any more."

"Oh?"

"It should be the wizard's tower."

"Crap." Goldenrod stepped carefully over the roiled stone. "I don't own it. Nobody else was here so it was a good spot for privacy."

"Yep. Especially since moms don't let their kids play here any more."

"What the hell? I'm not going to cook and eat them."

"I think they're more worried about you exploding."

Goldenrod had to admit that was a reasonable fear after Rivet's accident.

They knelt on opposite sides of Goldenrod's usual seat with the stone between them. Their hands wrapped around, completely surrounding the stone. Goldenrod sang the words of the spell, making the stone quiver.

"Now sing it with me."

They sang it together. No quiver.

"No, you have to slide the notes exactly."

Redinkle said, "Give it to me a piece at a time."

They practiced the individual syllables, then separate halves of the spell. When Redinkle was confident they joined hands again.

The first time through the complete spell wasn't perfect. The second time the stone vanished.

Goldenrod let out an exultant "Ha!"

Redinkle grinned, thrilled to be doing a new kind of magic. "Where did it go?" she asked.

"I don't know."

"Wait, you have no clue where it went?"

"It's not on this world. I didn't add a word to tell it where to go. I don't know if there's a default world or if it just went some random place in the multiverse."

"So." Deep breath. "You're casting spells without knowing what they do."

"I'm casting part of a spell to check if it does what I think it does."

"You don't know it went to a different world. It could have landed in the camp."

"That would have a different structure."

"How can you be sure?"

"Fine. I'll prove it. Wait here."

Goldenrod left her sitting by the outcropping. She picked her way through the twists of the keep—or tower—back down to the plateau.

This side of the island didn't have the handy path of the shoreward side. It was still rough enough to provide plenty of handholds. And it wasn't nearly as high as the cliff she'd scaled on the way to the elf village.

Once she was on the shore Goldenrod walked up to Lord Badelaire. He was reeling in a fish with his rod.

"Beg pardon, my lord. May I borrow a fish for a moment?"

"Um, okay?" His concentration was still on the line.

"Thank you."

Goldenrod took a fish from the bucket. She gripped it firmly. The fish flailed so hard she was amazed it hadn't jumped out of the bucket.

A few precisely sung words left her hands empty.

"There. Do you want me to bring it back down here or send it somewhere up top?"

Badelaire had shuffled a few feet farther away. "Um, you can keep it, Your Excellency."

"Thanks!"

The fish slime on her hands made it hard to keep a good grip on the way back up but after a few yards it was all gone.

Redinkle no longer wore her concerned expression. She was disgusted and angry. One hand covered an eye.

"See? That was a completely different spell."

"That damn fish smacked me in the eye."

The fish was flopping about in a crease in the rock a few yards from Goldenrod's perch.

Redinkle lifted her hand to show a bright red mark where the fish had bounced into her.

"Oh. Sorry. I thought it would just lie there. Verbena could heal that right up, I bet."

"She won't. She's saving all her juice for the fighters. Civilians have to be dying to get a heal."

Which Goldenrod would know if she wasn't in her tower all the time.

"What are you going to do with the fish?"

Goldenrod glanced down as the creature flipped over again. "I don't know. Badelaire said I could keep it."

"It's not that big."

Mages were still kept in reserve, so they only ate civilian rations instead of the larger portions going to the fighters. Pernach and Pinecone had offered to share but Goldenrod and Redinkle had refused. Which made the fish look very tasty.

Their belt knives were sufficient for gutting it. It was messy but neither woman cared. Redinkle heated the rock under it and sprayed flames across the top until it looked done.

They both burned their lips. They were just too hungry to wait for it to cool.

**

Downstream of the camp they saw bands of orcs. They were on top of the river bluff, following the evacuation trail.

"So much for our mission," said Whippet.

"No, we did good," said Newman firmly. "There's not many there. I expect there'd be three or four times as many if we hadn't diverted them."

He hoped the orcs were still spreading out upstream, searching for prey going away from the river. If not—the horde would be late to the siege. Delayed reinforcements had decided more than one battle in his deployments.

The raft outpaced the orc bands. Some greeted the patrol with hostile war cries. None bothered climbing down the bluff to throw spears at them.

The farther downstream they went the faster the current flowed. As the jagged mountains reared up before them Newman watched for the lake on their left.

For all the worrying he did about the current carrying them over the waterfall the actual maneuver was anticlimactic. The port paddles stroked backwards until the raft pivoted ninety degrees. Then they all thrashed the water until they'd pushed into the stagnant water of the lake.

It was swampier than Newman and Joyeuse remembered. They'd only looked hard enough to find their way around.

Now what they'd thought was algae-covered water was a mix of dense floating mats, low trees, and hummocks built from dead piles of one or both. The setting sun sent long shadows through the tangled swamp.

Navigating through that in the dark was hopeless.

"Let's spend the night on that island," said Newman. "We'll cross the rim in the morning."

Despite the raft's lack of maneuverability they put it ashore on the smooth green mound, right where they'd aimed for.

Instead of sliding into mud, the front two feet of the raft disappeared into the mound with a sickening squelch. A jello-like wave wobbled across the island. Then the wave wiggled back, making the raft shiver.

Pliers prodded the mound with his paddle and pronounced it "Plant goop."

"Let's camp someplace else," said Deadeye.

Newman laughed. "You want to pull up to Orc Highway One or try to cross the river twice?"

"Well . . . shit."

"You've been in the infantry long enough to sleep anywhere. It's time you proved it." Newman unfolded the sawblade from his multitool. He cut off a few of the broken branches at the stern of the raft.

Joyeuse asked, "May I borrow that when you're done?"

"Sure." He cut a few more then passed the tool on.

The spot he'd carved out was only big enough to let Newman lie on his side, half curled up. One arm was his pillow.

They'd all brought blankets but abandoned them after the first few days. Cold dirt was restful enough when you were as exhausted as the patrollers.

Joyeuse sawing away was enough of a lullabye for Newman.

***

"Excuse me, Lord Parchment?" asked Goldenrod.

"Yes, Your Excellency?" The grey haired man turned to face her. The crafters he'd been chatting with fell silent.

"Do you have any ink with you?"

He didn't answer for a few moments. He swallowed a couple of times. "No, I'm sorry, I do not."

"Thank you anyway." Goldenrod walked away.

At least that one hadn't given her a two minute rant on how dare she accuse him of being stupid enough to bring calligraphy supplies on an evacuation.

Ink was out. Goldenrod tried to think of alternate writing materials. Blood? Lady Burnout would object. And it dries quickly. Orc blood? She'd have to wait until the next attack was over. Anything food-related was out. She'd wind up in front of Duchess Roseblossom for violating rationing.

Goldenrod decided she'd have to write elf-style, cutting into the blank leather pages. The elves burned their symbols with heated bone. Not an option here. There wasn't even lichen to burn on the island. Redinkle wouldn't do it. She was saving her "juice" to be ready for the next attack.

That left actually carving the leather. She had a splendid set of leatherworking tools. . . back on Earth. Her belt knife was too dull to cut smoothly. She needed something small and sharp.

She studied the clinic before walking up to it. Burnout and Verbena were both calm. The lines of wounded were just resting, not needing treatment. Helpers were giving them food and water.

Lady Burnout looked up as she approached. "Goldenrod. How's your gut?"

"Just fine." She hadn't needed any healing since they reached the island. "I was hoping for a small favor."

The chirurgeon made a little "go on" wave.

"I need to borrow a scalpel. Or something else I can carve leather with."

"Why?"

"I need to write up my notes on the elvish spells."

"You're not going to cast anything, are you?"

"I'm not making any wishes. I'm being careful. I just want to write down the useful stuff in one place."

Burnout still had a dubious expression. But she reached into her medical bag. "Here. Bring it back when the next attack starts."

"I will. Thank you."

Back at the wizard's tower she spread the books around her, all open to a different spell. Belladonna's scroll was unrolled in the center. The newest book was half blank. Goldenrod opened it to the first blank page and prepared to write.

If she understood the grammar of elvish correctly the spell she was creating needed four words: what—how—from—to. All of which she had if she understood this as well as she thought she did.

The point of casting this spell was to find out if she did understand it.

One word she had memorized. One came from Belladonna's scroll. The other two from different books. She worked slowly, not wanting to make an error. There was no backspace in leather carving.

The words weren't just the sounds of the letters but how they were to be sung. The pronunciation went in the center line with the singing instructions above and below.

It didn't help that the gouges in the leather weren't much lighter than the plain leather page. Goldenrod found herself tilting the book to create shadows as she checked her work.

After the first word an inspiration struck her. She slid down into the crease below her seat. Stroking her fingers along the bottom she found fine black sand, almost silt. She rubbed it on her new letters and wiped the page with her hand. It worked. The letters turned dark while the smooth page stayed clean.

She went more slowly as the task progressed, not wanting to risk all the letters she'd accumulated. When it was done she quadruple-checked it against the sources. It was right.

Or rather it was what she thought it should be. She wouldn't know it was right until casting it gave the results she'd planned.

It was safe to rehearse the words one at a time. She sang them, leaving gaps between each repetition. She didn't know what the minimum safe spacing was. That was likely in one of the old books she hadn't stolen.

Re-arranging the order wouldn't keep the spell from working. It would be a different spell. The tales of apprentices killed by botched spells made her not want to experiment with that.

This experiment was a necessary step if they were ever going to see Earth again.

At some point rehearsing became procrastinating. Goldenrod

stopped, took three deep breaths to compose herself, and knelt facing her seat. She began to sing.

The spell flowed out smoothly. The words felt right. They fit together.

Goldenrod sang the last note, closed her mouth, and fainted.

When she woke she checked the sun. Hadn't moved much.

Goldenrod looked at the outcrop and laughed. She'd expected water, in a bottle or just a blob splashing onto the rock. Instead a red and white can sat there.

"I guess 'thirst cure' taps into more of my memory than I thought," she said.

The can was colder than Plane's ice sculptures. Those were small and melted at her touch. The can filled her hand and sucked the warmth out of her skin.

It looked like the ones she was used to. She checked the ingredients. "High fructose corn syrup." The can was from Earth, or someplace very similar.

Goldenrod couldn't resist the temptation any longer. She popped the top and took a sip.

It shocked her.

The cold was harsher on her teeth than any stream water. The sweetness overwhelmed her taste buds. For nine months there'd been no sugars but scarce berries. This was pure.

She sucked down more of the brown fluid.

Her heart started racing.

A guilty pang reminded her this was stolen from someone. She hoped it was from a store, not someone picnicking in the park.

"Right. Caffeine," she muttered. Months without it had wiped out her tolerance for the stimulant. She raised a hand in front of her face. No jitters yet. But drinking the rest of the can was a bad idea.

Not as bad as walking into camp and offering it around. That would start a riot. Give it to Redinkle? She couldn't even remember if her bestie drank this brand. If anyone caught them, riot.

And, oh God, proof she'd cast a summoning spell would put Burnout into a screaming fit. With Cinnamon and Fennel on the chorus. The official leaders of the mage council had left supervising her to Burnout. They'd freak over the can.

Goldenrod started searching the seaward side of the tower for a hiding spot. She held the can close to her body to hide it from watchers. It was still cold.

There was a cranny filled with water, brackish from the sea spray. The water purifier hadn't needed to come up this high. She poured the soda into the puddle. The clear water turned brown. A few stomps left the can flat. A kick sent it to the bottom of the puddle.

Now her hands were jittering. Probably more from adrenaline than caffeine. But no more magic work for her today. She went back to gather up her books.

***

All the patrollers were awake before dawn. Some couldn't stand to stay in the cramped positions any longer. Others were startled awake by noises of the swamp.

Some damn critter made an annoyingly loud splash jumping out of the water. If it was doing that to avoid predators Newman hoped one caught it.

The air felt stagnant too. Scents of decay, murk, and cheap perfume attacked them. The water turned pea green away from the blue river.

Deadeye started peeing off the side of the raft. Someone cursed at him. He replied, "You didn't want to drink this anyway."

"Yeah, but we have to smell it."

"Here? You can't even notice piss in here."

It was a long wait until dawn. Newman shut down the bickering by reminding them that the orcs were waking up and listening.

Whippet sat up abruptly. "Something's sucking on me!"

"Put a ring on it," advised Deadeye.

"Crap." Whippet pulled up his pants leg. "Ewwww." He scraped at the slimy creature with his knife and flipped it into the water. Moonlight reflected off the ripples as it swam away.

"Are you bleeding?" asked Newman, just loud enough to be heard.

"No. Well, oozing a little. Don't need a bandage."

"Good. Everybody check yourself. Parasites are sneaky."

Newman followed his own order, running his hands under his clothes. No stowaways turned up.

When the dawn light touched the top of a nearby tree they all lifted their paddles and started stroking.

The bow made a slurping sound as it pulled free from the hummock. The mound jiggled in reaction. A waterfowl sleeping on top let out a hacking cough of protest.

They maneuvered the raft through the hummocks and trees of the swamp. It grew denser as they neared the mountains. Twice they had to back-paddle and find an alternate route.

As the raft drew closer to the rim mountains, more vegetation blocked their way. Some logs and hummocks moved aside when Crusher or Pliers pushed on them. More held firm. At last they faced a solid mass and couldn't spot an alternate route to shore.

Newman handed his paddle to Joyeuse. He swung his legs over the edge of the raft and slid down. He stood hip-deep in the water. "Okay. We'll wade from here. Packs on. Take a swig from your water bottles."

He didn't need to tell them to do it quietly. They could hear orc bands walking around the lake. Some gaps in the swamp foliage let them see orcs. None of the orcs had seemed to notice them. All the patrollers were doing the head on a swivel scan for ambushes.

Newman held them back before the shore. Gathering them in the cover of a tall clump of grass he whispered, "We have a clear view of the bend here. We'll watch for a gap in their line. When the gap gets here, we cross, using that pass."

He pointed to one the orcs were by-passing in favor of an easier climb.

"If we're chased keep your weapons, ditch anything else slowing you down."

They nodded. Then the patrol settled in for a long wait.

It was past noon when the bend in the lake shore went a quarter hour with no orcs passing by. They switched their attention to the shore above them, peeking through the swaying grass.

"That's it, I see the one with no left hand," whispered Pliers.

Newman answered, "Good. Wait five."

He started a timer on his wristwatch. It and his knife were souvenirs from the Sandbox.

The afternoon sun brought more smells out of the water. Midges swarmed around them. The bites were more aggravating with their nerves poised for action.

The watch buzzed against Newman's skin.

"Now now now." He whispered it instead of shouting, trying to stay stealthy.

They slogged as best they could to shore. Once on blessed, wonderful dry land the patrol cut diagonally left toward the pass they'd picked.

Pliers ran up the first foothill, stopping halfway up to wait for the rest.

Between sleeping on the raft and crouching in the muck most patrollers had cramped, aching legs. A brisk walk helped but they didn't want to run if they didn't have to.

The lake side of the foothill had patchy grass and a few shrubs. Towards the top that dwindled to moss and lichen. The crest was bare rock. As was the back side of the hill.

There was a little valley between the hill and the base of the mountains. A cluster of shrubs and a few trees lined its bottom. Then it was nothing but rock up to the top of the mountains.

Newman and his men went over the crest in a tight bunch. Not running, but a brisk walk. They'd seen too many orcs to relax.

Pliers ran ahead again. He stopped before the bottom. His hands scraped some drying mud and slime off his pants.

The rest caught up to him. They passed through the line of brush together.

Once through Newman looked around. His eyes met those of an orc.

It lay in the shade of a tree, gnawing on the leg bone of a deer. More orcs lay about, some with bones of their own, others napping in the shade. Three young orcs gnawed on the hips.

Newman could see at least thirty.

The one staring at him let out a howl. More orc heads popped up from the bushes.

The howl cut off as Deadeye put an arrow in its throat.

"Run!" yelled Newman. "Run for the pass!"

He broke into a run. They were between the orcs and the pass. They just needed to keep their lead. He undid the straps on his backpack.

Running wasn't an option when the slopes grew steeper. Newman needed both hands to keep steady. He didn't want to sling his bow. He held it in his fist, bracing his knuckles against the rock when he had to.

The knuckles were already bleeding.

Newman looked around. All the men were ahead of him but one. "Crusher! Keep up!"

The fighter pushed himself into a sprint for a few yards. Then he reached a steeper portion of the slope, went up a couple of steps, then slid back down. Crusher had been the slowest runner of the patrol from the beginning. He hadn't eaten well since that stunt with the slice of tentacle. Now he was too damn weak to catch up.

"Fuck it."

Crusher drew his sword. He charged down the slope shouting a war cry in some language Newman didn't know.

The sword slapped aside the first orc's spear thrust then slashed open its throat. The backswing caught the next orc on the neck.

He plunged between two more, still swinging.

Newman turned back to the pass. Now he needed to keep up.

The orcs took long enough dealing with Crusher that the patrol gained a fifty yard lead. Close to the pass the rock face steepened again. Deadeye fired back a couple arrows as they paused there.

Joyeuse sat down and took off his boots. "This stretch is going to be real rock climbing," he said. "Best to have bare feet for traction."

"Screw that," said Pliers. "This stuff would cut my feet up."

"Bleeding is better than falling," countered Joyeuse.

Newman sat down to imitate him. A spear bounced off the rock face below him. Rather than untie the complicated leather laces of his boots he drew his knife and slashed through them. He sheathed knife, slung his bow, and started climbing.

It was an easier ascent than the cliff he'd climbed on the way to the elf village. But he'd rather have a straight drop to bare rock under him than a horde of ravening orcs.

Borzhoi pulled Newman over the top. They flinched as a spear flew by.

The pass was narrow and filled with boulders fallen from the mountains on either side. They hopped through, risking broken ankles to get more speed.

Pliers reached the other side first. He looked over. "Oh, shit."

"What?" demanded Newman.

Pliers dropped flat as a spear passed over him. "The orcs from the other pass are walking under this one to get to the shore. They saw me. They're climbing up."

The war cries of the ocean side orcs were audible now. It was a different chant from the cries of the orcs chasing them from the lake side.

Newman looked around. He saw a ledge well above the pass. "Up there! Go!"

The patrol started climbing again.

The lake side orcs came over the edge of the pass. Their massive upper body strength let them climb faster than humans. Excited hoots greeted the sight of the trapped patrol.

Newman moved up the rock, settling for footholds he could only squeeze his toes into. Sometimes he had to wait for Borzhoi or Whippet to move their feet up so he could grab a handhold.

Those pauses let him look around. The orcs were gathered below them. A few were climbing up.

Pliers was lagging behind. His boots needed big cracks or bumps. Sometimes he had to shift sideways before he could go up.

Damn it, I should have ordered him to take his boots off.

The handhold Newman was waiting for was empty. He climbed more. With his nose pressed to the rock he could appreciate one part of their situation. The clean salt air blowing in from the sea smelled so much better than the swamp.

A rattle of wood on stone announced another flurry of spears. This time there was a scream.

Newman looked right. Where Pliers had been was only empty rock. He shifted handholds to let himself look straight down.

Orcs with red blood on their faces grinned back at him.

Newman looked up and reached for another handhold.

Joyeuse helped Deadeye onto the ledge. While the squire reached down for the Wolfheads Deadeye unslung his bow and started sending arrows down into the climbing orcs.

Once he was on the narrow ledge Newman looked at his feet. "Damn, look at all that blood. I'm amazed I didn't slip off."

"Nah, once it dries a bit it's sticky. So you get extra traction," said Joyeuse.

Deadeye's bow twanged. A howl came from below. He scooted back from the edge.

"Need more arrows?" asked Whippet.

"I'm good. The climbers are giving up."

A dozen spears soared into view. The patrollers curled into balls as spears bounced off the mountainside above them and onto the ledge.

Borzhoi grabbed one as it rattled on the stone. "Hey, we can throw these back. It's like dodgeball."

"Only pointy," said Newman. "Hold onto them for now. We'll save them for when they make a rush."

The five patrollers left weren't badly hurt. The scraped hands and feet scabbed over fast enough to not need bandaging.

As the afternoon wore on the orcs made several attempts to storm the ledge. Deadeye used up all the remaining arrows picking them off as they climbed. When he ran out the whole patrol threw volleys of spears.

When the orcs gave up they had seven spears left. The orcs didn't throw more to restock them this time.

Whippet peeked over the edge. "Hey, they really are cannibals."

"You didn't expect that?" asked Borzhoi.

"Seeing it is different."

Then all was quiet for a while.

Deadeye broke the silence. "Forgive me if this is a rude question, but do we have a plan?"

"I have three," said Newman. "Plan A is the orcs get bored, go away, and we go on our way. Plan B is after dark we go down the side of the mountain. Which likely ends in falling to our deaths. Plan C is dying of thirst up here. Which is a longer life than being down there. If anyone has a Plan D I'm all ears."

Silence resumed.

"No, I don't have anything better," said Deadeye after some thought. "I was just hoping you did." He went back to sharpening the point of his spear.

The other patrollers chuckled.

"Hi! Hey, don't point that at me!"

Deadeye lowered the spear. "Sorry. Wasn't expecting any friendlies up here."

"Good day, Lady Aster," said Newman.

The mage was hovering by the ocean side of the ledge, out of sight of the orcs. She was clean, decently fed, and healthy. Newman looked at his men. He hadn't realized how thin and worn they'd become until he had a normal person to compare them to.

"We weren't expecting you either," said Aster. "But we saw the fuss up here so I wanted to take a look."

"Can you bring us more arrows?" asked Deadeye.

"I'm going to take you to the island."

Hope spread through the patrollers again. Lines vanished from their faces.

Newman smiled tightly, the best he could do. "Whippet first. He took a spear in the leg."

Whippet held out his arms to be picked up.

"No way, boy," said Aster. "My magic is strong enough to carry you. My muscles aren't."

She landed on the ledge on hands and knees. "Climb onto my back. Hold on tight. Touch anything sensitive and I drop you in the ocean."

He obeyed. His arms slid under her shoulders and his legs wrapped around her.

They lifted into the air and vanished around the curve of the mountain.

Deadeye started laughing. He rolled onto his back and laughed harder.

"What's so funny?" asked Joyeuse.

"I was just thinking, 'it would take a miracle to save us', and bam, miracle."

"That's how it works for Goldenrod," said Newman. "You should have thought that sooner."

That started the rest of them laughing.

Borzhoi didn't object to going next. When he and Aster were out of sight the rest started proposing each other for the next trip.

"I'm the commander. I'm last," said Newman. "You two settle it however you want."

Joyeuse offered, "Rock paper scissors?"

He chose rock to Deadeye's paper and was Aster's next passenger.

"Mind if I chuck these spears before we go?" asked Deadeye.

"Don't. I don't want Aster flying through retaliation."

"Yeah, okay."

Then the mage took Deadeye off, leaving Newman alone.

More alone than he'd been in years. There probably wasn't a human around for miles.

He thought on the men he'd lost. Leadsmith was just random chance. Or his decision to taunt the orcs instead of running for the woods. Crusher . . . he knew Crusher wasn't as fit as the others. He should have put Crusher up front where the patrol could prod him to keep going.

And damn it, he'd taken his own boots off but he hadn't made it an order. Pliers was good about orders. If anyone but Joyeuse had told him to do it Pliers would have obeyed.

Newman snapped out of his brooding to find Aster next to him. He climbed onto her back. After his long rough time on the patrol she was very warm and soft. He carefully put his hands on her shoulders.

Aster lifted off and went around the mountain. On the ocean side she made a slow twirl. "Dragon check," she explained. "They don't like sharing the air."

Then she faced the ocean and plunged down.

Newman squawked in surprise. She was dropping faster than they could fall. His grip slipped as she pulled away from him. He clutched her tight to keep from being left behind in mid-air.

Then g-force pushed him firmly onto her back as Aster pulled out of the dive and skimmed over the waves.

Sea spray splattered against Newman's face, delightfully cold. He tasted salt.

Then they were over the island. A line of armored men stood on the clifftop.

Aster rose up the side and flew to the center. There was Goldenrod, looking tall and strong, not the shattered vessel he'd left behind. Aster stood up, depositing Newman on his feet.

"Here you go, Your Excellency. I didn't give him any worse a ride than he deserved."

Then she stepped out of the way as the couple lunged for each other.

***

Count Dirk focused his binoculars on the orcs walking out on the causeway as the water receded. "They came on in the same old way," he said to Newman.

The younger man nodded.

Dirk glanced at him. "Not a fan of Wellington?"

"I was never a history buff, sir."

"Then what are you doing here?"

"Goldenrod asked me."

Dirk chuckled and went back to his binoculars.

Newman studied the orcs. He could see them well enough from the edge of the plateau. Trickles of fresh arrivals came through three passes. The slope was covered with bands. Each low tide let some through but not enough to balance the influx. The mob was growing larger.

The water fell low enough to reveal the orcs tossed into the water after yesterday's battle. Newman had done his share of corpse-flinging. Nasty, smelly work.

Dirk kept brooding through his binoculars. Newman thought the commander was wasting his time. Maybe he was just trying to look on top of the situation. Newman stuck to stroking a grindstone along the edge of his axe to sharpen it. House Applesmile had carried it with their essentials.

A wave of stench rolled over the island. Newman gagged. The tide had gone out far enough to uncover the rotting corpses from earlier in the week. Fighters across the island began gearing up for the impending battle. The low tide smell now took the place of herald announcements.

Newman's squad all reported in before the orcs crossed the middle of the causeway. It was officially Sharpedge's squad, but the squire was laid up with a hole through his thigh. Lady Burnout kept him from bleeding to death but it would take more magical healing for Sharpedge to be back on his feet.

The fighters knew their jobs. They were a mix of royal guards, Wolfheads, and a couple of crafters who'd learned quickly. Newman didn't have to do any training, just provide confidence and steadiness.

Steadiness was easy. Secure flanks and rear were a much more comfortable situation than the long range patrol.

Confidence . . . he could fake. Newman couldn't help having doubts when he looked at the swarming orcs waiting for their turn to cross. The humans could slaughter orcs, no doubt. Everyone here had lost count of how many they'd killed. As long as high tide ended the fight before they ran out of unwounded men or the energy to lift their arms, they'd survive.

The orcs were attacking the center now. Their deployment didn't have a plan. They just spread out from the causeway like swarming ants. Newman was on the right flank. It would be a few more minutes before any orcs reached him.

This time there were some eddies in the flow, orcs staying at the water's edge. Were they turning coward? Newman was fine with that.

As his first orc of the day approached Newman carefully judged its speed. He had a reputation. His squad expected him to open with something spectacular.

The custom was to swing from high left to low right. That way no one risked entangling their weapon with a neighbor swinging at the opposite angle. Newman hefted the lochaber axe.

The orc held its spear in its left hand as it climbed. It didn't try to attack Newman as it came in range, just clutched handholds and footholds to hurry over the edge where it could fight effectively.

Newman swung his axe like a guillotine. The width of the blade vanished into the orc's neck where it met the shoulder. It spasmed, dropping the spear.

He twisted the axe, levering open the cut. Orange blood sprayed out. The body fell, knocking down another orc halfway up the wall.

The familiar bitter scent of orc blood filled his nose. It was pleasant under the circumstances. Anything would be better than the stench of rotting corpses.

A glance to the side showed Newman his men were dispatching orcs competently enough. His next orc was being slow. He looked to the causeway.

The orcs eddying along the shore were picking corpses off the piles. They slung a dead orc on each shoulder and started back across the causeway. To Newman's surprise they didn't face resistance. The oncoming orcs made way, slowing down to make the causeway two way.

Well, good, he thought. *Less to fight.* He repeated the neck chop blow.

His squad let two orcs get over the top. Newman didn't have to deal with them. He just covered more of the edge while the squad surrounded and killed them.

Crisis over, he looked at the causeway again. The line of dead orc bearers was marching on. He wondered why. Orcs didn't bury their dead. Rations for the horde? It hardly seemed like enough.

A green hand grabbed the edge. Chopping through it would chip his blade against the rock. Newman flipped the axe around and smacked the hand with the haft of the axe. Bone crunched.

The orc poked its spear at him one-handed. He caught the spear with the hook of his blade and pulled. The orc lost its balance, slipped, and slid down the wall.

Newman looked at the causeway again. The corpse-carriers had stopped. No, they were moving. They just reached the center of the causeway, dropped their bodies, and rejoined the incoming line.

Another neck chop. Then one who wanted to fence with its spear while its feet braced it on the wall. After a few parries Newman stuck the tip of his axe in the orc's eye. Didn't seem to bother it at all. When he ruptured the other eye it stopped aiming. Then he put his weight on the axe and shoved it away.

The orc below it held on as the blind orc bounced off it. No bowling a strike this time.

More bodies were laid down on the causeway. The oncoming orcs stepped on them as they marched along. Some body carriers went past the midpoint, dropping their corpses on the far half of the causeway.

The squad was holding steady. Not wasting energy. Dropping each orc with two or three blows. Helping each other out when an orc became a threat.

He looked back at the causeway. Something bothered him about it.

Oh, shit.

"Count Dirk!" he called.

The next orc came in reach of his axe before he could call again. Newman swung early, chopping off an ear.

The orc snarled and thrust with its spear.

Newman deflected the weapon with the flat of his axe and swung down, severing two fingers.

The orc just grunted and kept climbing. Its head tilted to protect the wounded side.

He glanced to his right. Husky held his weapon high, clear of a reverse blow. Newman chopped the orc on the other side of its head, spraying blood from the neck.

A glance over his shoulder showed Count Dirk was pushing through the reserves.

"What is it?" demanded the commander.

Newman pointed at the corpse-carriers with his axe. "They're laying bodies down on the causeway. Stack enough of them and they'll be able to cross at high tide."

Count Dirk said nothing for five seconds, staring at the causeway. Then ten seconds. Then he shouted, "Archers!"

Deadeye trotted up in moments. He was desperate for action.

"Take down the ones carrying corpses," ordered Dirk.

More archers arrived. Deadeye relayed the orders, ending with, "Try not to shoot the dead ones."

Newman couldn't watch the first shots. He had to deal with another orc. When he looked up nothing had changed on the causeway.

Deadeye's bow twanged next to his ear. The arrow hit a body-carrier at the base of the neck. It pitched forward, dropping the two bodies. Orcs in the oncoming lane grabbed all three corpses before they could slide into deep water. Then they joined the line of body-carriers, one carrying two old corpses, another a fresh one.

More arrows flew overhead while Newman chopped the next climber.

"Cease fire," ordered Count Dirk. "Stubborn bastards."

Deadeye obeyed, reinforcing the command to a couple of his men who let extra arrows fly. He addressed the count in a lowered tone. "What are we being saved for, Your Excellency?"

"When orcs break through the line, take down as many as you can while we bring up the reserves."

Newman noted that it was now "when" instead of "if".

He rotated some of his men out for rest. Second-liners stepped up and did their share of carnage.

A gust blew putrid air over the island. Pulling rotten corpses out of the water and waving them in the air spread their stench. But the bitter smell of drying orc blood dominated the island when the wind wasn't blowing.

Now orcs were taking bodies from the pile at the base of the wall. Well, they probably made better traction than the wet ones.

***

King Ironhelm patted Sharpedge on the shoulder. "Hang in there."

He moved down the row to the next wounded fighter. "Hello, Falchion. How are you feeling?"

"Can't complain, Your Majesty. All things considered."

Falchion had three wounds. One through the shin, another in the belly. The third wound was impressive. A spearpoint had caught the side of his head, opening the cheek and mangling the ear.

Only the belly wound was bandaged.

Ironhelm made his tone hearty and encouraging. "The chicks will dig you when they see that scar. You'll have to fight them off."

"Ivy doesn't mind." Only the unwounded side of his mouth moved as he talked. "She says I never listened anyway."

The king laughed. "She's a good woman. She'll stick with you."

Falchion nodded.

Ironhelm moved to the next wounded man. After a few more chats he took a moment to study the battle at the island's edge. It was stable at the moment. There were enough reserve squads standing around that the royal troops wouldn't be needed soon.

He'd rather be fighting than doing this. But duty meant doing what he had to, not what he wanted.

Another wounded man was laid down in the row. The ones who'd carried him went back to their reserve squad. Lady Burnout rinsed her hands in a bucket.

King Ironhelm walked up to her. "I noticed you're not bandaging all the wounds."

She matched his quiet pitch. "There's no fuel for boiling cloth here. I'm saving sterile bandages for wounds most likely to rupture."

"You'd been healing people all the way before."

Burnout held up her hands. "When a fight stops I use all the magic I have left to close up wounds. If I do that now I might not have enough left in me to stop bleeding. Same for Verbena."

"Of course. I shouldn't be distracting you from your work."

She gave him a head dip and turned back to the wounded.

King Ironhelm stood brooding for a moment. *We're running out*, he thought. *Out of bandages, out of magic, out of men, out of time.*

He shook himself to cast off the gloom. Put on a confident smile. Then walked over to the new arrival. "Well! You're going to have a story to tell."

***

Goldenrod tossed some silt onto the page and rubbed off the excess. The spell was complete. Enclosed—world switch—here—origin point. If she understood the sorcerer's notes correctly . . . that was a big if.

The key insight was that she could use 'origin point,' the place that she personally remembered coming from, as a substitute for the matching spell that Belladonna had cast to tell the sorcerer where to pull them from. Instead of needing someone to understand a scroll and be a homing beacon for them Goldenrod would take them back to the park where they started. If she had correctly worked out the logic.

Elvish sorcery followed logical rules. Do this, that happens. If you do the wrong this, something else happens. Possibly a lethal something else.

Her own magic didn't work that way. She could ask for anything. It would happen . . . with a price. After much thought she'd concluded the price wasn't driven by the magnitude of the request but the probability. Something likely to happen, such as being attacked while wandering an orc infested forest, had no noticeable price. Magical power leaping from one person to another was so improbable she'd nearly died.

She'd thought of wishing everyone home. It would kill her. She considered it a fair sacrifice. This place was slowly killing them all anyway. If she felt any certainty that the wish would still work through her death she'd've done it. But her gut feeling was she'd just drop dead with no results.

What kept her from trying more wishes was that she couldn't be sure of the probability before she made the wish. She'd hurt herself badly with experiments. It was too risky to do more.

Or it had been. Goldenrod lifted her eyes to the line of men fighting at the cliff edge. She couldn't pick out Newman through the other men standing around. Now was the time for risks.

She laid both hands on the newly carved words. She carefully spoke aloud, "This spell does exactly what I want it to."

Her chest twinged. Maybe a little worse than killing an orc in the middle of a battle.

Goldenrod lifted her hands and looked over the spell. It didn't seem to have changed. But then the most parsimonious way for the wish to work would be to retroactively correct what she'd planned to write.

The wish had also given her some useful information. It was a high probability that she'd written the spell correctly. She could have more confidence going forward.

***

"Milord, you should take a break," said a second-liner.

Newman twisted the axe blade out of an orc's chest. The guy was right. He was tired. And thirsty. He'd just been too busy to think about it.

He waved the boy to his spot and took a few paces back.

"I've got it, sir," said Husky. The Wolfhead was the only first-liner still on the edge. That would make him acting squad leader.

"Get some," answered Newman. He turned around, looking for water.

The usual water bearer wasn't there. Instead Goldenrod stood holding a canvas bucket. A fighter finished draining a pewter mug and handed it back to her. She dipped the mug into the bucket and held it out to Newman.

He took it, drained it, handed it back. She filled it for him to empty again. "What are you doing here?" he asked as he handed it back.

"Queen Dalia asked for volunteers. The old crew needed a break."

Goldenrod handed him the refilled mug.

Newman poured it down his throat. "I thought you were working on some research."

She refilled it again. "I finished it. I think. I hope."

Newman just swallowed a third of the water this time. It tasted like orc blood. Or maybe that was just the smell of it getting into everything. "Congrats."

He drank a bit more. Looked over his shoulder at the continuing slaughter. "Damn, I wish those bastards would give up."

"The sorcerer put too much hate into them," said Goldenrod. She pulled a piece of dried fish from a bag on her belt. "Eat this."

Newman leaned forward to let her pop it in his mouth. With an axe in one hand and mug in the other he couldn't reach for it. He wasn't going to put down the axe. He sipped some water to soften the chewy piece of fish.

After much chewing he managed to swallow it all. He chased the fish with the last of the water in the mug. "Would be nice if you could break that spell."

Goldenrod froze as she took the empty mug. "Oh crap. One of the books had a section on mind control but I ditched it because I was just looking for teleportation. Damn. Damn."

She shook herself and refilled the mug. Newman sipped it. He didn't have anything to say to that.

Count Dirk called, "Newman! Take a squad and refuse the right flank. They're coming around."

He answered with a wave of his axe. A gulp emptied the mug. His squad was short a few heads. Husky and another were on the front line. Cuirass had taken a leg wound and been carried back to Burnout. A few second and third liners filled out the squad.

Newman led them right at a trot. At the corner of the island he could see the problem. So many orcs were waiting for their turn to climb to their deaths there wasn't room for them all. The overflow was coming around the corner where the wall was undefended.

If Newman had commanded the orcs he would have surrounded the island first then sent them up every side at once. There'd been barely enough humans to cover that much perimeter before all the casualties they'd taken.

Instead the orcs were just rushing at the first enemy they could reach. Berserk? Enspelled? Too used to fighting in small numbers? He didn't understand it.

Only a handful were walking along the side of the island. When Newman's men appeared at the top of the wall the orcs turned and started climbing. The one farthest down the shore ran back to get underneath a human before ascending.

Outflanking is just not a concept for these guys, thought Newman.

The orcs hooted as they climbed. More came around the corner in response. Newman wished he could plug the narrow gap between wall and water. Not with these raw militias. *If I had a dozen veteran pikemen, maybe. Even then on the flat the orcs could just pile bodies on top of us.*

The squad fell into the routine of chopping orcs as they reached the top. They were more spread out than the main line. Newman roved along the line, supplying extra muscle as needed.

A pair of orcs pulled themselves over the edge in front of a second-liner, blocking his blows with their spears. The weapons locked together. They knocked the boy onto his back.

The orcs stood over him, raising spears for a death blow. Newman sprinted and took the head off one. The other thrust down.

The boy had dropped his weapon in the fall. He pushed his hands toward the orc. Before the blow landed the orc flew off the island.

Newman watched the orc sail into the water, at least fifteen yards offshore. Splash. It didn't reappear.

He gave the boy—Spearpoint? Yes, Spearpoint was the name—a hand up. "Nice trick. But use the pikeaxe first."

"Yes, Your Excellency. Um, do I have to stand with the mages now?"

"No. We'll talk about it tomorrow." Count Dirk might disagree, but Newman wanted to keep all the men he could. They were more spread out here than in the center. One missing fighter would leave a big hole.

When a lull happened in the orc surge Newman walked over to the reserve and grabbed a couple of third-liners. The second-liners were almost all on the front line now. The line of wounded at Burnout's aid station was twice as long as when he'd last looked.

He felt a quiver as Count Dirk came toward him. A justification for taking the reserves for his squad sprang to his lips.

The commander said, "Brace for a push. They've finished laying their corpse bridge. Now it's one-way again."

"Yes, sir." That was the only non-screaming in panic answer he could give.

He could hear when the surge hit. More shouts of pain and cries for help. Massed war chants from the orcs. It focused on the center.

His squad was only a little busier. Spearpoint didn't need to do his new trick again.

Orcs screeched in triumph. Newman looked left. A dozen orcs had broken through the line nearby. More climbed over the edge behind them. Some third-liners ran up to plug the gap but they weren't in formation. The orcs knocked them aside before they could support each other.

Newman never decided to attack. He realized he was running towards the orcs, lochaber axe cocked back.

The first orc's head came clean off. The momentum of his charge added to the swing let the blow continue through to the next orc, catching it on the back of the neck. It dropped dead.

An orc turned to face him. Newman slashed the orc's belly open. He skidded on intestines as he pressed forward. That let an orc dodge his swing and bring its spear around for a thrust. He deflected it with the haft of the axe then pressed the blade into the orcs face. The shallow cut hurt enough to make the orc step back.

That gave him enough room for a real swing. Blood splattered his face as he chopped its neck.

When Newman wiped his eyes clear an orc's spear was coming straight at his heart. He twirled to avoid it. As the orc rushed past he swung the blade into the back of its thighs.

It collapsed. He looked for a new target. Somebody else could finish it off.

Two orcs approached actually moving as a pair. The spears aimed at his belly.

A sweeping blow of the axe caught their tips and pushed both spears to the side. The backswing took both heads off together.

The orc standing behind them gaped in astonishment. Newman didn't give it time to recover.

He could feel more humans coming toward him, diverting the orcs that could have stabbed him in the back. Ahead the fighters on the edge were closing the gap from both sides.

An orc held its spear at port arms to block the axe. Newman stepped in and swung the blade up between its legs.

It yelled like a human suffering the same wound. Newman pushed it aside.

The orc behind it took a step back as Newman advanced. Its foot landed on empty air. It fell, taking one climbing up with it.

Arriving at the edge he chopped left and right at the ones coming over the edge. Then he had no targets in reach.

A glance behind showed the last orcs falling to the reserves.

Newman looked over the battle.

The wall below him was coated in orange blood. A tangle of orcs was trying to sort themselves out on top of a pile of bodies. To the left orcs were braced in a pyramid. Others used them as a ladder, climbing faster than clinging to the blood-soaked wall would let them. More stood on the shore waiting their turn. The water was orange well away from the island. The corpse bridge held more orcs rushing toward the fight. Past that he could see more coming through the mountain passes.

"Back to your post, son," said King Ironhelm. "We've got this."

Newman started as he realized who was beside him. Duke Mace had stepped up on his other side, steel sword dripping with blood.

He nodded and turned away from the edge. Dukes and squires were finishing off the orcs and hauling bodies to the edge.

Burnout and Verbena were crawling from casualty to casualty. They were covered with red blood. At each body they pressed their hands on wounds for a quick moment, long enough to stop the bleeding, and then went on to the next one. More women followed after to carry casualties to the aid station.

Newman stared at them. Both healers looked like they'd aged years. They'd lost weight, more than he thought one could in a week.

He trudged back to his squad, suddenly cold and shaky as the adrenaline spike passed. They were holding the edge. Not easily. There was a frantic note as they rushed back and forth just barely keeping up with the whack a mole.

As an orc popped up in a gap Newman chopped its neck. He walked along the edge efficiently dispatching climbers. His men panted as they leaned on their weapons.

"Mages!" bellowed Count Dirk. "Do your worst!"

Newman looked back. He could see across the island to his counterparts on the other flank. There were no reserves but the mages. Now they were spreading out to join the line. Redinkle held a ball of fire in her hands. Plane reached into a puddle and pulled out a ludicrously oversized sword of ice.

"Anime fan," muttered Newman.

"Mage Rivet, reporting for duty." The one-eyed mage actually saluted. Badly.

Newman returned it. "Welcome. Let them have it."

Rivet carried three rocks, the smallest two fists in size. He dropped two and tossed the largest over the edge.

The rock swooped through the air. It smacked into the side of an orc's head. The jolt made it lose its grip. It slid down to the pile of corpses at the base of the wall, yelling the whole way.

The mage waved his hand. The rock streaked into another orc, hitting it under the ear. It fell onto the bodies and lay still.

Newman muttered, "Aim for the neck and the bottom of the skull. Those are the most vulnerable places."

Rivet obliged. More orcs fell, knocked out or dead.

An orc by the water hefted a spear as it stared at the mage.

"Crap." Newman tackled Rivet. They fell flat as a spear flew over them.

Rivet said, "Ow. What was that for? You made me drop the rock.

It's too far away to pick up again."

"Spearpoint, bring me a pikeaxe," ordered Newman.

The fighter waved. There were plenty of abandoned weapons lying about next to puddles of red blood.

Newman put a hand on the mage. "Stay down. You didn't have a weapon so you had to be a mage. Guess they'd fought enough elves to figure that out."

He turned toward the front line. "Archer!"

Bodkin trotted over. "Yeah?"

"Need you to take down a smart orc." Newman pointed.

"The one with the diagonal streak of dirt on his chest?"

Nod.

The arrow caught the orc in the throat. It fell and lay still.

"Good shot," said Newman. Bodkin hadn't been any good at moving targets when they arrived here.

"Thanks." The archer went back to his post.

Spearpoint came back with a pikeaxe. The blade was covered with orange blood. The previous owner hadn't gone down easily.

"Take it," ordered Newman.

Rivet held it with the blade toward him. "I don't really know how to use this."

"You don't have to. It's camouflage. Now do the magic."

Another stone lifted up and flew over the edge. An orc yelped as Rivet hit it, then fell after a harder blow.

Newman took the hand off an orc climbing over the edge.

A quarter hour of practice let Rivet clear off half the orcs climbing the wall. Most of them started climbing up again. That fraction was reduced as Rivet learned to break knees and elbows. Orcs would keep climbing with one broken joint but two put them out of action.

A fighter sidled up to Newman. "Sir, we're less busy now. Can I ask a favor?"

"What?"

"Can I go. . ." He gestured at the back of the island designated for the privy. "Go pee?"

"Just piss over the edge. It's not like they don't deserve it."

The bashful fighter wanted to protest. Newman's glare just left him stuttering. He undid his fly and let a stream out over the edge.

The orc underneath did not feel it deserved that. It expressed the reaction with screeches that were clearly curses, not battlecries. Rivet shut it up.

Goldenrod came by with a fresh bucket of water. She made every member of the squad drink at least one mug.

After she went by Newman looked over the front line. The sun was setting. Redinkle's fire and Sparrow's lightning stood out against the darkening sky. Pikeaxes still rose and fell. Not at the frantic pace of before, but still enough to tire men out.

"Sir?" asked Rivet. "Do orcs fight at night?"

Newman said, "Not well. Our night vision is better, at least some of us. I doubt they'll stop fighting."

"Oh."

"Getting tired?"

"Not physically. But I can only do so much magic in a day."

"Ah." This didn't surprise Newman. He'd heard plenty of discussions among mages finding their limits. "Conserve your strength. Just hit the ones doubling up on a fighter."

"Aye-aye."

Newman looked at the far shore. There were still orcs waiting to cross.

A clink announced Rivet broke another orc skull. The stone flew back to his hand. The orc fell onto the corpse pile.

That's going to be a ramp for them, thought Newman. *It must be nearly to the top in the center.*

Trying to wrap his mind around the piles of dead meat boggled Newman. This was beyond anything he'd experienced.

A woman screamed. He pivoted to locate her.

Not one of the reserves in the center. A civilian? Yes.

Aster stood by the aid center pointing at the sky. Mistress Cinnamon tried to calm her but the young woman kept screaming.

Newman followed the line of her arm.

He couldn't recognize the shape at first. It was dark. The scales were shiny enough to reflect red sunlight. The flickers of light shifted confusingly.

Then the wings flapped.

Newman's throat froze. He wet his lips. Took a deep breath. Shouted, "Dragon!"

The monster grew in the sky as it descended. More humans took up the cry of "Dragon". Orcish battle cries dissolved into hoots that must mean the same thing.

Civilians dropped flat. Some crawled under blankets. The battle line fell back a few steps as desperate orcs came heedlessly over the edge.

Then the dragon landed. On the orcs, thankfully. Spears flew through the air and bounced off the scales.

"Back up! Back up!" ordered Count Dirk.

Fighters who'd shoved the last rush of orcs back to the edge retreated a few steps.

Gouts of flame washed the front of the island from left to right.

Then the island was silent. No hoots, screeches, or war cries. The humans were all silent. And prone. No one ordered it. They just fell to their bellies by instinct.

Another blast of flame struck the center. Then there was noise. A slurping, crunching sound.

Like a toddler eating French fries, thought Newman.

He lifted his head to peek at the mainland. Orcs were fleeing over the mountains. *Nice to know something can scare them.*

Burnt orc didn't smell like pork or chicken. More like a grease fire. Rancid grease.

All the orcs on the flank had run back to be incinerated. Newman's squad was crawling to the middle where everyone else was gathering. He followed them.

The dragon flamed the mound of dead orcs again then resumed gobbling. Nothing was audible but the dragon eating and the distant waterfall.

Newman caught up to Goldenrod. She'd been slowed by her bucket of water, still a third full. "What's that spell you came up with?" he whispered in her ear.

She answered with her lips to his ear. "Will take us home. If it works."

The munching noise stopped. The dragon's head rose above the edge of the plateau. The vertical pupils shifted as they scanned the island.

Maximus was closest to the edge. He stood, leaving his weapon on the ground. He doffed his helmet as he walked forward. "Hi! We want to be friends!"

The monster stared at him. A puff of flame crisped him in place. Then the head darted forward. It left only his boots behind.

"Damn it!" shouted Rivet.

Newman could see the rock as it accelerated toward the dragon. It smacked into the eye just before the lids closed.

The dragon's head pointed straight up. It roared.

The sound hurt Newman's ears even after he pressed his hands over them. The bass rumble shook his bowels. He clamped down to keep control of them. A sharp odor said someone else had failed.

It launched into the air, still roaring. The wind from its wings sent skinny people rolling across the rock.

"Did I scare it or just piss it off?" asked Rivet.

The dragon flew up into the rays of the just-set sun and kept climbing. The roars continued as it rose. When it was smaller than the tip of Newman's little finger it started circling. Jets of flame flickered.

"Pissed," said Newman. "Very pissed."

Everyone was babbling in relief now. Even if the dragon was going to come back and kill them later it was the first time all day nothing was trying to kill them right then.

Lady Burnout's voice cut through the chatter. "Move away from the wounded! I need room for triage!"

The crowd expanded a bit but kept churning as people tried to find loved ones they'd been separated from during the battle.

Newman pulled Goldenrod to her feet. "Do you have the spell memorized?"

"Mostly. I have it written down."

"Let's get it."

Her spell book was safely wrapped in her bedroll. As soon as she straightened up Newman chivvied her back toward the crowd.

"I don't know if it will work," protested Goldenrod.

"We don't have anything better to do."

King Ironhelm was surrounded six-deep by men arguing how best to fight a dragon.

"You can't charge it," snarled Wolfhead Alpha. "Rhinos charged it and it just flew over."

Captain Spear said, "We soak blankets in seawater and drape them over our heads as we line up—"

"No lines, we need skirmish order," interrupted a duke.

Newman started trying to force his way into the press.

Deadeye was standing outside the scrum atop a boulder. "Your Majesty," he said loudly. "We need a plan for more than one dragon."

People turned to where he pointed. Curses followed. At this distance it could be mistaken for an airliner, but it was coming this way. Then a glow of flame proved it was a dragon.

"Another!" said someone.

Turning, Newman saw another speck of flame in the opposite direction.

Count Dirk looked up. "Wimp. One poke and you had to call for mom and dad."

The chuckles were gallows-grim.

Newman began working his way toward the king again. "Excuse me," didn't persuade anyone to move. Saying it while pulling them out of the way likely reduced the chances of violence.

His other hand was on Goldenrod's bicep. She wasn't willing to force herself into the narrow gaps he created. He pulled her after him, ignoring the squeaks as she was bumped by armored men.

Squire Falchion shoved back against the hand on his shoulder. Newman snapped, "I must speak to His Majesty."

Falchion turned to look at him. When he met Newman's eyes the squire gave way.

Was I persuasive? Or do I just look like I want to unsling the axe from my back and start cutting my way through? 'Cause that's tempting me.

Forcing his way through the next rank required adding "Your Grace," to "Excuse me, I must speak to his Majesty." And eye contact.

Count Dirk was the last obstacle. When he heard Newman's voice he stepped back to make room.

King Ironhelm turned to see the disturbance. "Ah. Baron. And Baroness."

His voice was calm, confident, regal. Stance relaxed. The exact image needed to keep morale up in a hopeless situation. Only the way his eyes flickered between them betrayed desperation.

"Goldenrod has a spell that can take us home," declared Newman.

The king's lips quirked. "I was just thinking we needed a miracle."

Goldenrod wiped a few drops of blood off her cheek where someone's pauldron had scratched her. "I don't know if it will work. I've studied the elvish—"

Ironhelm raised his hand. "We don't have time for the tale. The odds are a million to one. It might not work. Any failure is not your fault. If you want my permission, you have it."

When she didn't respond immediately he continued, "If you need more, what is it?"

His face locked onto hers, filled with firm confidence. Goldenrod drew strength from it.

"The spell needs all the mages to form a ring with the rest of us inside. The mages sing the spell together. And then we go home." Goldenrod held up the book open to the spell.

"Very well." King Ironhelm waved his arms as if shooing flies. "Fighters, away. Away!"

The armored men backed up in confusion.

The royal baritone raised up in a herald's carrying cry. "All mages to the King! Mages to the King!"

The churn of the crowd changed as people absorbed the sudden command. The king repeated the order.

Newman followed with "Anyone with hidden magical talent come too! Spearpoint, this means you!"

The fighters moved faster to make room for the mages. The space around the king stayed just as crowded.

When more than two dozen had arrived Ironhelm declared, "Mages of the kingdom, I command you to follow the orders of Baroness Goldenrod."

He took two steps back.

All eyes shifted to Goldenrod. The expressions ranged among anger, fear, curiosity, and hope.

"I've used the elf sorcerer's books to create a spell to take us home," began Goldenrod. "We need to cast it as a group. Holding hands in a circle, singing the spell together. Then the circle and everyone inside goes back to the Earth."

Now the most common expression was doubt.

"It'll work. I made another spell to test the theory. It brought a coke can from Earth."

"Show me!" said someone in the mob of mages.

Goldenrod glanced at the corner of the island where she'd hidden it. "There's no time."

Duchess Roseblossom spoke over the murmurs. "She's telling the truth."

That drew astonished stares. Roseblossom never came to a mage council meeting.

"It's my gift," said the duchess. "It came to me two months ago. I can tell who's lying or not."

Countess Fennel demanded, "Just how does this—"

She broke off as she felt the king's gaze. Fennel lifted her eyes to him, then flinched at the glare. "What do we have to do?" she asked Goldenrod.

"It's easy. We just hold hands in a circle and sing." Goldenrod gave them a summary of the spell's structure then began teaching the song. It was only twelve syllables. It was the intricate changes in pitch that gave the assembled mages fits.

They began rehearsing three syllables at a time.

King Ironhelm turned to herding his cats into a circle. Convincing Lady Elderberry her patients had to stand required royal persuasion as well as authority.

Dragon watchers were standing at the edge of the plateau for better views. Newman went to round them up. It was easier than he'd feared. Saying, "We're using magic to go back to Earth. Be in the crowd if you want to come along," sent them scurrying.

He took a moment for dragon watching of his own. All three moons were up, one full and two gibbous. They provided enough light to spot the monsters even when they weren't flaming.

They were close enough he felt confident in judging them both to be bigger than the first dragon.

Newman glanced at Goldenrod. The rehearsal was over. The mages were spreading out around the crowd.

"If you are not a mage, get inside the circle," ordered King Ironhelm.

Newman trotted to obey. He ducked under Goldenrod's arm and stood just inside of her. Deadeye and his homely girlfriend were next to him.

Deadeye gave Newman a nod. He was still clutching his bow. Well, Newman hadn't dropped his axe.

"Everyone holding hands?" called Goldenrod.

Shouts of "Yes" came from around the circle.

"Sing all four pieces together. Three, two, one." Then Goldenrod led them in the chorus of the spell.

The music was beautiful. But Newman scarcely noticed it. Goldenrod was *fading*. Her whole body went translucent. He could see moonlight glinting off waves through her head.

The mages beside her were see-through too.

Then the song ended and everyone was solid again.

"We all need to sing it perfectly," said Goldenrod. "I'll sing the whole thing solo, then we'll do it together."

She went translucent again as she sang. The listening mages didn't.

Through the song Newman could hear distant dragon roars. All three were circling together over the island now. Doubtless discussing which recipe to use for insolent humans.

Goldenrod became solid again as she finished the song then faded as the chorus began. Newman looked to the side. Not all the mages were translucent. Most were. Some faded in and out.

The song ended. They were still on the island.

"We need to sing this precisely," commanded Goldenrod. "Listen closely. Get every note right."

She sang it for them again. Then the mages sang together.

The dragons flew lower. The biggest was below the other two.

The song ended. Goldenrod lectured on the mistakes she'd heard.

"Papa dragon, mama dragon, baby dragon," muttered Deadeye. "This island was just right."

Newman twitched a lip. He was too tense to appreciate humor.

"Screw it." Deadeye ducked under Goldenrod and Redinkle's linked arms. He nocked an arrow as he ran toward the edge.

Newman grabbed Deadeye's girlfriend to keep her from following. "Shhh," he whispered into her ear.

Goldenrod started singing the spell again.

Papa Dragon made his next loop low enough for Newman to feel the breeze off his wings. The beast moved out over the water then turned straight toward the island.

Newman saw the ash-gray palate as the dragon opened his mouth. Smoke trickled from the nostrils.

The circle of mages started the spell together.

An arrow flew from Deadeye's bow. It shot into the open maw and stuck in the inside of the left cheek.

The dragon roared. It lifted in the air and hovered. Talons reached into the fanged mouth to scrape at the cheek.

The song ended and they were all still on the island.

"Okay, if you can't get it right, get out of the circle," snapped Goldenrod. "Everybody squeeze together. Quickly, people."

Newman backed up a couple of paces. People were rearranging themselves without much fuss. Children went up on men's shoulders. Lady Buttercup was on Joyeuse's shoulders and looking very pleased to be there.

When shouts around the circle confirmed everyone was holding hands again Goldenrod sang it for the mages.

After a few puffs of flame Papa Dragon stopped writhing and flew back up to join baby. Mama Dragon dived down toward the island.

The circle began singing together.

Deadeye fired arrow after arrow at the dragon. It held its head high, hiding eyes and nose from the archer.

The arrows bounced off scales. Even ones hitting joints didn't penetrate.

Deadeye held his position, looking for the dragon to expose a weak point. He realized its intent too late.

Scales rasped as the dragon belly-flopped onto the rock. It slid across the island, pulling itself along with its talons.

Then a wing flap lifted it into the air. Moonlight gleamed whitely off the black scales. A few glinted red.

There was no sign of Deadeye. His girlfriend whimpered. Newman looked left and right at the mages. Most were transparent. A few stayed opaque.

The song ended.

Nothing happened.

Newman shouted, "If a mage didn't go transparent, pull him out of the circle."

People complied eagerly. Strained nerves were soothed by action. Protests by tone-deaf mages were ignored. Half a dozen gaps appeared in the circle.

Mages strained to reach each other's hands. Goldenrod pressed against Newman. It would be pleasant under other circumstances. He stepped back. Again.

"Ow. Watch that axe!" complained the person behind him.

People pressed against each other. Short people found themselves crowdsurfing, held up by multiple hands. Some wounded were held up as well.

Newman watched Goldenrod and Redinkle try to hold hands, unable to reach. They settled for cupping their fingers and hooking them together.

Mama Dragon finished a loop around the island. She roared as she closed in.

Goldenrod called, "On zero, three, two, one." The mages sang in chorus. Twelve syllables in unison.

The dragon spewed flame over empty rock.

***

Goldenrod closed her eyes and sagged. Newman caught her in both arms, lowering her gently to the grass.

The rest of the mages also fainted. Only half were caught.

Newman wasn't worried about them. The grass was soft. He ran his hand over the plants. Just like Earth grass. His fingertips slipped into a gap between two pieces of sod. Someone laid a new lawn here.

The crowd spread out. Some just wanted room to breathe. Others to explore the new place.

"There's the pond!" said an excited voice.

"I see the parking lot streetlights!"

"Sidewalks!"

"We're back! We're back!"

Newman leaned over Goldenrod to make sure no one dancing in celebration stepped on her.

"Calm down, people," barked Elderberry. "We still have wounded to treat."

A quick argument sent the wounded to the streetlights in the arms of young men. As others saw work happening they came over and joined in.

Newman carried Goldenrod after them. They passed through a belt of trees and a gravel lot before reaching the pavement. Elderberry directed casualties to different spots as triage.

He laid Goldenrod with the other unpunctured sleepers. The axe kept him from sitting. He unslung it and laid it across his lap, edge out. She breathed steadily. He hoped she'd wake soon.

There were no cars in the parking lot. Goldenrod's must have been towed months ago along with everyone else's. Couldn't be a weekend. There'd be some cars here if it was.

Volunteers were putting pressure on the wounds of the worst wounded. Spear punctures had reopened when they were carried, or in the squeeze of the crowd. Tearing cloth announced clothes being sacrificed as bandages.

Some people stood in the road ready to flag down any passing car. Others debated what direction would be the shortest walk to a phone. Children ran among them, celebrating their escape.

Mages were waking up. Not Goldenrod. But others sat up or stood. They repeated the delight of finding themselves on Earth. Their exclamations had a smug proprietary note.

Autocrat Sharpquill slapped his forehead. "I'm an idiot!"

He dug into the pouch at his belt. A smartphone came out. "I've just been using this as a reference library and notepad. Forgot it's a phone. Still half charged, bless Sparrow. I'll call Halberd, he can bring his church bus and—shit. Account suspended for overdue payments. Please visit our website to update your payment information. Shit."

He drew his arm back to throw the phone away.

Duchess Roseblossom intercepted him. "We can still call 911."

Sharpquill looked at her in disbelief. "What would you even say to them?"

"Anything, if it gets the wounded into the hospital."

He handed it over.

"Hi, several people have been injured at Atkinson Park. They were trying to build a tall bonfire and it collapsed. A dozen with deep punctures and some more with minor injuries. The east parking lot of Atkinson Park. By the road."

Duchess Roseblossom kept giving the 911 dispatcher real details on the injuries and fanciful ones on the accident. After a few minutes her imagination ran dry.

"Oh crap, my low battery warning just beeped, I'm going to—"

She pressed the disconnect button. "Stupid conversation anyway."

Sharpquill said, "We're going to have company."

A gasp and cough jerked Newman's attention back to Goldenrod. She sat up and looked around.

"Did it work?" she asked. "Oh. Parking lot. It did work. Heh. I wonder why we landed in the parking lot."

Newman kissed her forehead. "We arrived at the campsite. I carried you here."

Goldenrod turned and laid her head on his thigh. "Tired."

He stroked her hair.

Lady Burnout heaved herself to her feet. Elderberry met her halfway and helped her over to the worst of the wounded. The chiurgeon knelt next to the volunteer putting pressure on the wound.

Burnout laid her hand over the volunteer's. "Damn."

The volunteer startled. "Did he die?"

"No, no. You're doing good. Keep the pressure on. It's—I can sense the damage. You're on the right place. But I can't do anything to it. Can't clot, can't join."

"Too tired from the teleport?" asked Elderberry.

"No. I've been too tired to cast. Then I can't sense wounds. We're back on Earth. Magic doesn't work as well here."

Headlights and flashing red and blue lights announced an approaching police car. Duchess Roseblossom moved over to stand near the most severely wounded. The Autocrat, King Ironhelm, and their hangers-on trailed after her.

The commotion woke Goldenrod. "What's going on?"

"Police are coming," answered Newman.

"Oh, oh. Kingdom people aren't good at dealing with cops."

"I'll go hang around in case they need an interpreter." Newman eased Goldenrod onto the grass around the streetlight, picked up his axe, and walked over to Roseblossom.

The duchess waved her arms to attract the police car.

It pulled up facing her. The headlights shone on the lines of wounded.

The cop emerged, standing behind the open door. "What's the problem?"

"We have a lot of hurt people. The structure they were building collapsed."

Lady Burnout broke in. "Do you have a first aid kit?"

"Yeah, sure." The cop popped his trunk open. He tossed the red and white box to Joyeuse. The squire trotted over to Burnout.

The cop looked around the carless parking lot. He spoke at length into the microphone clipped to his shirt. Listened, talked some more.

"How did you people get here?"

Roseblossom answered, "By bus."

The cop made a 'go on' gesture.

"The party organizers dropped us off. They'll come back for us tomorrow."

Newman listened as the duchess tried to deal with the cop's questions. He wouldn't want to try telling the truth either. She was handling the cop smoothly. Having a lawyer for a husband must have given her practice with them.

The problem was this cop could smell bullshit. He didn't like it. Anything Roseblossom gave him he poked holes in.

The truth would just convince him everyone was on LSD.

"Look, let's focus on the important thing." The duchess spread her hands wide as she came closer. "We have people bleeding who need to go to the hospital."

The cop whipped out his gun and leveled it. "Back off, lady!"

Newman reflexively raised his axe and stepped forward. So did the king and his squire.

The muzzle swept side to side. "All of you, back off!"

Duchess Roseblossom backed up, waving down the fighters. "Stand easy, gentlemen. Stand easy."

Swords and axes were lowered.

Once the cop lowered his weapon she said, "I'm sorry, sir. I apologize for startling you."

"Yeah, yeah. You people just stay where you are."

The cop was right to be afraid, Newman thought. Even if he was a better shot than most cops, he'd only wound half the fighters before they took him down.

I shouldn't think about decapitating cops, Newman told himself. *That's bad.*

The one way to *guarantee* his safety would be to not point weapons at Duchess Roseblossom. But there was no explaining that to a cop.

More flashing lights signaled a convoy coming down the road. Three police SUVs. Two police vans. And, thank God, three ambulances.

The convoy pulled into the parking lot. They parked in a line abreast behind the first police car. The bank of headlights made Newman squint against the glare.

The ambulances stayed behind the police vehicles.

Doors and boots sounded. There were a lot of cops. They were carrying carbines and shotguns. One had a sniper rifle with a bipod. He braced it on the hood of an SUV.

The first cop declared, "Right. You guys are all under arrest for brandishing a knife longer than six inches."

He pointed at King Ironhelm, his squires, and Newman.

"This is bullshit," muttered a squire.

Duchess Roseblossom spoke firmly. "Gentlemen. Please cooperate. We need to get past this quickly so we can get medical help. In the morning I'll have every lawyer in Stonefist's firm there to bail you out. And it won't be a bad night compared to where we were."

King Ironhelm tossed his sword behind him and lifted his hands. The rest followed suit. Newman laid the axe down gently as he could.

Helmeted police officers came forward to cuff them. In a few minutes Newman was in the back of a van going down the road. He'd seen gurneys passing by as he was loaded in, so hopefully this was worthwhile.

"What are we going to tell them?" asked Joyeuse.

The king answered, "We're waiting for our lawyers to show up."

"I hope that works on my parents," quipped another squire.

They all laughed, tension amplifying the humor.

Newman hoped they'd be issued a prison jumpsuit soon. His tunic was stiff with dried orc blood. It itched.

And probably stank, given how the cops reacted. He didn't notice it anymore.

No such luck. Their in-processing was abbreviated by the word "lawyer". The cops noticed who liked to stand with whom and broke up the sets.

Newman was sent into the same holding cell as King Ironhelm. The cell held a dozen men ranging from thugs to drunks. The two scanned the room for threats. Finding none, they relaxed.

One young thug stood up from the bench and stomped toward them.

"Hey! Show some respect. It can be dangerous in here."

Newman and Ironhelm looked at each other, confirming they'd heard right. They started laughing. Full-throated belly-laughs.

Ironhelm kept his back against the wall. As the laughter weakened his knees he slid down to sit on the floor.

Laughing equally hard, Newman kept himself upright by hooking an arm through the bars of the open grill making the door. Tears ran down his face.

Another thug popped up from the bench and grabbed his friend's shoulder. "C'mon, homes. Ain't no green in messing with crazy people."

About the Author

Karl Gallagher has earned engineering degrees from MIT and USC, controlled weather satellites for the Air Force, designed weather satellites for TRW, designed a rocketship for a start-up, and done systems engineering for a fighter plane. He has, on a few occasions, put on armor and been hit in the head with a stick. His sole moment of martial fame was being one-shot in Crown so efficiently there was a three paragraph write up in the kingdom newsletter. He is husband to Laura and father to Maggie, James, and dearly missed Alanna.

About Kelt Haven Press

Kelt Haven Press is releasing print, ebook, and audiobooks by Karl K. Gallagher. For updates see:

www.kelthavenpress.com

Subscribe to the newsletter for updates on new releases.

Other Works by Karl K. Gallagher

Science fiction fans, check out <u>Torchship</u>, a working-class hard SF
adventure.

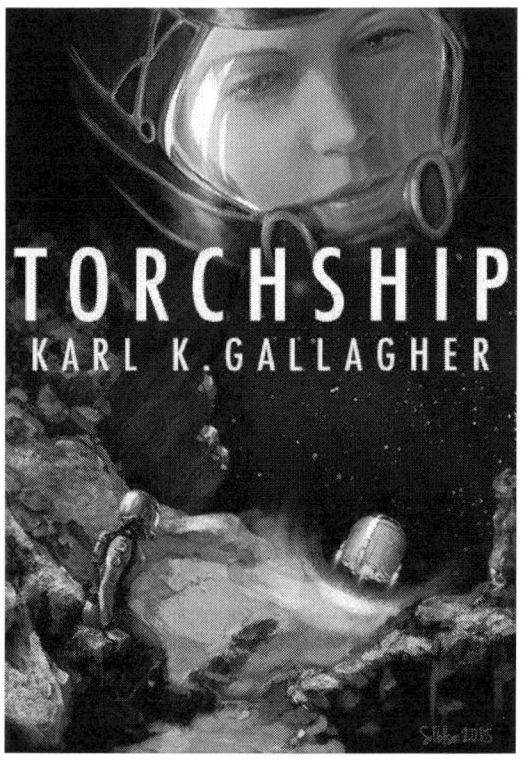

The sequels Torchship Pilot and Torchship Captain are included in the Torchship Trilogy omnibus.

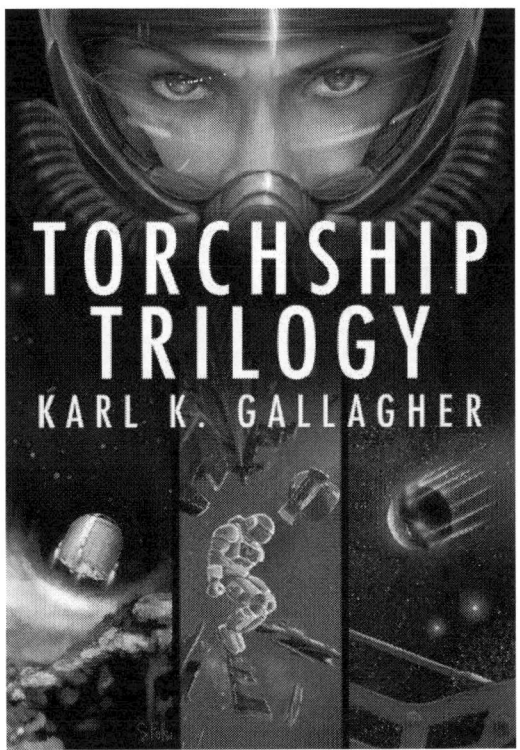

Made in the USA
Columbia, SC
15 May 2019